Birds of Passage

Joe Giordano

JUDY
thanks for your
support
Joe Giordano
1-11-16

Harvard Square Editions
New York
2015

Published in the United States by
Harvard Square Editions
www.HarvardSquareEditions.org

ISBN: 978-1-941861-08-0

Printed in the United States of America

For my parents

Chapter 1

MORETTI'S ARM WRAPPED around Leonardo's neck like a snake. "*Walyo*, young Leonardo, why the long face? Still no job?"

Leonardo hung his head. "Nobody's hiring in Naples," he said in a monotone.

Moretti considered Leonardo. The younger man had sculpted features, and hazel eyes under curly black hair. Women gave Leonardo furtive glances as they passed. Moretti stroked his chin. The elbows on Leonardo's dark jacket were shiny and the sole of his right shoe was loose. Leonardo didn't look up at Moretti, who was in his forties, with a mustache like smeared lampblack. His mousy brown hair was parted in the middle, and his chinless face sunk into a white collar. His checkered suit jacket was buttoned over a wide floral tie.

They stood at Moretti's kiosk under the sign "*Norddeutscher* Lloyd Steamship Line, *Porto di Napoli*." Moretti was an agent for the steamship company, recruiting Italians to work in New York. Near the marina, horses clomped, steel-rimmed carriage wheels rumbled, and a Lohner-Porsche electric car hummed along the cobblestone street that fronted the wharf. The late afternoon sun stretched the men's shadows like black crepe paper. Beyond the turquoise sparkle of the Bay of Naples, bulbous clouds cast blue-green shadows across the double-humped caldera of Vesuvius. The air smelled of raw sewage, treated wood, and brine.

Leonardo said, "Even the fishmongers told me to come back next week, but I've heard that for three months." Leonardo moved out of Moretti's grasp. He looked at the sky.

Seagulls floated on a cooling breeze and squawked down at him like teasing children.

Moretti said, "I'm amazed that no one will hire a capable man like you."

A waiter in his fifties with slick black hair and sleepy eyes dodged horses and an open top 1905 Fiat with red spoke wheels and crossed the boulevard carrying two small coffees on a wooden tray. He placed them on the ledge of the kiosk, and Moretti paid.

Moretti put three spoons of sugar into his coffee. Leonardo left his bitter.

Leonardo said, "There's a shoemaker in the village, Signor Felicio, who wants me as his apprentice."

Moretti raised his hands. "Shoemaking is an excellent trade."

Leonardo grimaced. "Perhaps. But Signor Felicio; he likes boys."

"Ah. I see." Moretti took his coffee in a gulp. He smacked his lips and replaced the cup on the saucer with a click. His gaze evaluated Leonardo. "I believe your father is a tenant farmer on Don Salvatore Mazzi's property. Can't he help get you a small farm to work on the estate?"

"My father asked, but Don Mazzi told him I wouldn't be hired. He didn't even offer me a job shoveling manure."

"I wonder why?"

Leonardo shrugged. "I saw Don Mazzi once, when I was a boy. He rode up to our house. My mother was there. He stared at me but didn't speak."

"That's strange. Well, no matter. I have your answer. You must go to the United States. America's where a young man can make his fortune." Moretti's voice dropped to a conspiratorial tone. "In New York you can get a job and make two dollars a day. That's many times what a tenant farmer makes, right?" Moretti placed his hand on Leonardo's shoulder. "And once a man like you finds his way, there's no limit to the opportunity. Like heaven in the bible, New York's streets are paved with gold. Perhaps you'll become rich enough to buy Don Mazzi's *fattoria* when you return to Italy."

Leonardo shook his head. "I can't leave my mother. She's devoted to me."

Moretti nodded. "Of course, the bond with your mother is strong. You're the sun, and she's orbiting Venus, the most beautiful woman in the world. But a mother wants success for her son."

"She'd rather I stay in the village and become a shoemaker." Leonardo shook his head.

Moretti spread his palms. "How is life in your father's house when you don't work? Leonardo, you're not a boy anymore. A man must have the dignity of his own income. Listen." Moretti leaned close, and Leonardo felt the scratch of Moretti's whiskers on his ear. "This is what I'll do for a special friend. I'll advance you a steamship ticket."

Leonardo's eyebrows rose. "A steamship ticket. What do you mean, 'advance'?"

"It's an investment. You'll pay it back from your wages in New York."

Leonardo tilted his head. "I don't know. I don't want to be in debt."

"Would I send you to America if I didn't think you'd make money? And that's not all." Moretti released Leonardo. He walked inside the kiosk. He was framed like a wanted poster. Moretti shuffled inside a small wooden drawer and came out with a stamp and ink pad. He opened a silver metal box and took out a steamship ticket. With a flourish Moretti rolled the stamp on the inked pad and pressed it to the back of the paper. His face beamed when he showed it to Leonardo. *Diritto di vitto e d'alloggio.* "This entitles you to food and lodging. My colleague in New York, Signor Gentile, will arrange for you to have a place to stay." Moretti extended the ticket to Leonardo. "This is an offer you can't refuse. No?"

Leonardo stared at the paper. America would be an adventure. His mother would resist, but he had no better option. He took the ticket.

Moretti smiled. "My friend, America is your future."

* * *

Leonardo's father, Nunzio Robustelli, dropped his mud-crusted shoes at the door and trudged into the kitchen. His three-day grisly beard was as coarse as a Rhino's skin. He was a short, wiry man with a full head of black swept-back hair. The shape of his eyes had earned him the nickname Chinaman from his fellow tenant farmers. He reeked of dirt and sweat. He headed straight for the jug of homemade red wine, grabbed a chunk of goat cheese, some bread, and plopped down at a wooden table next to Leonardo without a word. He carved off a slice of cheese and poured himself a tumbler of wine.

Leonardo's mother, Anna, didn't look up when his father entered. Her black hair was streaked with gray; her eyes were as blue as the Mediterranean. She stirred a black kettle of simmering tomato sauce on a wood-burning stove. The smell of garlic filled the house. A gray-stone fireplace was opposite the table, and a beat-up pot filled with warmed water for washing hung from an embedded cleat. Atop the crude-beam mantle was a tiny oval tintype picture of Nunzio in a military uniform. There were steps that led to a loft, Leonardo's parents' bedroom, with some simple wood furniture and a straw mattress. Leonardo slept on a narrow bed in the corner next to the fireplace.

Leonardo never heard his father laugh. No matter how hard Leonardo tried, his father was never pleased. Every day Nunzio was off at dawn and home at dusk. In the evening when Nunzio wanted sex with Anna, he'd order Leonardo to bed. Although Leonardo pressed his hands to his ears like a vice, his father's muffled grunts would drive him into a fetal position. More recently, when Leonardo heard his parents make love, he'd leave the house and sleep outside.

Leonardo fidgeted in his chair. His eyes shifted between his parents. He took a deep breath and stood. "I'm going to America."

His mother put down her ladle and turned. His father's face chewed itself into a smirk, but his gaze didn't rise.

Anna's blue eyes crinkled into a frown. The creases in her face deepened. She wiped her hands on the linen apron over her ankle-length blue skirt. "I don't understand."

"There's no work in Naples. There are so many competing tenant farmers that you slave all day and can't afford bread. There's no future for me here."

Leonardo's mother was rigid. His father sliced off another piece of cheese.

"There are jobs in New York. I'll make good money."

Anna took a step toward her son. "But Signor Felicio wants you as his apprentice. Shoemaking is a good trade. Everyone wears shoes."

Leonardo's eyes rolled. "Mama, I don't want to be a shoemaker."

Anna moved closer to her son. "What about Rozalia Valentini? She likes you. I can see it in her eyes. Her parents have promised her a house and some farmland for a dowry."

"I don't love Rozalia."

Nunzio drained his glass. He glanced at his wife. "There are worse reasons to marry than for money."

Anna's mouth pursed. She looked at her son. "New York is so far. You've never been away from me."

"Mama, you taught me that the bird leaves the nest. It's time."

"Is New York safe?"

Leonardo put his arm around his mother. "I'm old enough to take care of myself." He squeezed her shoulders. She turned away. "Mama, come on. I talked to Signor Moretti in Naples. He's an agent for the steamship line. He gets jobs for Italians in New York. He's advanced me a steamship ticket. Look." Leonardo took the paper out of his pocket and read the stamped message aloud.

Anna glanced at the paper in her son's hand. "Moretti was a barker in Chiarini's Italian circus. Now he recruits unemployed Italians to leave their homes. He's a moneylender and a *girovaghi*. He's traveled and trades in his experience like it was jewels. Why do you trust him?"

"I don't, but a man needs to make his own way."

Nunzio leaned back. His chair creaked. He spoke slowly as if to an idiot. "Moretti would steal breast milk from a baby. He'll profit from you, not the other way around." He poured himself another glass of wine.

Leonardo said, "You don't want me to have my own money. You want me to remain under your control."

Nunzio's face reddened. "A few *lire* in your pocket won't make you a man. When will you complete your military service? The government won't forget you."

"When I come home."

Nunzio faced Anna. "I told you no good would come from his studying English." He waved at Leonardo. "I've warned you. Do what you want."

Leonardo turned to his mother. "Mama, it's 1905. Lots of Italians are emigrating to America. I'll make some money in New York. With steamships I can be home in ten days." He kissed her cheek. "You won't even know I'm gone."

Anna's eyes glistened. She nodded to him, but sobbed in the night. She awoke to each sunrise with dread. Every new light was one day closer to when Leonardo would leave.

Chapter 2

ON THE DAY Leonardo was to leave home, Anna couldn't get out of bed. Whenever she tried to raise her head, the thought of his going prostrated her. Nunzio had trudged out to the fields before first light. She heard Leonardo's shuffling, uncertain steps below her loft bedroom. He's struggling too, she thought. He has a restless nature, just as she did. Anna sighed, and closed her eyes.

Anna's mother, Silvia, was forty when she was born, and her father, Pasquale's, hair was gray. Silvia had suffered multiple miscarriages, but after a series of *novenas* to Saint Anne, the Virgin Mary's mother, Anna arrived. Anna was eight when she took Dante's *The Divine Comedy* from its shelf and asked her father to teach her how to read. Her mother frowned. "Women need to learn how to cook and keep house. A man wants a reliable and loyal wife, one who adheres to the wedding vow to love, honor, and obey."

Anna was more interested in wildflowers and butterflies than sewing for her dowry. At sixteen, the sight of Anna stopped conversations in the village. Pasquale and Silvia had the responsibility to arrange a husband for her. They understood that Anna's intelligence and curiosity weren't traits attractive to everyone and pondered which young man would be the best match. Marriage was forever, divorce was inconceivable, and they wanted Anna to be happy with their choice.

Pasquale was a tenant farmer on the Mazzi Estate. The young Salvatore Mazzi, now the Don of the estate where Nunzio worked, was often seen riding a black stallion around the countryside. Mazzi was married, but known in the village as a fisherman of women. One morning, Pasquale spotted Mazzi ride up to his daughter while she walked to the market. Mazzi leaned over in his saddle. Pasquale couldn't hear the conversation, but Anna smiled and stroked the horse's muzzle. To Pasquale's eyes Anna was far too friendly. He and Silvia agreed that it was urgent that they decide on a husband for Anna.

When families with eligible men came to call, Silvia told Anna, "Let them see you doing housework," but Anna insisted to greet them with the open copy of Dante in her lap. The families would sit around the table while the young men shot glances at Anna, but she gave no indication of preference and showed little interest in marriage. Silvia wrung her hands.

Nunzio Robustelli was born with dirty fingernails. His father was a tenant farmer on the Mazzi estate as generations of Robustellis had been before them. Nunzio grew to be the strongest man in the village, always called upon to carry the saint's statue on feast days. Nunzio first saw Anna on the day of a *festa* procession. She smiled at Nunzio and stopped his heart. Soon after, he asked his father to arrange a visit to her parents. Pasquale was impressed with Nunzio's farm skills. Silvia was encouraged that Nunzio Robustelli could be a steadying influence on Anna.

When Nunzio was formally introduced to her, he bowed and mumbled, "Pleased to meet you," and was silent.

Anna shifted on her feet and raised her eyebrows to her father.

Nonetheless Pasquale approached Nunzio's father, offered a modest dowry, and the match was agreed.

When Pasquale announced his decision to his daughter, she blanched.

"I don't love Nunzio. We've hardly spoken."

Her father replied, "He has calloused hands. You'll never starve."

Anna resisted. She woke up sick every morning.

Silvia pleaded with Anna to relent. "You'll bring shame upon this family."

Finally, Anna acquiesced to her parents' choice.

In honor of the marriage, Salvatore Mazzi's father gave Nunzio a desirable plot to farm that included a small house. The gift was unusual, but townspeople viewed it as a sign of the respect the Mazzis had for the Robustellis. The match was agreed in February, but weddings were never held during the Lenten period, so the ceremony took place immediately after Easter. Leonardo arrived eight months later. Nunzio swallowed his surprise; he had Anna. Although Leonardo was eight pounds, the village was told that he was a premature baby.

Leonardo clung to Anna like a shadow. She taught him what she knew about nature, the names of flowers and the birds that darted overhead. She had a vegetable garden and raised chickens. The hens were her pets, and Leonardo would squeal with delight when one would lay an egg in her hand. She read Dante to him.

Leonardo was a child in constant motion. Anna always kept one eye on him as she went about her chores. One afternoon the wildflowers were in bloom and the fields were alive with smudges of red, white and yellow, like finger-paints on the green hills. Leonardo played in front of the house. Anna on her knees weeded the garden. A man, ramrod straight in his saddle, quietly walked his black stallion up to them. The horse's forehooves trod on some basil, and the animal snorted. Leonardo stopped and looked up. The man stared at him with steel gray eyes. Anna rose from the dirt and wiped her hands. She walked over to Leonardo and put her arm around his shoulders. She met the man's gaze with a raised chin. She smoothed Leonardo's hair and cupped his face with her hand. Nothing was said. After a few moments the man wheeled his horse and rode off. Later Leonardo learned the rider was Salvatore Mazzi.

Chapter 3

AT THE NAPLES MARINA the sun broiled humanity like chops on the grill. Leonardo and Anna were on the street at the edge of the crowd. Peasant men in brimmed caps and ill-fitting vests and women in white blouses and billowing ankle-length skirts held onto wide-eyed children and waited to be called for pre-board inspection. Many churned aimlessly around the concrete apron of the port like confused inmates in a mental hospital. Fruit vendors and cheap watch peddlers called out their offers. Mendicant Franciscans solicited alms and competed with threadbare beggars with open palms. Stress sweat vied with rotted fish and raw sewage for the dominant odor. Every baby cried. *Carretas* choked the *Vico di Via Porta* entrance to the marina. Prospective passengers' mule carts were loaded with the bureaus, tables, chairs, casks of wine, kegs of olives, rounds of cheese, and huge cloth bundles tied with grass ropes they intended to take aboard ship. *Carabinieri* in blue uniforms with silver belts and swords at their sides, wagged their fingers at the owners. Furniture was not permitted; protests were ignored.

A shout of pain turned heads. A dentist in a white smock held a bloody tooth in a pair of pliers. A man was doubled over and held his jaw. The dentist raised his voice for the next person who wanted to board ship toothache free.

Leonardo clutched a cloth satchel that contained the copy of Dante's *The Divine Comedy* his mother had given him, plus some shirts and underwear. He looked over his mother's shoulder.

Anna took Leonardo's hand. "Your father's not coming." She had on her only jewelry, gold earrings with antique coral centers.

Leonardo took in a breath and nodded. Anna's face was wet with perspiration. She patted her forehead. Leonardo called out to a buxom woman who carried an earthenware pot. She sold drinks of water in a common glass. Leonardo paid her, and Anna drank with hands gnarled from heavy toil. The water was warm and flavored with the slight taste of licorice. Leonardo put his arm around his mother. She clung to his waist.

A call rose from the pier, "*Germanese.*" Passengers for the *Norddeutscher* Lloyd ocean liner were told to make their final farewells to family and pass through the iron spear pickets of the border control area. The moored *Prinzessin Irene's* gray 172-meter length loomed on the horizon. The steamship's twin stacks smoked black; the whistle let out a long hollow moan. Passengers who'd sailed to Naples from Genoa, the ship's port of origin, looked down from the railings like gargoyles.

Leonardo hugged his mother tight. She said into his ear, "Be careful in New York." Her tears dampened his cheek. She pressed a blue envelope to Leonardo's chest.

He saw the folded edges and raised his eyebrows. "Mama, where did you get money? And dollars?"

She squeezed his hand. "You'll need this."

"I don't want your money."

She pushed the envelope into his jacket. She shoved a small wrapped package into his satchel. "It's some bread and dry sausage for you to eat on the boat." She gave him a wet kiss on his cheek.

Leonardo's eyes were damp. He hugged her. "I'll be fine."

Their hands slipped slowly from each other's grasp. He picked up his bag. His mother's blue eyes welled up. As he walked away from Anna toward the enclosure, he shot looks at her over his shoulder. Anna's hands held her face. The crowd filled in behind him. He lost sight of her, and emptiness filled his heart.

Other passengers made final hugs of farewell. Men and women's faces had tracks of tears. Murmured prayers for safe passage were in the air, along with cries of, *"Buon viaggio e buona fortuna."*

At the black-gated entrance, a gruff inspector stopped a child, eyes red-rimmed with trachoma, and she was turned away with her mother. A woman whispered it was their third attempt to emigrate. Fear rose on many faces that they might also be stopped from boarding. Leonardo brushed aside dark men who offered to sell him fake passes for the health inspection and counterfeit baggage-fumigation tags. Leonardo shook his head, but some passengers paid. Inside the *capitaneria*, officials in white uniforms emerged from a dark building like conjured ghosts. They shoved Leonardo along into the steamship broker's office where his passport was verified, and the American consular agent confirmed his name on the manifest. An official grabbed his sleeve, and he was hustled to the next stop. Before he realized what was happening a doctor roughly peeled up his eyelids to check for trachoma and tousled Leonardo's curly hair to detect the yellow crust of favus. After he was cleared, an official pushed Leonardo ahead. Behind him officials rejected an older couple as unfit for travel. Another official jerked Leonardo into the vaccination station. Women shrieked and children wailed around him. Leonardo removed his shirt, and the doctor inoculated him for smallpox. Leonardo was pushed ahead before he was dressed. A rotund clean-shaven official behind a table looked into Leonardo's satchel. He grabbed the cloth-wrapped sausage and bread and held it to his nose.

Leonardo said, "My mother gave me that."

"Not allowed." He dumped the food into the trash.

Leonardo gasped. "What did you do?"

"All hand luggage is fumigated."

The bag was dusted and thrown back in Leonardo's face. His ears turned scarlet. "Give the food back."

"Next."

"You bastard."

Rotund raised his finger. "Another word and you don't board."

Heat spread across Leonardo's face. He showed a skeleton's grin.

The man gulped and leaned back. His voice cracked. "It's the rules."

Leonardo took two breaths and the sea breeze cooled his face. He moved on.

Alongside the gangplank, six derricks slung steamer trunks onto the deck above. Leonardo scaled the steep incline like Mount Calvary among passengers dressed in farm clothes, some in Roman refinery, shod or barefoot. The people toted bulbous cloth-wrapped bundles, valises, and fiber baskets. The procession resembled an army of industrious ants.

On deck, Leonardo pushed to the railing and peered out. He saw his mother on the street. Aside him, passengers waved handkerchiefs, parasols, and hats. Leonardo stretched and waved his arms, hoping she could spot him, but Anna didn't respond. He struck a wooden match, lit a crumpled bit of paper, and held it overhead like a torch to draw her attention, but the wind blew out the flame. He shouted, "Mama," but she couldn't hear him. On the pier the high-pitched voice of a young tenor rose with a plaintive song, *Addio a Napoli.* Other voices tried to join in, but cracked with sadness. Leonardo looked at his mother, standing alone, and clutching a handkerchief to her mouth. Tears streamed down both their faces.

When all the compartment baggage was stowed, the first and second-class passengers were escorted aboard to the decks above Leonardo and the other third-class passengers in steerage. The gangplank was withdrawn. The ship's horn gave a long blast, and the metallic metronome of twisting engine gears began. The screw turned, and the ship was underway. The fading light of day turned Vesuvius purple and gave the gray-blue clouds pink underbellies. As the ship cut through the Bay and passed Capri, the sight of the white buildings of Naples dissolved to black.

An official with a fireplug physique in a black-luster coat and dirty pique cap with a megaphone announced the distribution of ration tickets. He gave Leonardo a jute-wool blanket roll. Inside Leonardo found a tin spoon, fork, cup, a small pan, and a little red card that read, "Good for One Ration."

Below deck, Leonardo found the men's sleeping section, hundreds of double-tiered iron bunks in blocks of eight. The mid-ship bunks were steadier when the ship rolled. Those close to portholes with better air and light were already piled high with baggage. Leonardo felt his way into a dark section and found an upper berth above a Turk, who wore a red fez and embroidered jacket. A burlap-covered jute mattress was thrown over the iron slats of the bunk. It was as lumpy as a bag of rocks. A cork-filled life vest was a makeshift pillow. Leonardo's nose crinkled at the stench of coal fumes. He lay back and closed his eyes.

Soon after the ship reached full speed, sixteen knots, the dinner bell jolted Leonardo awake. He grabbed his tin pan and utensils and squeezed along the companionway with dozens of other men. Atop the steep iron stairs women and children emerged from their sleeping section and converged with the men on deck. The cooks and stewards lugged great troughs of food and baskets of bread, which they lined up along a narrow passageway so that the mass of people were forced to form a rough line to receive their meal.

Above Leonardo on the first class deck, Horatio Branden, a partner in an uptown Manhattan law firm and his wife, Edith, stood surveying the dinner scene below. He said, "Look at that mob. The Italians are dirtier than the Negro, and the children are diseased." Branden banged his hand on the ship's railing. "The policy that allows this rabble to come to our shores is pure folly."

Edith said, "Horatio, how can you be so cold?"

Branden sensed something in his wife. "Edith, what are you thinking to do?"

"I've talked to the other women. We can't abide the children not having something decent to eat while we feast up here. We'll drop some fruit and candy down to them."

"Edith, don't. There's a steerage class for a reason. The crew won't allow it. Don't embarrass me."

"You're too easily embarrassed." She walked away.

As Leonardo moved past the tanks of food, cooks ladled out macaroni, a chunk of beef, and boiled potatoes on the same small plate topped with a slice of bread. Red acid-flavored wine was poured into his cup. It took Leonardo an hour to be served. He shrugged at the first mouthful. The food was cold, but he hadn't eaten for twelve hours, and he wolfed down the meal.

By the time he'd finished eating, Mrs. Branden and a number of other women were calling for the attention of the children and dropping apples and oranges into their hands. The children screamed in delight. An officer wearing a black coat went up to the women. His palms were raised as he tried to stop them. The ladies ignored him and only left the rail when their fruit supply ran out.

Leonardo rinsed his utensils in the cold seawater provided. A sailor was stationed to limit each passenger to one cup of drinking water. Leonardo filled his cup with potable water, swished some in his mouth, and swallowed. There'd be no baths until he was again on shore. When they finished eating, many passengers dumped the leftover scraps onto the deck for the crew to swab and hose away. The stewards did a half-hearted job, and Leonardo almost fell in the slippery mess. Some passengers had taken their meals back to the bunks. Morsels littered the floor and mattresses. A few tried to throw food through portholes, many missed the mark. The smell of strewn food mixed with the now active use of the toilets. At night the deck watch required everyone to stay below. In his bunk, Leonardo tossed and turned in the stinking miasma around him.

The next morning the ship's hatches were open, and a stab of sunlight awakened Leonardo. His hand went to his face. His left eye was sore and swollen half closed, the effect of a bedbug bite during the night. His right arm throbbed with vaccination aftereffect. He was groggy, but the breakfast bell got him out of bed. Topside, Leonardo waited his turn in the food line. He was given a biscuit and coffee. He plopped down onto the deck beside two middle-aged men. The coffee was weak. He tried to crack the biscuit in half without success. He said, "These things are like tufa."

The first man had a three-day beard and bushy eyebrows. He put the biscuit between his teeth and gnawed. He grabbed his face. "I think I broke a tooth."

The third man had a scar from ear to chin. He took out a stiletto and cleaved off a chunk. He popped it into his mouth. His face crinkled, and he spit out the crumbs. "It tastes like seawater."

The three men looked at each other, and they sailed their biscuits over the side of the ship. They laughed.

Bushy brow's extended his hand. "I'm Beppo Lucchese from Messina."

The man with the scar said, "I'm Giuseppe Fontana from Naples."

After Leonardo introduced himself, Beppo said, "This is my third trip to America. I'm headed for a coal mine in Pennsylvania."

Giuseppe said, "This is the first time for me. I was promised a job as a mason in New York."

"You two are lucky. I'm not sure what I'll be doing."

Giuseppe asked Beppo, "What are the women like in America?"

"The Americans won't look at you, and the Italians want to get married. I have two wives, one in America and a second in Italy."

Leonardo's eyebrows rose.

Beppo shrugged. "It was a practical necessity."

They all laughed.

As the *Prinzessin Irene* sailed along the south of France, the wind raised whitecaps and soon the ship rolled along deep swells. Leonardo's face turned white, and he grabbed a cleat to steady himself. His gut rose to his throat. The sensation he felt was both uncomfortable and unknown, and sweat glistened on his forehead. He retched, and what was in his stomach spewed out like a fountain. The putrid smell of vomit compounded his misery. The ship pitched savagely, and he was thrown to the starboard deck. He crawled to the hatch. Many other passengers were in a similar state. They made use of the handrail to stumble down the stairs. The darkness and disorientation of the lower deck as the ship rolled caused Leonardo to retch again. No one could control themselves, and vomit sprayed everywhere. Leonardo clawed like a blind man along the line of bunks and managed to reach his. He pulled himself onto the jute mattress. Prostrate, he felt some relief from the nausea. But the roll of the ship threatened to throw him down to the floor. He urgently grasped the iron edges of the bunk. Some passengers reeled from the odor of the vomit and the toilets and tried to make their way back on deck. They collided with those coming down the steps, and the stairs were clogged with tangled bodies struggling in opposite directions. There were cries of anguish for God to help them. Some moaned. Leonardo wondered if his misery would ever end. He was sure that if Dante had sailed in the *Prinzessin Irene*, *The Inferno's* deepest circle of hell would've been seasick victims in steerage.

When the dinner bell sounded, Leonardo lifted his head, but his stomach rose, and he fell back onto the bunk with a thud. Leonardo's heart pounded. Few passengers were able to leave their bunks to claim the evening meal. Those who struggled to get on deck collected the pile of macaroni, beef, and potatoes, but managed to swallow only a few mouthfuls. The officers decided to make a health inspection. Stewards held scented cloths to their noses as they walked through the bunks and shouted for people to come on deck. Leonardo didn't move. A burly steward stabbed Leonardo in the side with a baton. He flushed red. He climbed shakily down from the bunk. The face of the Turk in the lower bed was yellow. Slick smudges of vomit covered the floor and some men fell. Leonardo walked hand over hand, bunk to bunk, as if he traversed the side of a cliff. Step by step, up the stairs he went. On deck, he fell to his knees. Around him, men, women, and children spilled on top of each other like straw. Below deck, the crew swabbed and hosed as much as was possible. Stewards pulled people to their feet for the doctor to examine. A steward roughly grabbed a woman by the left arm. She cried out in pain. Leonardo's ears turned red, and he rose. The woman saw his face and begged him not to retaliate for fear she'd be barred from entering America. Leonardo's death's head grin caused the steward to take a step backward.

The next morning the ship anchored near Gibraltar. The Mediterranean was calm, and Leonardo decided he could go on living. Bumboats arrived carrying Spanish and Portuguese passengers as well as some additional provisions. The ship was underway in an hour. That evening Leonardo ate some of his macaroni and afterwards practiced English phrases with Beppo and Giuseppe.

On the third day's sail in the Atlantic they hit a gale. Clouds rushed toward the ship like galloping horses. The ship's bow rose up a gray wall of water and plunged down into the swell. The captain ordered passengers below. Sailors battened down the hatches, but seawater washed over the ship and flowed into steerage. The high winds brought some ventilation, but the stench from the toilets, vomit, and coal soot overwhelmed all. The ship rolled to port as if it would founder. The Turkish man below Leonardo fell out of his bunk. His eyes were open, but he didn't rise. Leonardo watched him slide back and forth with the roll of the ship until the storm passed. A doctor arrived, pronounced the Turk dead, and two sailors removed the body. Leonardo relieved his seasickness by lying prostrate. Every time he lifted his head, the specter of nausea rose in his gut. He left his bunk for a nibble of food, the toilet or, when demanded for a health inspection. After four days, Giuseppe shouted down to him that Sandy Hook was sighted. Leonardo struggled up. He had to see land.

Chapter 4

LEONARDO'S MOUTH tasted like an army had trampled his tongue with hobnailed boots. He trudged up the stairs and pressed himself to the rail. The air was crisp, and a shiver went through him. Sandy Hook's white lighthouse was off the port bow. The hazy skylines of Brooklyn and Staten Island were ahead. The *Prinzessin Irene* slowed, and a small boat motored toward them. Beppo and Giuseppe came to his side.

Beppo fidgeted. His voice had a tone of concern. "That's the American doctors. This is only the quarantine inspection to allow the ship into New York harbor. There's more ahead."

Giuseppe was haggard, pale, and had sweat on his brow. "Do I look sick?"

Leonardo put a hand on his shoulder. "You look fine."

Leonardo had hardly eaten for days. His vomit-wipe sleeve jacket hung on him like he was a wire hanger. He was light-headed. He breathed in the sea air and straightened his back. He'd endured too much. He wouldn't let the doctors return him to Italy. Leonardo unfolded the paper that Moretti had given him with the Ellis Island inspection questions. Beppo and Giuseppe read over his shoulder.

Giuseppe said, "I'll lie about the money I have. If they think I'm poor, they won't let me in."

Beppo said, "I'll only tell them about my American wife."

Giuseppe asked Beppo, "How much should I bribe the inspector? How much for the doctor?"

Beppo shrugged. "I got in without paying the last two times. If necessary, give them everything you have." Beppo turned to Leonardo. "I have American naturalization papers. If the inspectors give me trouble, I'll use them." He showed the two men.

Leonardo said, "But the name on the documents is 'Tizianno Vecelli.'"

Beppo colored. "Well, they're just for emergency. I bought them in Naples." He tucked the papers carefully into his pocket.

Giuseppe pulled Leonardo aside. "I'm afraid they'll find out I was in prison."

Leonardo's eyes widened.

Giuseppe moved closer. "There was no work in Naples, and the money ran out. I met a woman whose clan was Camorra. Her brother gave me a job extorting protection money from importers. The police picked me up. They beat me, but the gang would've killed me if I talked. I was in jail six months when the police chief decided to empty the prison. He gave us each a steamship ticket and a clean passport to get out of Italy. I'm not the only former prisoner on this ship."

Leonardo said, "How would the American authorities know you were in prison? Italy won't tell them."

Giuseppe's face relaxed.

Leonardo looked around. Mothers cleaned children's faces with rags dipped into their single cup of fresh water. Men dry shaved. The crew brought cabin baggage on deck.

Above, Horatio Branden prodded Edith. "Look at those people. As if a few swabs with a dirty rag would scrape the dirt off that urchin's face."

Edith said, "Those people have hope for a better life. They want to present their precious children to their new home as best they can."

"It's pathetic."

"Jesus was born in a manger. Do you think Mary cleaned His face before the Wise Men arrived? Was that pathetic?"

Branden closed his mouth.

The skiff pulled alongside, and the crew lowered a ladder. Officers with U.S. gold eagles on their white caps climbed aboard. They headed for the upper deck and checked the first and second-class passengers. When they finished, the doctors stationed themselves aft, and the steerage immigrants paraded past them. A man hadn't removed his hat, and a steward knocked it off. The doctors peered at Leonardo, Beppo, and Giuseppe, but they weren't stopped. They breathed a collective sigh of relief. The doctors returned to their boat, and the *Prinzessin Irene* steamed into New York Harbor.

As the ship skirted the western Manhattan shore, the immigrants gaped at the gigantic skyscrapers. Many buildings were more than twenty stories tall. Giuseppe said, "Beppo, you didn't lie. It's magnificent. How can you leave such a city?"

As the ship approached the Statue of Liberty, the immigrants flowed like a wave for a closer look. Children were hoisted atop shoulders. The passengers stared in silence until a girl asked if that was the Virgin Mary. Her mother told her that the statue was the goddess of America.

The *Prinzessin Irene* steamed north past Ellis Island and docked at the *Norddeutscher* Pier at the Port of Hoboken for customs clearance. Horatio and Edith Branden and the other first and second-class passengers were ushered off the ship. They quickly passed through customs and headed either for inland trains or the ferries to Manhattan. When the gangplank was cleared for steerage passengers, Leonardo pressed forward. His memories of the *Prinzessin Irene* were seasickness, overflowed toilets, coal ash fumes, and the unwashed stink of his fellow travelers. He clomped down the steamship's wooden gangplank as fast as the crowd allowed. The ship's stewards hustled people along. A woman whose bag slipped hesitated, and a steward grabbed her right arm and threw her forward. Leonardo clenched his fists but stopped himself. He was glad to leave the ruffian bastards behind. On land, Leonardo's legs were rubbery, as if he was still at sea.

Crew members extracted baggage from the hold and dumped it onto the pier. Thousands of immigrants churned with customs inspectors, stevedores, and dockhands. People pushed and families scattered. Mothers screamed out the names of children who'd been separated from them. Men with keys in their hands anxiously searched for their trunks so they could be opened and inspected. Wide-eyed children were piled atop baggage. Babies screamed. Customs officials threatened immigrants and poked them with batons to establish a line. English and Italian curses filled the air. Next to Leonardo, a customs official argued with an immigrant over the duty to be assessed on a mandolin. A broken-English protest was futile. Cheese wheels, wine casks, and other food were assessed duties. Leonardo's satchel was examined, passed, and marked with chalk. He sought out Beppo and Giuseppe.

Beppo said, "We get barged to Ellis Island next."

Leonardo dreaded another boat ride and prayed that the river would be calm.

A vendor of fruit approached Giuseppe and offered him an apple for five cents.

Beppo said, "*Ladro*. An apple sells for one cent on any corner in New York." Giuseppe had silver *lire* coins in his hand. Beppo cautioned that he'd be cheated on the exchange.

Giuseppe looked at the shiny red apple and chewed his lip. He shook his head.

After two hours to complete customs inspection, Leonardo and the others were directed to a barge. Immigrants were loaded down with burdensome bundles and struggled up the gangplank of the boat that would take them to Ellis Island. Once aboard, people collapsed on the floor or atop their baggage. Leonardo went to a rail. When the barge set off, every wave slap on the hull clenched his stomach. At the Ellis Island wharf, Leonardo's mouth gaped. The expansive four-tower red brick building was worthy of a king's palace. Leonardo decided that if New York could afford a castle just to receive immigrants, there surely was a way to make money here.

The crew announced that other barges would be unloaded first and people needed to wait on board. Children cried that they were hungry. Impatient boys threatened to jump ashore, but were warned off by officials. As the sun lowered on the horizon, babies sobbed themselves to sleep. Heads drooped. Men and women leaned against each other. Leonardo sat on the deck and closed his eyes.

The sound of chains woke Leonardo as the crew dragged the gangplank to shore. Wearied faces without a smile lifted their heavy luggage bundles and piled off the boat. Officials in black uniforms counted and grouped the people. In front of Ellis Island's cavernous grand entrance the cry went out for immigrants to get their ship health tickets ready. Immigrants overburdened by baggage held the papers in their teeth. Mothers carried babies in their arms and balanced bundles on their heads. Officials ushered everyone up the stairs to the registry floor. The great hall was as wide as St. Peter's Basilica. The noise of anxious conversation buzzed like a hornet's nest. Leonardo was directed to sit at one of the rows of benches beside the stairs.

When called forward, Leonardo's first stop was a health inspector in a black cap whom he'd seen lift hats and push back shawls in search of favus. The official scrutinized faces for disease. Those who limped, he marked with chalk. Next Leonardo approached a doctor in a gray coat. People cried in anticipation of the trachoma examination. The doctor rinsed his hands in disinfectant, then turned up Leonardo's eyelids with a metal instrument. Leonardo groaned. The doctor spoke in gruff gobbledygook to a tall man with a black mustache who marked Leonardo with a "C" in blue chalk. Leonardo's heart sank. Perhaps he'd be sent back to Italy. Leonardo was told he'd be detained in quarantine. Behind him a child was diagnosed with trachoma, and her mother was marked with a "T."

Beppo and Giuseppe weren't chalked and continued ahead to an inspector in a black uniform who sat on a stool at a wooden desk. A translator was beside him. Their papers were inspected and the list of questions asked. When they passed muster, their faces brightened with relief. They were pushed forward. Beppo bought a railroad ticket for Pennsylvania and was shunted toward the stairs for the trains. Giuseppe was directed to another staircase for the ferries to the Battery. No delay for goodbyes was permitted. All Leonardo could do was wave. They called out to each other, "*Buona fortuna.*" Leonardo saw his friends' backs go downstairs. He looked around, saw only strangers, and swallowed. It hit him that he knew not a single person in New York. He wondered how long it would take him to make friends.

Some immigrant families misread signs and took the wrong stairs. They wailed at officials who blocked their return.

Leonardo's "C" indicated conjunctivitis. A doctor admitted him to the Ellis Island Hospital quarantine.

Chapter 5

CARLO MAZZI, Don Salvatore Mazzi's son, had blond wavy hair, gray eyes, and walked with the stride of the moneyed invincible. While Leonardo endured steerage travel to New York, Carlo was about to return to his father's Naples estate from the University of Bologna, where he majored in Roman History, fencing, and women.

In Bologna, Caprice Sacco was fulsome with pomegranate lips, the fantasy of every male at the university. She'd been pursued by a score of frustrated admirers, and the field had narrowed down to Carlo and Aldo Paladino. Aldo had a high forehead, and not a stitch or hair was ever out of place. He was nephew to a cabinet head in Prime Minister Alessandro Fortis's Historical Left government, and his post-graduation political career was assured.

One afternoon Carlo and Aldo were vying for Caprice's attention over a bottle of Prosecco at an outdoor café.

Caprice crossed her legs. "It's a shame that the tradition of knights jousting to win a lady's heart are over."

Aldo's eyebrows rose. "What do you mean?"

Caprice smiled slyly. "You both pursue me, but you don't fight to prove your love."

Carlo smiled. "What an intriguing idea. Aldo, let's duel for our lady. First blood will settle the issue."

Caprice twirled a black curl and shifted in her seat. "I'll await the victor in my apartment."

Carlo and Aldo left Caprice and retrieved their fencing gear. Their triangular shaped epée blades had small protruding spikes near the tips that ripped flesh or clothing registering a "hit." Carlo and Aldo found a green section of a quiet park near campus, and they squared off. A roost of gray and white pigeons waddled over to view the spectacle. They ruffled their feathers in anticipation.

As was his mental preparation for every match, Carlo imagined Aldo as a slice of beef to be carved, chewed, and spit out.

"En garde."

A series of unsuccessful lunges, reprises, and ripostes ensued, then Carlo's epée sliced across Aldo's neck. Aldo screamed in pain, and a rivulet of blood flowed. Carlo removed his mask and laughed. Aldo's face glowed red, and he lunged at Carlo. Carlo parried him aside. The two men collided and wrestled to the ground. Carlo ripped off Aldo's mask and pounded him into unconsciousness. Before leaving to claim a luxurious afternoon with Caprice, Carlo unbuttoned his pants and urinated on his opponent. The pigeons cooed.

In Naples, Carlo played. Some afternoons he galloped the countryside around the Mazzi estate astride a black stallion like Marcus Aurelius plucking peasant girls who caught his eye. Other days he caroused in town with the sons of other rich men.

His father the Don, Salvatore Mazzi, had salt and pepper hair and walked with a slight limp due to a recent stroke. Carlo was the Don's only child. His mother had doted on him, but she passed away. His father compensated for Carlo's loss by catering to his every whim.

On a particularly hot afternoon Carlo was in a Naples café with rat-faced Dino Lombardi. They wore well-tailored jackets. They slouched on wooden chairs and drank beer under a Peroni sign. The discussion turned to Italian politics.

Carlo said, "What good was Garibaldi and the unification of Italy?" He spread his arms. "King Victor Emmanuel raised our taxes and Rome's economic policies are a disaster. The *Mezzogiorno* has been impoverished. That's why the port is filled with people leaving Naples."

Dino nodded.

Carlo continued. "Italy isn't a nation. We don't speak the same language, and our northern keepers hold us in disdain. We're just ..." He searched for the phrase. "A geographic expression, the boot of Europe. The South should go its own way."

A shadow fell over the men and four eyes rose to see Pero Silvestri with hands on hips. Silvestri was a large man with a dominant nose, short gray hair, in his fifties, with the erect bearing of a former general.

Silvestri's eyes blazed at Carlo. "That's treasonous talk."

The blood left Carlo's face.

Silvestri said, "That's what I thought; a coward, just like your father." He gave the men a hard stare and moved on.

Carlo's jaw tightened.

Dino leaned close. "How can you accept such an insult?"

Carlo glowered, and his voice was flat. "I don't."

The Mazzi estate contained hundreds of acres of terraced vineyards, olive, chestnut and walnut groves, tomatoes and other vegetables, herbs, and watermelons. Silvestri owned the large farm that abutted Mazzi's, and they were engaged in a bitter legal fight over water rights. A stream meandered over both properties and was critical for irrigation. A worker alerted the senior Mazzi that Silvestri had diverted the flow, and the two Mazzis rode out to investigate. Salvatore was on a bay gelding, Carlo on his black stallion. Silvestri carried a shotgun and supervised the work of a dozen men who finalized a dam. The water that flowed onto the Mazzi property was down to a trickle.

Salvatore shouted at Silvestri, "Have you lost your mind? You have no right to steal our water."

Silvestri jutted his chin at them. "I've retained the water that flows on my property. If you object, go to court." Silvestri turned his back on Mazzi and called out to one of his workmen, "More stones. Raise the wall level. Some water is getting out."

Salvatore was red-faced. "You'll destroy our harvest."

Over his shoulder Silvestri sneered. "That's not my problem."

Carlo said, "You won't get away with this."

Silvestri looked at Carlo like he was *merda*. His voice was a growl. "Why don't you try and stop me?"

Salvatore's voice sputtered. He broke into a cold sweat. His breathing became rapid. He faltered. Carlo caught him.

"Papa, we need to get you back to the house."

Salvatore nodded. Carlo led him home. Salvatore was put into bed, and a doctor was called.

Doctor Sprandio, a short fastidious man, examined Salvatore. He took Carlo aside. "I don't know what put your father into this state of agitation, but these episodes are a grave risk to his health. I've given him amyl nitrite, but he needs to rest."

When the doctor left, Carlo sat on the edge of his father's bed. "Shall I go to our *avvocato*?"

Salvatore shook his head. "The courts would take months. Meanwhile, our crops will wither and die." He flushed. "That bastard Silvestri wants to be the death of me."

Carlo stiffened. He placed his hand on his father's forehead. "Papa, please rest."

Salvatore nodded, closed his eyes, and slept.

Thunder rumbled ahead of a towering gray cloud. The morning was hot, the air smelled heavy, and the humidity deposited a trace of moisture on the black barrel of the sawed-off shotgun in Carlo Mazzi's hands. Carlo had risen before dawn and chosen a route to the Silvestri estate that would keep his approach hidden. Carlo passed one of the signs at the border of his father and Pero Silvestri's property, "*Vietato L'Accesso Proprietà Privata.*" Carlo crouched in a field and waited for sufficient daylight to see ahead. Along a beige dirt road a seventeenth-century stone farmhouse with a salmon-tiled roof was nestled on a rolling hill. Carlo spotted the flash of a white shirt. He peered around some trees and saw Silvestri at the head of a row of terraced grape vines. As Carlo stealthily moved forward, he saw that Silvestri was bent over examining a blood red rose planted as an early warning for pests that would attack the fruit. He carried a shotgun under his arm. As Carlo neared Silvestri's position, his boot crushed a stone. A flock of ravens took flight and cawed loudly. Silvestri's head came up. He saw Carlo and raised his weapon, but a nervous finger betrayed Silvestri. He pulled the trigger prematurely and both barrels fired off target. Carlo shouldered his shotgun and moved forward. Silvestri backed away. His mouth stretched in fear like a tragic theater mask. He raised his palms.

"*Schifoso.*" Carlo fired. Silvestri's skull exploded in a blur of red. The old general was thrown into the vines, and his back hit the ground. His white-haired head was a bloody hole with the glint of gold from a tooth in his lower jaw.

The Mazzi beige stucco and stone farmhouse stood high in a countryside of nuanced dark and lighter green hills under a dazzling blue, sunlit horizon mantled by puffy cumulus clouds that blended with the azure of the Mediterranean in the distance. Blazing thirty-foot tall Bougainvilleas of crimson, magenta, lavender, and white crept around and over the farmhouse walls.

Salvatore Mazzi stood outside the house with Father Paulo, a young priest in a black cassock with a wide-brimmed hat and beard. Salvatore was the largest benefactor to the local church. He was a man politicians approached for funds. At Christmas and Easter he made a great display to help the poor and was a reliable source of patronage for local people.

Salvatore said, "Father, thanks for coming."

The priest placed his hand on Salvatore's shoulder. "I was worried when I heard you fell ill. I'm delighted to see you back on your feet. *Vai con Dio*."

The priest climbed onto his donkey cart and shook the reins to start the animal moving. When the priest was out of sight, Salvatore drifted toward the house. He looked at the gold pocket watch he kept in his vest and wondered where Carlo had gone earlier that morning.

Salvatore looked up to see Carlo cutting through the fields toward him, his shotgun hung low at his side. When Carlo reached him, his son's face was pale, and he was sweating. Carlo's eyes darted.

Salvatore put his arm around his son and pulled him inside the columned portico of the house. "Tell me what happened."

"I killed Silvestri. He fired first, and I shot him."

"Where?"

"On his estate."

Salvatore stiffened. "Are you sure he's dead?"

Carlo nodded.

"Did anyone see you?"

"I don't think so."

"Good." Salvatore kneaded his chin. "Silvestri's workmen heard us both argue with him." His gaze drifted out to the horizon, then his eyes returned to meet his son's. "The *carabinieri* will come here. I can handle them, but I don't want you to be questioned." Salvatore squeezed his son's shoulder.

"I need to get you out of Italy. A little time and a lot of money will solve this problem. Then you can come back."

Carlo nodded.

Salvatore said, "I'll take you to Vincenzo."

"Are you sure you can travel? I can go on my own."

"I don't want anyone to see you on the road." Salvatore patted his son's cheek. "Don't worry about me. You just removed a thorn from my side."

They embraced.

"You'll wait with your uncle until I can make arrangements in Naples for your travel. Our attorney will get you new papers. I want you someplace the *carabinieri* can't reach. America. Lots of Italians are in New York. You'll blend in until I send for you. Okay?"

"Yes, Papa."

"Put together some things. I'll change into farm clothes. We'll travel by mule cart. No one will see you under the blanket in back." Salvatore kissed his son's cheek. "Don't worry. Everything will be okay."

"*Grazie*, Papa."

The springless mule cart bounced on every rock and rut on the dirt road that led toward the sea. Salvatore and Carlo arrived at Vincenzo's home in the afternoon. The yellow stone house with terracotta roof near the shore was small, on one level with a planked wooden door. A ceramic window box burst with red and pink flowers. Vincenzo Mazzi was Salvatore's younger brother. He heard them arrive and came out of his house. He was shorter than Salvatore, well muscled with black hair. The skin on his face was deeply tanned and weather-beaten like boot leather from the hours he spent at sea on his commercial fishing boat. The three men embraced each other. Salvatore explained the reason for their sudden arrival.

Vincenzo shrugged. He said to Carlo. "Pero Silvestri, good riddance."

Salvatore said, "You'll need fuel for a trip."

"I'm always ready."

Salvatore mounted the mule cart and left for Naples.

Vincenzo put his arm around his nephew. "Don't look so concerned. Your father will make arrangements. America will be a nice adventure. You'll tell me all about it when you've returned home."

They walked out to the pier where Vincenzo's boat was docked. The craft had a length of fifteen meters with a wheelhouse some paces from the stern. The hatches were covered with canvas. The deck was planked and the polished cleats glinted in the afternoon sun. A single engine powered the ship. Six steel drums of liquid fuel were lashed together on deck, and gravity fed the main tank. The vessel's hold had a capacity of two tons of ice. Vincenzo cast his nets far beyond the range of other commercial fishermen, and the ice insured his catch would be fresh and command a premium from fishmongers in Naples. The ship was painted sea blue below the water line and spotless white above. On the mahogany stern was the name, *Odissea*.

Vincenzo said, "We'll take a boat ride. Like when you were a kid."

Carlo hugged his uncle. "*Grazie*."

Vincenzo patted Carlo's cheek. "Let's have something to eat. I have a beautiful *Branzino* to grill for us. A little lemon and olive oil." Vincenzo winked. "*Delicioso*." Inside the house he pulled out a white wine, *Lacryma Christi*. "We'll have a bottle from your father's vineyard."

The next day, Vincenzo and Carlo heard the rumble of the mule cart's return and they greeted Salvatore outside. The three men embraced and entered the house. The furniture was simple and wooden. They sat around a table.

Salvatore handed a set of documents to Carlo. "You're Enzo Di Stefano, and you work on a freighter." Carlo perused the passport and a card that identified him as a seaman. "Vincenzo will take you to Palermo. You'll find the freighter, *Dinnamare* of the Creole Line, on Tuesday at Pier 12. The captain, a man named Diehl, will have been paid by the time you arrive. A seaman will meet you on the quay and take you aboard. Don't leave your cabin during the voyage. They'll bring your meals. When you arrive in New York the captain will give you a shore pass to leave the ship. I've cabled a cousin on your mother's side, Alberto Leggiéri. You've never met him. He's lived in New York since he was a child. He'll meet you when you disembark. But he knows nothing of what happened in Italy. *Capisci?*"

"How long will I need to be away?"

"Some months at least. Alberto will take you to the Italian ghetto in lower Manhattan. You've learned English from your university studies, but there you can speak Italian. Alberto will help you rent a place to stay." Salvatore leaned closer to his son. "Keep a low profile. No carousing, no flaunting your money. No one must suspect you're on the run. Informers are everywhere. If the authorities catch you and deport you, everything is lost. Silvestri's family may suspect you killed the old man, but if they receive confirmation there'll be a vendetta for sure. They'll come after you. Do you understand?"

"Yes, Papa."

Salvatore handed Carlo a belt. "This has two strips of leather. Between them are two hundred U.S. dollars. When you need more money, go to the Bank of Napoli in New York. If necessary, contact our attorney in Naples. I'll wire you money. If you must cable me directly, use the name Di Stefano or Leggiéri. Do you have any questions?"

Carlo shook his head.

Salvatore waved his hand. "*Non ti preoccupare*. When I believe you can return to Naples I'll let you know."

The three men stood. Carlo's eyes were red. His father embraced him and kissed his cheek.

"I need to get back to the estate. I don't want the *carabinieri* to wonder where I've gone." He turned to Vincenzo. "Leave as soon as you can."

Carlo and Vincenzo were underway in less than an hour. The *Odissea* slapped swells along the slate-colored Mediterranean under an overcast sky. Vincenzo was at the helm. Carlo's gaze was distant.

Vincenzo noted the shadow on Carlo's face. "You're troubled by the killing. But you did what was necessary. I'm proud of you."

"*Grazie*, Uncle. The image of that bastard dead on the ground is stuck in my head. I can't shake it."

"It's natural. You'll have a few rough nights."

"I appreciate your taking me to Palermo. I know it's a risk for you. I'm sorry you're involved."

Vincenzo spread his hands. "Carlo, please, blood is all. We'd risk everything for our family." He slapped his nephew on the back.

They were a few hours out of Naples and made good progress. The day cooled toward evening. On the horizon Vincenzo spotted towering clouds roll toward them with a sneer, and the muscles in his jaw bulged. He pointed. Carlo nodded, and his gut soured.

Vincenzo said, "This will be rough. Attach a jackline to your waist."

Vincenzo gave the helm to Carlo and sidled around the ship to secure the hatches. Vincenzo took the wheel and attached his jackline. Carlo crouched next to him. They rode into the storm. The wind rose and rattled the metal fittings. Flags and rope riggings snapped like whips. The green and white-foamed sea levitated the bow skyward, then plunged them down and the horizon disappeared. Rain pelted the men in horizontal sheets. Black clouds blotted out the sun. Lightning flashed, illuminating the men in a bright frozen image like a match strike. Thunder exploded overhead. Vincenzo's hand lifted from the wheel to shield his eyes from the wind and rain. The boat lurched, and he lost balance. He tottered backwards and tumbled over the transom into the sea. Instantly his jackline snapped off the deck and stretched like a rubber band.

Carlo jumped up. "Uncle." In the strobe of lightning flashes Carlo saw Vincenzo floundering in the heavy seas. The wheel spun out of control. Carlo righted the course and slipped loops of rope onto the spokes to keep the wheel steady. Vincenzo tried to pull on the line to reel himself back to the boat, but it was futile. Carlo grabbed for Vincenzo's rope, but the ship rolled, and Carlo slipped to his knees.

Vincenzo went under a wave and came up sputtering for air. Carlo took hold of Vincenzo's jackline, pressed his feet against the transom for leverage, and pulled. The boat dove into a trough and a huge wave washed onboard and hit Carlo in the back like a rabbit punch. His head hit the stern. He tasted blood. His hands had loosened, and the gain he'd made on Vincenzo's rope paid out. Carlo took hold and restarted the tug of war against the sea. His back strained. He pushed with his legs and stretched to make headway. The line cut his fingers and palms, and he shouted curses into the wind for the lack of gloves. Hand-over-hand, Carlo reeled Vincenzo toward the boat. His biceps and thighs burned with exhaustion. He saw Vincenzo's hand clutch the transom. Carlo tied off his jackline on a cleat, reached over the stern, and grabbed his uncle's belt with both hands. He hauled him onto the boat and tumbled backwards. Vincenzo retched and vomited seawater. Carlo crawled over to the helm and kept the throttle at slow power. It seemed an eternity before the storm passed and was a growl in the distance.

Vincenzo's head lolled, his back against the port side. He lifted his hand to Carlo. "*Grazie.*" His voice sounded like he'd gargled with ground glass.

Carlo nodded and swallowed. His mouth felt dry as a cactus. He got them both some water. "I thought I lost you. It took all my strength."

"Blood is all."

Carlo nodded. "Can you get up?"

Vincenzo smiled. "*Uno momento.*" He took a breath and struggled to his feet.

During the night they took turns at the helm and slept as they could. Sunrise opened Carlo's eyes. The Port of Palermo was ahead.

Chapter 6

A FEW DAYS after Carlo and Vincenzo set off for Palermo, Captain Baldassare Ceruti of the *carabinieri* arrived at the Mazzi estate astride a chestnut stallion with a white star on its forehead. Ceruti's uniform was dark blue with silver accents. He wore black calf-length boots, and his brimmed cap had a brocade image of King Victor Emmanuelle III. He wore a silver sword and scabbard around his waist. Ceruti earned his rank fighting marauding gangs of thieves in Scanno, Antrodoco, and brigands in Chieti, but his bravery and accomplishments threatened superiors, and he was exiled to Naples where they hoped he'd lose himself fighting the Camorra families' organized crime labyrinth.

Salvatore Mazzi came out to meet Ceruti at the gate and invited the captain to sit on the portico. A servant placed a ceramic pitcher of blood orange juice on a low stone table.

Mazzi said, "Captain, would you like some juice, or perhaps you prefer coffee?"

"*Grazie*, Don Mazzi. Nothing for me."

Mazzi poured some pulpy red liquid into a glass and sat back in his chair. A black cat wandered onto the portico from the garden, sat, and surveyed the two men. It rose, rubbed itself against a column, and left the loggia to hunt mice.

Ceruti looked at Mazzi with a pleasant gaze. "Don Mazzi, perhaps you've heard that Pero Silvestri is dead."

"Ah, yes. Father Paulo mentioned it to me after the Sunday church service. He said Silvestri died on Friday." Mazzi took a sip of juice.

"Did Father Paulo tell you how he died?"

Mazzi shrugged. "I assumed he committed suicide. After a lifetime of disappointments I imagined he put an end to it."

Ceruti tilted his head. "It wasn't suicide. Silvestri's shotgun had been fired, but his body was too distant from the weapon for the wound to have been self-inflicted. It was murder."

"Ah."

Ceruti said, "You have another theory?"

"Out here we need to worry about thieves. No one wanders far without a weapon."

"A gold watch was still on the body, and he had *lire* in his pocket. This wasn't a robbery by some vagabond. He was shot in the face at close range. This suggests the murder was personal."

Mazzi took a sip of juice.

Ceruti said, "You don't seem surprised."

"Captain, Silvestri was a man who made enemies like a dark suit collects lint. Everyone he came in contact with learned to detest him. So no, I'm not shocked."

Ceruti shifted in his chair. "Don Mazzi it's well known that there was bad blood between you and Silvestri. I must ask where you were Friday morning?"

"I was at home speaking with Father Paulo about church finances."

"I see."

"Are you sure I can't get you a coffee?"

"Is your son Carlo around?"

"Carlo? Why?"

"I've spoken with one of Carlo's friends. He said that Carlo argued with Silvestri at a café the previous afternoon. There are also witnesses who said you and Carlo fought with Silvestri when you were on his farm the evening before the murder."

"Carlo was at home that Friday morning. Silvestri would quarrel with a statue. He was a disagreeable man. If your suspect list includes people who had words with Silvestri, you'll need to interview every family in Naples."

Ceruti smiled. "Did Father Paulo also speak with Carlo that Friday?"

"No. Carlo slept in. You know young men."

"May I speak to Carlo?"

Mazzi slapped his thigh. "You just missed him. Carlo's gone to Europe on business."

"That's too bad." Ceruti kneaded his ear.

Mazzi put his glass down. "Your son, how is he?"

"He's away on military service."

"Wonderful. Will he join you in the *carabinieri* afterwards?"

"He says not."

"Have him come see me. I'm sure I can find him an opportunity. There's a shoemaker in the village who's looking for an apprentice. My brother Vincenzo needs strong backs on his commercial fishing boat. I've encouraged Father Paulo to channel church funds toward the young men in the community. Perhaps help them attend university."

Ceruti said, "When will Carlo return?"

"His trip is a combination of business and pleasure, so it's open ended."

"I'll need to speak with him when he's back." Ceruti rose. "Don Mazzi, thanks for your hospitality."

Mazzi watched Ceruti ride away, and a cloud covered the sun.

Domenico and Bartolomeo Silvestri were heavy set like their father. With bald heads and handlebar mustaches, they looked like strong men at the circus. Both had completed their military service, and Domenico, the eldest by three years, was considered an expert with a pistol. They received Captain Baldassare Ceruti at their home, and the three drank coffee on a shaded veranda.

Domenico said, "The dam my father built to block the water flow onto the Mazzi property has been destroyed. I'm certain that one of the Mazzis either killed my father, or they paid to have him murdered."

Ceruti put down his cup. "Signor Silvestri, we've not completed our investigation."

Bartolomeo's cheeks flushed. "Investigation? What's to investigate? My father wasn't robbed. He was shot in the face." Bartolomeo caught a sob in his throat.

Domenico put a hand on his brother's shoulder. "Captain, what Bartolomeo is saying is that the murder was both brutal and personal. Salvatore Mazzi hated my father. We believe that he's responsible."

"Mazzi was with Father Paulo the morning your father was killed."

"And what about Carlo and Vincenzo Mazzi? I understand that Carlo hasn't been seen since the murder. His father claims he's in Europe, but no one has heard from him."

"The *carabinieri* throughout Italy have been alerted to help find him. Our inquiries extend to other countries as well. If Carlo Mazzi is guilty, he'll be brought to justice."

"Excuse me, but you're well aware that the Neapolitan judicial system is so corrupt, the law doesn't operate at all. Salvatore Mazzi is a rich man. His son will never be found guilty."

"I don't agree. While I respect the love you had for your father and understand the grief you suffer because of his death, I must caution you not to try and take the law into your own hands. Despite your father's murder, I would be forced to put you both on trial."

Bartolomeo started to speak, but his brother put up his hand. "In Italy people accept that men have the right to redress the murder of their father. Captain, we mean you no offense, but we'll be hiring someone to make our own inquiries."

Ceruti stood. "That's regrettable. If you intend a vendetta, the result, I believe, will be more tears for your family."

Chapter 7

PALERMO'S EARLY MORNING CLOUDS covered the horizon like a burial shroud, and the sea was a dull green. The *Odissea* motored into port, cruised along the channel and tied up.

Vincenzo and Carlo stepped out of the boat. "In a couple of weeks you'll be in New York." Vincenzo pulled out a nine-inch stiletto. "Merchant ships are rough. Take this for protection."

Carlo slipped the blade into his pack. "Maybe you should rest before you head back to Naples?"

"I want the *carabinieri* to find me at home. I don't want them to suspect that I've taken you away."

The men embraced. Vincenzo climbed back into the *Odissea* and gunned the boat toward Naples.

At Pier 12 the *Dinnamare* was a hulking gray slug with rust accents. Carlo found a sailor leaning against a pile at the edge of a wooden gangplank that rose and fell with the lap of the waves. Erik Lund was a Swede in his thirties with a crooked smile and dirty blond hair. He wore a blue wool cap and a short black jacket.

Carlo showed his papers, and Erik led him up the gangplank. On deck were drums of olive oil and stenciled burlap bags of grain. Black smoke curled from the stack. Erik saluted a brown-haired heavyset man with a ruddy complexion. On the man's white and black cap, was embroidered *Chefingenieur* in gold brocade. He eyed Carlo as he passed. Erik and Carlo went below to an aft cabin. It was the size of a closet, no porthole, with two bunk beds.

Erik said in English, "I come later." He moved his fingers to his mouth and Carlo understood he'd bring a meal.

Carlo closed the door and sat on the bed. He decided that if he had to stay inside this cell for the entire voyage as his father instructed, he'd go insane. He yawned, laid his head back, and quickly fell asleep. He was awoken by loud knocks on the door. Carlo sat up too quickly and hit his head on the bunk above. He rubbed his forehead and opened the door. Erik had a distressed look. Next to him, with a fist raised to bang the door again, was the chief engineer.

The man said in heavily German-accented English, "Did we disturb your sleep?"

Carlo could hardly understand, but recoiled at the tone.

The engineer turned to Erik, "Get this dago into the boiler room."

Carlo stiffened.

The man stormed away.

Erik had a sheepish look. He held up two forearm-length leather gloves.

Carlo said, "What's this?"

Erik made a shoveling motion. "Coal. Boiler."

Carlo heard the engines and realized the ship had left port. "Who is he?"

"Krause. Boss me." Erik grimaced. "*Merda.*"

"I'll stay here." Carlo started to close the door.

Erik stopped the door with his hand. "Shovel or no eat." He pantomimed thrusting his fingers toward his mouth with a negative shake of his head.

Carlo's eyes narrowed. "*Figlio di puttana.*"

Erik shrugged.

Carlo said, "Does Captain Diehl speak Italian?"

Erik shook his head. "German only."

Carlo puffed out a breath. "Okay, let's go."

Erik led the way.

Carlo climbed down the dark steel steps to the coal-crusted and cramped boiler room like an *Inferno* circle of hell. Heat radiated on his face, and the roar of the furnaces filled his ears. The furnaces and boilers were surrounded by a tangle of pipes, valves, chains, and riveted bulkheads. Coal chunks, some as large as a man's torso, were heaped on the floor. Two men toted wheelbarrows filled with coal and dumped them into piles. The soot that covered their faces gave them the look of players in a minstrel show. When they saw Erik and Carlo, they dropped their wheelbarrows and left.

Krause entered the boiler room and stood with arms crossed.

Erik glanced at Krause. He picked up a shovel and turned to Carlo. "Watch." Erik stabbed a large lump of coal repeatedly with the shovel's edge until the chunk was broken into small pieces. He swung open the large iron firebox door.

Carlo looked into the white-hot furnace, and flames imprinted an image on his retina like the sun. Sweat dripped down his forehead.

Erik took a shovelful of coal. He timed himself with the roll of the ship and thrust his load atop the fire-grate. Erik continued to stoke the furnace. When finished, he raked residue ashes that had fallen under the grate into a pit. He slammed the furnace door shut with a clang. He wiped his brow with a red rag. Erik pointed to the second furnace. "You."

Carlo hesitated. He was grimy and sweaty.

Krause said, "What's the matter, dago, afraid of work? Lund, didn't you tell him no work, no food?"

Carlo considered his options. If he could communicate with Captain Diehl, he'd get out of this drudgery, but how? If he started trouble with Krause, he risked being turned over to the authorities in New York, or worse, detained and returned to the Italian *carabinieri*. It was clear that Krause wouldn't give him food unless he worked. He reflected on his father's advice. Carlo put on the leather gloves and picked up a shovel.

Krause smirked. He pointed to the glass pressure gauge. "See?" Krause picked up a piece of coal and scribbled on a bulkhead wall, "180." He walked close to Carlo. "Understand?"

Carlo saw the burst capillaries in his cheeks and felt Krause's sour breath on his face. Sweat dripped coal dust into Carlo's eyes, and it burned. Pressure started to rise up his throat and into his ears. He pictured Krause as a side of beef. Carlo lifted the shovel.

Erik inserted himself between the two men. "Okay, okay."

Krause maintained his smirk. "Fine." He sidled over to the speaking tube. He blew the whistle attached to the tube and barked orders to the engine room through the mouthpiece. He turned on his heel and left.

Four hours later the two minstrel players relieved Carlo and Erik. Carlo collapsed into his bunk without eating. The next thing he heard was Erik at his door summoning him for the next shift.

Two days later Krause showed up toting a half-finished bottle of schnapps. He plopped himself onto the coal pile and took a swig. Krause's speech was slurred and, when he yelled, spittle flew. "Captain Diehl says you're a special passenger. Not to be touched." A small smile came to his lips. He continued as an aside. "Bullshit. You're some sort of dumb dago thief from down in the boot with a rich papa who'll pay for his son to be smuggled into America."

Carlo broke coal chunks with his shovel. He understood the gist of Krause's words through the German accent. A tingle went up his back.

"Okay, I won't touch you." Krause picked up a lump of coal and threw it. It bounced off Carlo's shoulder.

Carlo stiffened. Krause picked up another chunk, but Erik stepped in the way. Krause sniffed. He rose and walked unsteadily out of the area.

Erik waved his hand. "Krause no like Italians. *Merda.*"

The next day, Krause was in the boiler room with a bottle of booze. He took his perch atop a coal pile. He slapped his chest. "Below deck Krause is captain. Understand?"

Carlo ignored him.

Krause said, "The pressure's too low. Shovel faster."

Erik walked over to the glass gauge. "Pressure good."

"I said shovel faster." Krause picked up a jagged-edged piece of coal and hurled it at Carlo. The chunk struck him behind the ear and drew blood.

Carlo squared with Krause. His face looked like he'd eat him raw. Erik pushed Krause out of the boiler room. He stumbled and cursed as he left.

On their last shift before entering the Port of New York, Erik handed Carlo a shore pass. A sly smile crept across Erik's face. "We find women."

Carlo laughed.

Krause hadn't returned to the boiler room since the last incident, but on this day he appeared. He swaggered in with a brown-handled Luger pistol on his belt. "So, dago thief, you think you'll escape into New York?" Krause patted the weapon. "Maybe not after I talk to the police."

Carlo's face darkened and he fingered his stiletto.

Two short blasts from a tug's whistle announced the *Dinnamare* was being towed into New York harbor. Most of the crew went topside to get a sight of the Statue of Liberty and their first glimpse of a city in a couple of weeks.

The whistles were a signal for Carlo. He rose from his bunk. He wore his sweater inside out. The stiletto was in his belt. He shouldered his gear and slid along the passageway toward the chief engineer's cabin. Krause's door was ajar. He sat at a table looking over some papers. The Luger lay alongside. Carlo quietly put down his pack outside the door and pulled out his knife. He slipped on the boiler room gloves. Carlo burst into Krause's cabin. Krause saw him and reached for the pistol, but Carlo closed with him quickly and knocked Krause to the floor. He plunged the knife into Krause's side. The engineer struggled like a bull, but Carlo stabbed him repeatedly. As a coup de grace, Carlo put his knee into Krause's back, pulled his head by the hair, and dragged the stiletto across Krause's throat like he slaughtered a pig. Carlo stood. The pool of blood around Krause's head spread wide. Carlo wiped the knife onto Krause's shirt. He dropped the bloodied gloves. He reversed his sweater to hide the bloodstains underneath. His heart pounded. His sweat smelled sour. He paused at Krause's cabin door and took deep breaths to slow his pulse. He glanced down the passageway to confirm it was deserted. He grabbed his pack, closed the door, and walked purposely toward the iron ladder to get on deck. He presented his shore pass and strode down the gangplank.

On the pier Carlo saw a man in a tweed suit and bowler hat. "Are you here for Enzo Di Stefano?"

Alberto Leggiéri smirked. "Well, I'm not waiting for a sea breeze."

Chapter 8

THE DAY AFTER Carlo Mazzi arrived in New York, Leonardo was released from the Ellis Island quarantine. Hot baths, decent food, and a daily saline rinse had cleared his conjunctivitis. Leonardo banged open the hospital door. The sky and sea were gray, and he turned up his jacket collar to a stiff breeze. He strode toward the ferry. On the boat to the Battery some immigrant Irish girls sat nearby and smiled at him. They were chaperoned by a priest who would place them as servants with rich uptown New York families.

At Battery Park, Leonardo scanned the tall buildings on the perimeter. An elevated train hissed steam and roared up 6th Avenue. A trolley's bell clanged, and passengers for Broadway boarded. Cabbies in top hats picked up well-dressed fares and snapped whips to drive their horse-drawn carriages forward.

Inside a twenty-story gray building, Leonardo found the office for the *Norddeutscher* Lloyd Steamship Line. A man in a brown suit with jowls that pulled his mustache into a frown wrote a note for a teenager wearing a newsboy cap beside him.

Leonardo said, "Signor Gentile?"

The man held up his palm, "*Uno momento.*" He finished a scribble in pencil, spewed out English instructions, and handed the note to the boy who sped off like a shot. He turned to Leonardo. The bags under Gentile's brown eyes gave him the look of a Basset Hound. "*Sí?*"

I'm Leonardo Robustelli. Signor Moretti in Naples said I should ask for you."

Gentile grabbed a clipboard. "Which ship were you on?"

"The *Prinzessin Irene.*"

Gentile looked up. "That landed two weeks ago. Where have you been?"

"I was detained in quarantine."

Gentile took a half step back.

"I had pinkeye. It's okay now, see?"

Gentile squinted at Leonardo, but kept his distance. He raised his clipboard. "Ah, I see your name on the manifest. I have nothing for you today. Come back tomorrow morning before seven."

"Signor Moretti said you'd help me find room and board." Leonardo unfolded the steamship ticket carefully. He showed Gentile the stamped message.

"Did Signor Moretti explain how we work?"

"Not in detail."

"Well then let me tell you. I represent the Emigrants Industrial Savings Bank. The bank's only clients are Italians. Prospective employers approach the bank and request men for work. As the bank's agent, I dispatch you to jobs. The employer pays the bank, and we pay you. Signor Moretti advanced you a steamship ticket. That's $35. You should have the cost with interest repaid in six months. We take a finder's fee commission from your wages. If we arrange for room and board that's deducted as well. The net wage is paid to you in cash, or you have the option to leave your savings safely on deposit. Many of our clients make use of the bank's facility to send money to their families in Italy."

"Signor Moretti said that some jobs pay $2 per day. How much will I get?"

"Do you speak English?"

"Not well."

"Do you have any skills? For example, do you have experience as a mason, a seaman, or a shoemaker?"

"No."

"Well then you fall under the category of general laborer. The good news is that there are lots of jobs, but the pay is less than for a skilled worker. You'll receive about fifty cents a day, net. Once you've paid for the steamship ticket, your take goes up. Of course we continue to deduct our agent's percentage."

Leonardo's brow furrowed. "That's far less than $2 per day."

"Many men work six or eight months and return to Italy with a hundred dollars in their pocket. That's more money than they could've earned in Italy if even they could find work."

"How much commission do you take?"

"That's confidential."

"I should receive more money."

"We don't negotiate."

Leonardo crossed his arms.

Gentile pulled at his chin. "You're new to New York. Why don't you walk around and get a sense of the place. You can find room and board at 10 Spring Street." Gentile wrote on a piece of paper he handed to Leonardo. "Ask for Senora Medina and mention my name. Come back tomorrow ready to work."

Gentile's direction led Leonardo past dirt playgrounds and back alleys toward the human crush of tenement row in the Italian ghetto. Mulberry Street was a tangle of people, bicycles, and horse-drawn carts. Men were in animated conversation. Women in shawls, some with babies in their arms, carried straw baskets and negotiated with vendors in cloth caps who manned pushcarts. Girls in pigtails and dirty-faced boys shouted as they ran through the maze. Leonardo's nostrils were filled with the odor of manure piled against the curb like snow drifts. Flies that hovered around the fruit, vegetables, and manure bounced off him like black raindrops. He kept his mouth closed so as not to ingest unwanted protein. Leonardo heard Neapolitan spoken, and his step lightened. He walked through open racks of wares offered by the ground floor shops that lined both sides of the street. People peered down at him from tenement windows. Fire escapes were draped with beaten rugs and aired out bedding.

Leonardo passed a blind man selling pencils. He heard a voice behind him say, "You must have just stepped off the boat."

Leonardo spun, but it wasn't the blind man who'd spoken. Instead, it was a man stooped over like Atlas carrying the world. He had a full beard and smoked a black pipe. He wore two hats, a wool cap under a brimmed fedora. He wrapped himself in two overcoats. White lint stuck to him from head to toe as if he'd been rolled in flour. He stood in front of a bakery with a large picture window. Round and long loaves of bread were offered behind a painted sign, "Bread 5¢."

Leonardo said "What makes you say that?"

"You're dressed old-country. Italians who've been here a while dress like Americans. They shed their old clothes. I know." He pointed to a rickety spoke-wheel cart piled over with bloated burlap bags. The man laughed. He had no front teeth and, when he smiled, he looked like a theater comedy mask. "I'm an expert in what people throw away. Where are you from?"

"Capodimonte."

"Ah, *paisano*; Caserta is my home. I'm Guido Basso."

"Leonardo Robustelli, *piacere*."

They shook hands.

Basso said, "Where are you going?"

"Spring Street."

"It's not far. I'll show you."

Basso grabbed the long handles and pulled his cart. Leonardo walked beside him. The cowbell on the cart clanged as they walked.

Leonardo said, "You can make a living with garbage?"

"It keeps a cellar roof over my head. You have a job?"

"Not yet."

"Work with me. I can use a young back. I'll teach you the business and give you a quarter per day. When you're ready you can go out on your own. I make eight to ten dollars per week. Sometimes more. It's amazing what people throw away."

Leonardo smiled. "*Grazie*, but it's not for me."

Basso tilted his head. "Too proud, or you have a better prospect?"

"I have a *padrone* in New York."

"Really? But you understand that the *padroni* are thieves? They hook you with an advanced steamship ticket and afterwards they collect a commission on everything. Your wages, your room and board, if you keep cash on deposit, or if you send money to Italy. If you're not a barber, a shoemaker, or a mason, the *padroni* pay you pennies for hard manual labor."

"Maybe I'll find something better."

"Where? You can't join a union. The Irish control them. An Irish boss wouldn't hire an Italian for a leprechaun's pot of gold."

"So that's why you became a garbage man?"

"Partly. My spine is crooked as you can see. Ellis Island would've rejected me, so I smuggled myself into America through Canada. I arrived in New York with no means to find a job. The money I brought soon ran out. I couldn't communicate with Americans, and their manner showed they considered me beneath contempt. I was on the street, alone."

"I understand. What did you do?"

"I had no talent to play an instrument for spare change. The blind already sold pencils on corners. The streets were full of men who hawked peanuts or bananas. There were hordes of beggars."

"I see that some Italians open shops."

"You need capital and a family to help you before you can open a bakery, a grocery, or an artificial flower shop. As a lone entrepreneur, my best option was garbage. I'm my own *padrone*."

"True. What do you collect?"

"Everything I can sell. Glass can be recycled, bones carved for knife handles, even dead animal fur can be sold for clothing. Rags are my mainstay. I sell them to make cardboard or paper."

"You dig through alleys and refuse dumps?"

"Everyone does. So I try to have an edge. If I hear someone has died, I go to their apartment and express sympathy to the family. They keep what's useable or wearable, but something always gets thrown away and I get first pick."

"Then what?"

"I hang remnants on rope lines. The rain washes away the lice, the crusted filth, and human waste. The sun bleaches the cloth, and they're ready for sale."

"It's all the lint from the rags. That's why you look snow covered."

Basso laughed. "I've sucked in my share of cotton dust." He pointed. "There it is, 10 Spring Street."

Chapter 9

LEONARDO AND BASSO shook hands, and the ragman turned toward the Bowery. The tinkle of his cowbell faded as he walked around the corner. Leonardo stood before the three-story brownstone tenement. The slatted window shutters were closed. Clothing and bedding hung on a crisscross of lines between tenements and waved on the breeze like pennants on a ship. Garbage cans filled to overflow lined the streets. Cats spit at each other in conflict for the contents. Leonardo walked through a low black iron gate. Staccato shouts rang out from the basement a few steps below street level. The door was ajar. The sign above it said, "Ciro's"

As Leonardo entered, a brown furry hand grabbed his face. He jerked away and put his fingers to the scratch on his cheek. The monkey screeched and bared his teeth. The animal was dressed in an elf's peaked cap. His organ grinder owner, a stocky man with a mustache and a straw hat, held the animal's tether.

A buxom middle-aged woman with bare arms and graying hair shouted to the organ grinder, "Take that animal outside. He's scaring the customers."

The organ grinder recoiled at the woman's rebuke. "*Sì*, Senora Medina." He gave her a slight bow. He turned to Leonardo with an embarrassed smile. "*Scuzi*." He tugged on the monkey's leash. "Let's go." They backed into the street.

The woman brushed away a forelock with a wrist. She had a on a red apron and held a rolling pin. A mound of dough was on a table. Her hands and forearms were crusted with flour. "Signore, sit anywhere. Azzura will be with you in a moment."

Leonardo surveyed the scene. The basement was one large room. Beyond Isabella Medina, her husband, Ciro, sweated at a sizeable iron cook stove. He had thinning hair. He was wearing a white apron and stirring a huge caldron of red sauce with simmering meat while boiling pasta in another large pot of water. On the shelves above and around the stove were stacks of white dishes and straw-covered bottles of wine. Isabella rolled out dough and cut it into strips of pasta for the pot. Arrayed on both sides of the kitchen area were twenty to thirty men in work clothes sitting on chairs at wooden tables. Some ate, some played cards. A crowd gathered around two men playing *morra*. One man shouted, "*Cinque*," the other "*Otto*," as they thrust hands at each other, each man trying to guess the combined number of fingers displayed. The group of men who surrounded the players delighted in the game and waited for their turn. Everyone drank wine or beer. Pipe and cigar smoke were thick and competed with garlic for the dominant odor in the room. Leonardo looked closer at the knot of men around the *morra* game and saw the scarred face of Giuseppe Fontana with a fist full of money peering over the shoulders of the group. Leonardo called out and ran over. When Giuseppe recognized Leonardo, his face brightened, softening his scar. The two men embraced.

Giuseppe said, "I thought you were on a boat back to Italy."

"I had a touch of pinkeye. I was cured, and they let me out. What are you doing here?"

"I made connection with a New York Camorra gang. The boss gave me this *morra* game. I also run the *banco di lotto*. Wait."

A round of competition had ended. Giuseppe paid the winner and a new opponent stepped forward. Both players put up money with Giuseppe.

He said, "I take a bite from every round." The men's hand-thrusts and staccato shouts began again. "Where are you staying?"

Leonardo shrugged.

Giuseppe said, "Sit. Have something to eat. I live in a room upstairs. Stay with me."

"*Grazie.*"

Shouts rang out. Another round of *morra* was finished. Giuseppe paid the winner, and the competition continued.

Leonardo moved away and sat at a table with two men engaged in animated conversation while they forked into mounds of spaghetti with red sauce.

A soft voice over his shoulder said, "What will you have?"

Leonardo looked into jade-green eyes and long black hair. The woman looked seventeen. She wore a white pleated blouse with a mandarin collar and long dark skirt. She smiled.

He swallowed. "How much for a plate of spaghetti and a glass of wine?"

"Fifteen cents."

Leonardo fingered his blue envelope. "Okay."

"Did you just get off the boat?"

"You can tell from my clothes?"

She nodded. "What's your name?"

"Leonardo Robustelli."

"Azzura Medina. *Piacere.*"

"*Piacere.*"

Azzura said, "You're from Naples?"

"Capodimonte."

"My parents are from a town near Sorrento. I was born in New York."

"Your Italian is excellent."

"*Grazie.*" She smiled. "I'll get your food."

While Leonardo waited for Azzura to return, tattered men straggled through the front door; peddlers of artificial flowers, bootblacks, and a dirty-faced boy of twelve who lugged a huge harp for an old man. They all looked cold.

Azzura returned with Leonardo's meal. Her hand lightly brushed Leonardo's back when she placed the plate and cup on the wooden table. The sensation of her touch lingered.

She said, "Where will you work in New York?"

"I'm not sure. I have a *padrone* who'll get me a job, but it doesn't pay very well."

"Where will you sleep?"

"Here with my friend Giuseppe." Leonardo pointed.

"So I'll see you tomorrow? In the restaurant I mean."

"Yes."

Isabella Medina's booming voice rang out. "Azzura. What are you doing?"

Azzura jumped. "Mama, the man needs to pay for his meal."

"Get the money and tend to the other customers."

Azzura said, "I'm sorry, my mother doesn't want me to fraternize with the men."

Leonardo took out his blue envelope and gave Azzura a dollar. "Could we meet outside somewhere?"

Azzura made change. "My parents don't like me out of their sight."

"But maybe you can get away?" He smiled.

Azzura's eyes went down.

Isabella shouted, "Azzura."

Azzura had an embarrassed smile when she left. Senora Medina rolled dough and gave Leonardo a hard look.

Chapter 10

THE NEXT MORNING Leonardo arrived at Gentile's office at six-thirty in the morning. There were ten men in line ahead of him. Gentile called off their names and gave them job assignments.

Gentile said, "Robustelli, go to Siegel & Cooper, Sixth Avenue and 18th Street. Ask for Mr. Carson. You'll be part of the porter crew." Gentile handed Leonardo the paper authorization. "Next."

Leonardo said, "Excuse me, Signor Gentile, how much does it pay?"

Gentile looked annoyed. He flipped back a page on his clipboard. "Let me see, gross amount less steamship loan. Are you staying at Senora Medina's?"

"Yes, but I found a friend. I'm in his apartment, and I bought my own dinner."

"So no room and board. All right, let me calculate. That's sixty cents per day. Six days."

Leonardo frowned.

Gentile looked over his shoulder. "Next."

When Leonardo arrived at the department store, he asked a sales clerk and was directed to Mr. Carson. Carson was thin, blond, and spoke in a high-pitched voice. Leonardo showed him Gentile's authorization. "Oh yes, the new man. Fine." Carson looked around the store. He pointed. "See that man in the brown coveralls? That's Mr. Mazzali. He's the crew boss. Go see him."

Leonardo understood Carson's point more than his words. He walked up to Mazzali. "Signor Gentile sent me here, and Signor Carson told me to see you."

Mazzali looked at the paper. His eyes narrowed. "Gentile was supposed to give this job to my Cousin Leilo."

Leonardo straightened.

Mazzali said, "Have you ever done porter work before?"

"No."

"Here's a broom. Keep the aisles clean, but stay out of the customers' way. *Capisce?*"

"*Sí* Signore."

About an hour later Mazzali found Leonardo. "Mr. Carson wants a meeting with the porter staff, fourth floor. Follow me."

Leonardo, Mazzali, and the others of the porter crew assembled before Carson in front of his office.

Carson said, "Gentlemen, I've decided to shift all porter work to nights starting this evening. You won't be in the customers' way, and it'll be easier and quicker for you to clean. So leave at noon and return to the store at eight o'clock. If this is a problem for anyone, we'll get a replacement from Mr. Gentile. Are there any questions?"

Mazzali turned to Leonardo. "Did you get that?"

"I'm sorry, my English. I'm not sure."

"Carson said you can leave at noon today, but be back in the store by eight tomorrow morning. Okay?"

"Do I still get paid for a full day?"

"Absolutely. See you tomorrow."

When Leonardo returned to the store the next day he couldn't find Mazzali. None of the porters were around. He approached Mr. Carson.

Carson said, "So there you are."

"Sorry?"

"You missed work last night. I can't have unreliable people. Mr. Mazzali anticipated we'd be short of crew because of the change in schedule so he brought his Cousin Leilo. He did fine. As you can see, the store is spotless. You're no longer employed here."

"I don't understand."

Carson walked away.

Leonardo's ears got hot. He went to Gentile's office.

Gentile said, "What are you doing here?"

"Mazzali at the department store lied to me about the hours of work. Signor Carson fired me and gave my job to Mazzali's cousin, Leilo."

Gentile spread his palms. "You didn't understand Carson's English?"

Leonardo huffed and shook his head.

Gentile said, "Come back tomorrow. U.S. Biscuit Company needs someone to move boxes. The pay is less than the department store, but it's the best I have at the moment. Come before seven and I'll have the authorization for you."

"Is that all you can do for me?"

Gentile rolled his eyes. "Signor Robustelli, may I say that you've been a difficult client."

"But I lost my job because I was lied to."

"I told you that your lack of English skills would cost you. What do you want me to do?"

"Explain to Carson that I was deceived."

"Excuse me, but I must say this: Carson doesn't care. He just wants his floors cleaned. Leonardo or Leilo is all the same to him."

"It's outrageous."

"I'm sorry you feel that way. You're free to return to Italy. Of course, you still owe us for your steamship ticket, and you'll need $35 for the steerage fare home."

Leonardo's face flushed.

Gentile's voice softened. "I understand. You're a young man, and disappointment is new to you. But it's part of growing up." Gentile extended his arm. Leonardo backed away. Gentile sighed. "Return to Senora Medina's. Have something to eat. Get some sleep. This won't be the last job you'll be fired from. You need to recover and go on. Calm down, and come back tomorrow."

Leonardo headed back to Siegel & Cooper before the night shift crew arrived. He spotted Mazzali on the street and confronted him.

As soon as Mazzali saw him, he raised his palms. "Don't start trouble. I did it for my cousin."

Leonardo's smile was cold. "Sure." His punch struck like a cobra, and Mazzali hit the concrete like he had rubber legs. Mazzali clutched his face, and blood flowed between his fingers.

Leonardo strode away.

When Leonardo walked into Ciro's, Giuseppe was running the *morra* game. He saw Leonardo. "How was work?"

Leonardo slumped into a chair. "I was fired."

"*Merda.* Is that what happened to your hand?"

Leonardo flexed his fingers. "Yeah."

A round of the game finished. Giuseppe paid the winner and took the next bets. Leonardo's chin rested in his hands.

Giuseppe said, "Hey, I have an idea. Tomorrow I see my *guappo*, Frank Rizzo. He's promised me a union card on the waterfront."

Leonardo raised his head. "Those are the best paying jobs. I thought Italians were frozen out of the union trades by the Irish?"

"*Sí.*" Giuseppe winked. "Unless you have a friend." He sat next to Leonardo. "Why don't we go together? Maybe he'll help you, too?"

Leonardo brightened. "That would be great."

Giuseppe grasped Leonardo shoulder. "Okay then." There were shouts of victory from the *morra* game. "Excuse me. I need to pay a winner."

When Giuseppe left Azzura came over to Leonardo's table. She smiled. "Did you find work today?"

Leonardo pursed his lips. "Found and lost."

"I'm sorry. You don't seem disappointed."

"Maybe it'll work out. My friend Giuseppe has a contact who could get both of us a union job."

"Really? That's good money."

"How about a glass of wine to celebrate?"

Azzura smiled. "Coming right up."

Chapter 11

WHEN CARLO MAZZI ARRIVED in New York, his cousin, Alberto Leggiéri brought him to his apartment. Leggiéri rested his feet atop a wooden crate next to the coal stove. His hair was oiled and neatly parted. He wore a wool vested suit and white shirt. A perfumed handkerchief was tucked into his breast pocket. His neck scarf was skewered with a ruby and diamond gold pin that in reality was red and clear glass set in brass. The *Bolletino Della Sera* was open on his lap. He read the headline to Carlo. "Murder of Freighter *Dinnamare* Engineer."

Carlo sat on a spindle-back wooden chair and leaned his chin on his palm.

Alberto continued. "Chief engineer, Günther Krause, was found stabbed to death in his cabin. Police suspect Enzo Di Stefano, a seaman who boarded in Palermo. Di Stefano was given a shore pass in New York and is missing." Alberto's eyes rose to meet Carlo's. "You killed the engineer?"

"The *sfacim* intended to alert the New York police about me. I would've been sent back to Italy."

Alberto frowned. "Maybe someone saw us meet on the pier. The cops will be after both of us."

Carlo said, "Don't worry. We weren't followed. I burned the Di Stefano papers in that coal stove. There's no way to trace me."

"Us, you mean." Alberto kneaded his chin. "So you need documents. I have an attorney who can help. Who will you be now?"

"How about Carlo Leggiéri?"

Alberto shrugged and nodded.

Carlo stretched. The men sat at a coarse-wooden table in the front room that featured the apartment's only window, streaked panes that overlooked a row of outhouses in the interior yard. A dinged tin pot sat atop the coal stove. In the chipped-paint room in the back, two burlap bags of rags lay on the floor as mattresses.

Carlo said, "Alberto, the pigs on my father's farm live better than you."

Alberto sniffed. "We don't all have rich fathers. Some of us work for a living."

"What sort of work?"

"You'll find out this morning."

Alberto and his father immigrated to New York from Naples and lived atop a Five Points Saloon, Black Billy's. When Alberto's father was killed falling off a scaffold, Billy gave Alberto a few coins to serve drunks five-cent rum. When he wasn't with Billy, Alberto earned a dollar a week blackening boots or delivering newspapers. As Alberto wandered farther from the tenement, he observed that the best-dressed teens weren't violent types, but the subtle players of the pickpocket trade. Alberto's age and doe brown eyes permitted him to get close to a mark. He'd spot a man who carried bank notes loosely or had a watch chain hung from his vest. Under the wave of a newspaper, Alberto would separate the man from his valuables. Black Billy taught him that everyone steals. The goal in life was to steal more than was stolen from you. But pickpocket work led to frequent arrests and juvenile work detention. Alberto turned to more sophisticated frauds that didn't expose him to risk. That's when he met Andrew Tucker.

The sign on the Broadway building third floor office said, "Andrew Tucker, Attorney at Law." Tucker was bald and wore a brown-checked suit that bulged everywhere.

Alberto introduced Carlo and they sat in padded chairs in front of Tucker's walnut desk.

Tucker said, "So you're without papers? Would you like me to create documents that prove you're an American citizen?"

Carlo shrugged. "I don't expect to be in New York that long."

"Even so, with citizenship you can vote. More to the point, you can sell your vote. Congressmen do favors for their friends."

"I see what you mean. Political help could come in handy."

"Exactly. We'll take care of that after our meeting with Mrs. Withers. Alberto, what have you told Carlo?"

"Nothing yet." Alberto turned to his cousin. "There's a little business we need to do with Mrs. Withers. Leave the talking to us."

There was a quiet tap at the door.

Tucker said, "She's here."

Evelyn Withers was thin, in her forties. She wore a white-feathered hat, high neckline printed dress, and carried a dark muff purse. Tucker pulled out a chair for her. Raw chapped hands and delicate fingers took out a small white handkerchief from her purse.

After introductions she said, "May I call you Carlo?"

"Of course."

"Alberto has been such a friend to me. I was walking in Central Park under the tree canopy near 59th Street. The wind sent a shiver through me, and before I knew it tears flowed. I couldn't stop myself even in broad daylight." Mrs. Withers's face colored. "I wanted to run and hide. Then Alberto spoke to me." She touched his forearm. Her voice cracked. "He asked what was wrong." She dabbed her eyes.

Alberto took her hand. "Unfortunately, Evelyn's husband, Herbert, had just passed away."

"It was sudden." She took a deep breath. "My husband left me two hundred dollars, but that wasn't enough. Before I was married I worked as a typist, and I was hopeful I could return to a clerical position. A company asked me to take a typing test." Her voice fell off. "It was a disaster. My eyes were worse than I realized."

Tucker had a pitcher of water on his desk. He poured her a glass.

"When I realized I couldn't work, God help me, I allowed myself to despair. Then, like an angel, Alberto appeared." She took a sip of water. "Alberto was kind. He walked me to a park bench nearby. We sat, and he listened."

Alberto said, "Once I understood Evelyn's problem, I thought that Mr. Tucker could help her, so I arranged a meeting."

Tucker said, "Yes, by a fortuitous set of circumstances, I've come to represent one of the owners of a property in Harlem, Joshua Cooke. He and his brother, Seth, own a nice house as tenants in common. Their mother passed and left them the home. Unfortunately, there's disagreement between the brothers. Joshua wants to sell the house, and Seth doesn't. I've been retained by Joshua to settle the matter in court. I'm authorized to borrow the money needed to pursue the case. Joshua put his share of the house up as collateral."

Alberto said, "I committed to lend $50 to Mr. Tucker, but I knew he needed more funds. When I understood Evelyn's dilemma, I suggested she invest as well."

Mrs. Withers managed a tight smile.

Tucker said, "Mrs. Withers, as I committed to you at our first meeting, here's the affidavit from Mr. Cooke that gives me the authority to borrow on his behalf pledging his share of the house as security." Tucker handed her the paper. She squinted at it. "And here's the promissory note, also signed by Mr. Cooke, which guarantees you $250 in four months' time in exchange for $200 today."

Mrs. Withers took both papers into her lap. She looked them over carefully. "Yes, this looks in order."

Tucker handed similar documents to Alberto, "You'll receive $62.50 in four months for the $50 you give me today."

Alberto took out his wallet, counted out $50, and placed it on the desk.

Tucker folded Alberto's money and placed the bills inside a metal case with a latch cover.

Alberto said, "Mr. Tucker, you indicated that there would be more opportunities to make loans on an ongoing basis."

"Absolutely, and for Mrs. Withers as well." Tucker turned toward her. "I have another real estate deal in the works that should bear fruit about the time this promissory note comes due. I expect your loans could profit you at least $100 this year."

Mrs. Withers's smile widened. "Very well." She reached into her purse and withdrew a stack of notes. She hesitated, then handed them to Tucker.

Tucker accepted the money with both hands with the solemnity of a priest. He placed Mrs. Withers's $200 into the metal box. "Congratulations to both of you." He rose and shook Alberto's hand. He made a small bow to Mrs. Withers.

Mrs. Withers stood. "Well, that's that." She turned to Alberto. "Will I see you later?"

"I promised I'd show Carlo around New York today. May I call on you at home tomorrow?"

"Yes, come for tea." She extended her hand to him.

He kissed it. "You're most kind." His eyes rose to meet hers. "Until tomorrow."

Mrs. Withers floated out of the office.

When her footfalls on the linoleum hallway faded, Tucker opened his metal box and took out Alberto's original fifty dollars plus twelve more. He pulled two quarters out of his vest pocket and handed the money to Alberto.

Carlo slapped his knee. "Alberto, you cheat widows for a living?"

Alberto grimaced.

Carlo said, "What happens in four months?"

Tucker said, "We postpone payment. We give her checks that bounce. What's she going to do, sue us?"

Carlo shook his head.

"Alberto, does your cousin want to do business with us?"

Carlo ignored Tucker.

Tucker said, "I don't want trouble. If we can't be friends, we can't do business together."

Alberto squeezed Carlo's arm. "Everything's okay, right?"

Carlo nodded.

Tucker said, "Good. Because you know that thing we talked about? The preacher will arrive tonight. Carlo can be part of it. If he wants."

"Yeah, great. We'll talk about it later." Alberto pulled Carlo's arm. "Let's go."

When they were on the street, Alberto confronted Carlo. "I can see you don't like Tucker. But I need him to make money in this city."

"Alberto, you're family, I won't interfere with your business. But stealing money from widows is wrong."

Alberto's voice rose. "You forget that your mother came from the poor side of the family. Rather than scrounge in the dirt on another man's land, my father came to America. When he died, I had a good mentor. After you're here a while you'll understand that the Germans, Irish, even northern Italians shut southern Italians out of work at decent pay. I don't beg for scraps; I take. You have a rich father. You went to university. Even so, you became Signor Di Stefano. You can't judge me."

Carlo's voice had an edge. "Don't mention that name. Di Stefano is a wanted man." Carlo softened his tone. "And whatever I did was for family or honor."

"Okay, okay."

"My father would've helped you if you'd approached him."

"Really? Why don't you help me now? You heard Tucker mention the deal? Read this." Alberto handed Carlo a paper.

Take Back Your Life!

Do you face financial ruin? You deserve a second chance.

I deal in a fungible commodity that will solve your financial problems. If you struggle emotionally with crushing indebtedness, strike a blow against a Federal Government that compounds your woes.

A minimum investment of $100 gets you $400. Maximum $5,000 returns $20,000. Act now. Stock is limited.

Think of your children.

I take an oath before God to supply you with the means to save your family and your fortune!

Reply by Telegraph ONLY with the words "Financial Freedom"

To: A. B. Andrew, 200 Broadway, New York

Carlo spread his hands. "What's this?"

"It's a circular I wrote. I send it all over the United States. *Bradstreet's* lists business failures. I send it to anyone in financial trouble. Word spreads."

"And what's the 'fungible commodity'?"

"What do you think?"

Carlo scratched his cheek. "Counterfeit money? There's a huge amount of counterfeit dollars sent to New York from Italy."

"Good guess. You're almost right. We tell responders that I'm in contact with an agent who has acquired discarded U.S.

Treasury plates. We offer to sell counterfeit money indistinguishable from genuine currency."

"But you don't possess old Treasury plates. So how does it work?"

"We tell the mark to come to New York and examine the merchandise. They can walk away if they don't approve the quality."

"But without Treasury plates, you risk they'll be disappointed and not pay."

Alberto laughed. "We show them notes produced from Treasury plates. There's no risk that they won't like the quality."

"Wait a minute."

"Carlo, we show them genuine currency. Most marks take one look and want to corner the market on our trade."

"Obviously you don't sell real money for twenty-five cents on the dollar."

"We pull a switch before they leave. The mark walks out with a bag full of blank paper."

"Who have you done this with?"

"Many people. Last week it was a bank employee from Chicago who'd embezzled funds and needed to square accounts."

"Aren't the authorities aware of what's going on? When you mail your flyers, you can't be sure to whom they're passed. You don't worry that your prospective clients might be police?"

"Of course. But there are two special aspects to this con. If a mark gives us a hard time, we have police on the payroll who come in and hustle him out of New York. If the mark's a cop, he's less likely to arrest one of his own. Also the mark's intent is to buy counterfeit money. That's a felony. The courts don't prosecute criminals who steal from criminals. Even if somehow we're arrested, we go free."

Carlo said, "So what do you need from me?"

"I get ten percent for writing and distributing the circular. If, in addition, I put cash at risk, my take goes up. I have $80. How much money do you have?"

"Two hundred dollars."

"Give it to me, and I'll split the profit with you."

"This is for the deal Tucker mentioned?"

"Yeah, a preacher from Buffalo needs to get his church out of debt."

"A pastor wants to purchase counterfeit money?"

Alberto smiled. "Everyone's a crook."

"All right. I'm in."

* * *

Pastor Isaiah Spencer was wire thin with little hair and a pallid complexion. Alberto brought Spencer to an office near Grand Central Station.

Tucker extended his hand. "Please call me Mr. Andrew. You've met Mr. Alberto, and that's Mr. Carlo."

"Err, of course." He smiled like he was greeting parishioners on Sunday.

Tucker took a wad of money from his pocket and handed it to Spencer. "Pastor, please examine the bills."

Spencer put on wire-rimmed glasses. He counted the money with a look of concentration. "These notes look like genuine currency. I'm impressed."

"Thank you." Tucker extended his palm, and Spencer handed back the bills. Tucker brought out two more stacks. He counted out the amount as Spencer watched. "That's sixteen hundred." Tucker produced a stack of butcher paper. "I'll hide the bills by wrapping them as three bundles. You understand that the authorities must not find this counterfeit money in your possession?"

"Of course."

"Right. Now I'll put them into this satchel." Tucker placed the bricks of money into a plain brown-cloth bag and closed it with a snap.

Alberto gave Carlo the sign.

Carlo stepped forward. "Excuse me, Pastor Spencer."

Spencer turned to Carlo and raised his eyebrows. "Yes?"

Carlo moved closer. "I'm sorry, but may I ask you a personal question?"

"Of course, my son."

Carlo pursed his lips. "I apologize for asking."

Spencer put his hand on Carlo's arm. "Please, ask your question."

Alberto moved to block the Pastor's view of Tucker. As he did, Tucker reached below the table and switched the bag with the money for an identical bag that contained bricks of blank paper.

Carlo said, "As a man of the cloth, how do you rationalize trading in counterfeit currency?"

Spencer's brow furrowed. "You're right. It was a difficult decision. The economic times hit my parishioners hard. They simply don't have the money to keep the church going. My choice was to abandon my flock or find the means to go on. I believe I've chosen the greater good."

"Of course. I understand. Thank you."

Spencer gave Carlo a wry smile.

Tucker cleared his throat. "Pastor Spencer, may I trouble you for payment?"

"By all means. That was twenty-five cents on the dollar." Spencer counted out the four hundred dollars and handed it to Tucker.

Alberto took Spencer's arm. "I'll walk you to the train. You may want to send the satchel to Buffalo by Adams Express. That way there's no chance the bills can be discovered on your person."

"Good idea."

"Their office is in this building. I'll take you."

Chapter 12

IN NAPLES, Captain Ceruti's case load included the *carabinieri's* investigation of Camorra criminal activities. The Camorra was an underworld of clan-based mobs often at odds with each other for the spoils of illegal activities in and around the city. The Zangara gang was the Camorra family located in the Torre Annunziata section of Naples. Giulietta Zangara, the *guappo* or head of the family, was a savior for most of the residents of Torre Annunziata. The clan was the primary employer in the district, and Zangara would personally hand out food to the poor. Some years before, a rival Naples gang, the Russomannos of Santa Lucia, attempted to decapitate and neutralize the Zangaras. Giulietta Zangara's father, then the *guappo*, was gunned down and her brother was stabbed to death in prison. Zangara took the reins amidst male derision that a woman could successfully lead a criminal enterprise. No woman had ever held a position of importance in any Camorra mob. Zangara had the man who shot her father captured and brought to her. She gutted him like a fish and had his body dumped at the *Fontana del Gigante*. She arranged to have her brother's killer strangled in prison. She unleashed the Torre Annunziata *soldati*, and more than twenty of the rival Russomanno clan were killed on the street. Having established her ruthlessness, Zangara sought compromise over the continued violence both with the Russomannos and in her dealings with the other Naples clans. She avoided confrontation with Ceruti and the *carabinieri*. If any Zangara gang members were arrested, their families were financially supported. Her motto was, "He who is silent will be rewarded. He who speaks will be killed."

* * *

As Carlo and Alberto completed their con of Pastor Spencer in New York, a grizzled farm worker on the Mazzi Estate in Naples sat on a brightly painted *carretta* that carried fifty-kilo sacks of flour intended for the market in Naples. Salvatore Mazzi slapped the donkey's rump and sent them off. Mazzi held a shotgun under his arm. He turned to supervise a new farm hand feeding a mare. The horse stomped and whinnied. "Put the feed bag straps over her ears. When she's finished, place a pail of water on the ground next to her."

The mare dropped manure. Mazzi looked up.

Captain Ceruti approached on his chestnut stallion. The captain dismounted and Mazzi invited him onto the portico. Ceruti accepted a glass of blood orange juice.

Ceruti said, "You're carrying a weapon. Expecting trouble?"

Mazzi said, "We live in dangerous times. After what happened to Pero Silvestri, I decided to take an extra precaution."

"I understand." Ceruti sipped some juice. "Any word on when Carlo will be home?"

"Ah, no. He's probably entertaining French ladies on the Champs-Elysees."

Mazzi's black cat sprung onto the loggia with a mouse in its mouth. He dropped it at his master's feet and purred.

Ceruti consulted his notepad. His tone was nonchalant. "I received an interesting report from Sicily this week. A murder was committed on the steamship, *Dinnamare*, sailing from Palermo to New York." He eyed Mazzi over the glass.

Mazzi was stoic.

Ceruti said, "The chief engineer, Krause, was stabbed to death in his cabin and found when the ship docked in America.

The New York police suspect a man who boarded the ship in Palermo, Enzo Di Stefano." Ceruti's eyes rose to meet Mazzi's. "The *Dinnamare* set sail again before I could speak to the captain, Diehl, a German."

"Why are you telling me this?"

"My counterpart in Palermo questioned a seaman who left the *Dinnamare*, Erik Lund. His description of Di Stefano was remarkably similar to Carlo's."

Mazzi said, "Carlo is in Europe."

"Of course. Even so, it's an odd coincidence. I'll speak to Diehl when the *Dinnamare* returns to Sicily." Ceruti looked out over the horizon. "I suppose that one way to smuggle someone out of Italy would be to bribe a freighter captain to take him on as a seaman. Once the ship arrived at its destination, a shore pass would get him into a new port, and he could disappear."

"That's an interesting theory. Would you like more juice?"

Ceruti smiled. "No, *grazie*." He put his notepad away. "Don Mazzi, I have another concern. The Silvestri brothers are making independent inquiries about their father's murder. They don't think I'm doing my job, and I'm afraid they're bitter. The dam that Pero Silvestri built to block the water from coming onto your property has been destroyed."

"It was an illegal structure."

"Perhaps. But the dam's removal and Carlo's disappearance have raised the Silvestris' suspicions that someone in the Mazzi clan either killed their father or ordered him murdered."

"Carlo didn't disappear. He's traveling on business."

Ceruti puffed out a breath. "I'll give you the same warning I gave the Silvestris. A vendetta between your two families will be disastrous for both."

"Thanks for your concern."

Ceruti stood. He looked like he wanted to say something, but he shook his head and strode to his horse.

Salvatore sent word for Vincenzo to come to the estate. He arrived in his donkey cart the next afternoon. The brothers sat on the portico.

Salvatore said, "Ceruti has all but confirmed that Carlo was on the *Dinnamare*. He murdered the chief engineer on the ship."

Vincenzo hit his knee with a fist. "You told him to keep to himself."

"I'm sure Carlo had a good reason for the killing. Could the Silvestris have known Carlo was on the boat and paid the engineer to assassinate him?"

Vincenzo sat back. "We acted quickly. Was there time for the Silvestris to know of our plan?"

Salvatore shrugged. "Maybe if the attorney talked to the Silvestris after I left."

"So Ceruti confirmed that the Silvestri brothers plot revenge against us. We need to warn Carlo that they know he's in New York."

"I'll contact Carlo through the bank. We must assume that even the rocks have been hired to kill us. We need to take extraordinary precautions."

"What do you propose?"

"The only solution is to kill the Silvestri brothers."

Vincenzo stiffened. He looked into the distance. "You're right. But you're not in shape for the job." He faced his brother. "I'll do it."

Salvatore shook his head. "I don't think the Silvestris will let you get near them. And there are two of them. We need to be subtle, and we need help. I'll go to the Torre Annunziata Camorra clan. The Zangaras are the most powerful mob in Naples."

Vincenzo's eyes widened. "Are you sure you want to cross that line?"

"I need to remove the Silvestris' threat against Carlo once and for all."

Vincenzo rubbed his cheek. He nodded.

When Vincenzo left the farm, Domenico and Bartolomeo Silvestri were on a hill that overlooked the road. Domenico said, "That's the brother."

Bartolomeo's gaze narrowed. He nodded.

Chapter 13

SALVATORE MAZZI walked slowly down the steps of a steep
Naples street in the Torre Annunziata neighborhood that
looked like a stretched accordion's bellows. A dozen playful
children shouted and dodged around him like spirits on the
wind. Garments flapped in the breeze on clotheslines strung
between multistory gray-faced buildings. Women stood on
balconies and stared down at Mazzi as they shook out rugs. He
passed a café. Three ragged men shoveled macaroni into their
mouths with fingers at an outdoor table. They paused their
meal and eyed him as he walked by. The open door at his
destination had a small overhang to keep out the rain. Two
Camorra thugs in rough clothes with suspicious eyes leaned on
the wall on either side of the door. Mazzi asked for "*La
Senora*," and one of the men motioned for him to follow. He
escorted him inside, and the second man followed. Mazzi
removed his hat. He was ushered into a living room. Giulietta
Zangara sat on a floral armchair like the Queen of Sheba. Her
white complexion was attractive under a mane of black hair.
She was in her forties. A long blue and white dress hung down
to her shoes. The room had a china cabinet against a wall with
dishes set on edge for display and a few ruby and cobalt
Murano glass vases inside. Behind Zangara were a window and
a door that opened to a courtyard garden. The scent in the air
was fresh cut roses. A quiet girl of about twelve with short
black hair, Zangara's niece, arranged the long stem red flowers
in a glass vase. She placed the arrangement on a stand next to
the *guappo* of the Camorra clan in Torre Annunziata. Mazzi

looked into Zangara's face and understood her nickname, eyes of stone.

Zangara gestured for Mazzi to sit in a chair across from her. The two men took wooden armchairs on either side of him. "Don Mazzi, would you like coffee or juice?"

"A small coffee."

While they waited to be served, Zangara gazed at Mazzi with a half smile. The two thugs on either side of him fidgeted. The room was hot. They sat in silence. A fly buzzed and banged against the closed window. Outside, Mazzi heard a mother call out for her son, "Carlo, Carlo."

When the coffees arrived, Zangara waved her niece from the room. "Don Mazzi, I'm honored by your visit."

"*Grazie*, Donna Zangara."

Zangara sipped her coffee. Her lips retained the enigmatic smile.

Mazzi said, "Donna Zangara, I have a problem. A family whose *pater familias* was murdered thinks that our clan had some involvement. The two sons can't be reasoned with. My family needs protection."

Zangara finished her coffee and replaced the cup in the saucer. The stone eyes skewered Mazzi. "The Silvestris want you dead."

Mazzi stiffened.

Zangara's smile widened. "We hear everything. The Silvestris have aligned themselves with the Russomannos from Santa Lucia. You're right to be concerned."

Mazzi swallowed.

Zangara leaned on her hand. "Fortunately for you the Santa Lucia mob has given us other reasons to oppose them. If we get involved, there will be blood, and that costs a lot of money."

"What do you want from me?"

"A man with your wealth and influence can help us in many ways. We'll ask for favors when we need them."

"In exchange, you'll eliminate the threat to my family?"

"We'll eliminate the source of the threat. Do we have a deal?"

Mazzi ran his hand through his hair. His palm was damp with sweat. He stood. "*Sí*, Senora."

Chapter 14

FRANK RIZZO was Giuseppe's *guappo*, head of the Mulberry Street Camorra gang. Like Giuseppe, Rizzo was put on a boat by the Naples chief of police with the warning never to return. Hungry, he had to make a living. He hit the Little Italy streets and became a rag picker. He had no cart, but carried his junk in a bloated burlap bag. Lugging loads strengthened him. Sometimes he fought other rag pickers for what could be scavenged. There was a garage on Delancey Street that held illegal boxing matches. On occasion he'd sneak a peek inside to watch one man impose his will on another. One morning he uncovered the rags of a diseased man who'd died steeped in his own filth. Rizzo retched at the odor. He tossed aside his junk, walked into the boxing garage, and up to the promoter, Maxie Shapiro. Shapiro had been a successful middleweight and scraped together enough money to buy the garage. He was a Jew in his mid-forties, with curly reddish brown hair, a cauliflower ear, and a nose nearly flattened on his face. Rizzo told him he'd had amateur bouts in Italy. Shapiro gave him a look like he wasn't that stupid, but threw some boxing gloves at him and told him to get into the ring. Rizzo was put up against a white-as-milk, skinny legs Irish kid. Rizzo charged and beat him into a cowering blob of sobbing flesh. Shapiro had to pull Rizzo off his bloodied opponent. Shapiro gave Rizzo a silver dollar and told him to come back the next evening ready to box. Rizzo's Friday night match was a tar-black semi-pro with the experience of twenty club fights. Rizzo took three punches for every one he gave. His face streamed blood, but he knocked his opponent out in the fifth round. Rizzo was the betting long shot, and he received tips from the gamblers who'd won. Rizzo earned more money in an hour than in six months toting rags. The back slaps and "atta boys" puffed out his chest. Shapiro told him that if he stuck around he'd teach him some defense.

Shapiro allowed Rizzo to sleep on a cot in the garage and gave him a few bucks a week to guard the place at night. During the next year, Rizzo had a series of successful bouts even against bigger, heavier kids, but then he drew a fight with an Orca-tough German light heavyweight who turned his face into a mass of blood and stopped him in the fifteenth round. That night, Shapiro talked to Rizzo while he patched his cuts.

"Look, Frank, you're a *mensch*. You know I love you, but if you keep taking these beatings, your brain will be scrambled, and all you'll be good for is to empty spittoons. You need work that requires your toughness but doesn't rip your face to shit. *Capeesh?*"

Rizzo's bruises cried out in his head. He nodded.

"Good. There's a guy I want you to meet. He's Camorra. You know, a *paisan*."

When Rizzo was inducted into the Mulberry Street mob, the head was Luca Pellegrino, a large clean-shaven man with eyes that stared like lit cigarettes. Rizzo's toughness was valued by Pellegrino, and he was recruited for personal protection. Pellegrino wore a neck to groin chain-mail vest that saved him from at least one stabbing assassination attempt. The job of protecting Pellegrino had become unattractive to most gang members as a string of previous bodyguards had been killed in failed attempts on his life. Rizzo found slip-streaming in the lifestyle of a boss attractive, eating, drinking, and carousing alongside Pellegrino while shadowing him around Manhattan. The experience tutored Rizzo in the gang's business and he learned how activities were administered. The main source of

Pellegrino's income was prostitution and running what was called the Manhattan branch of the Royal Italian Lottery, selling thousands of tickets in Little Italy for a monthly drawing. Pellegrino had a favorite working girl, dark and curvy with a fiery personality. She took a liking to Rizzo and, against his better judgment, Frank fell in love. One evening Pellegrino and the woman had a loud argument about the other men in her life, and in a drunken rage, Pellegrino slit her throat with a straight razor. When Rizzo came upon the scene, he drew his revolver. Pellegrino wasn't wearing his armor, and Rizzo shot him through the heart. Rizzo assumed command of the gang's activities and no one challenged him for *guappo* in the Lower East Side.

The sky was angry, and there were lightning flashes in the distance. The Italian social club on Mulberry Street was on the ground floor of a tenement. Overhead, an Italian flag snapped in the wind. A handful of men sat outside, drank coffee, and scowled at anyone who walked past. Giuseppe nodded to them as he and Leonardo reached the door.

Giuseppe stopped. "Frank Rizzo's nickname is 'hole in the head,' but nobody dares to call him that to his face. Speak when you're spoken to and address him as 'Signor Rizzo.'"

Two small windows limited the interior light. The wide room smelled of ten-cent cigars. A small bar was in the far corner. Men sat at round tables and talked with animated hand gestures. Some played cards. Some drank coffee or beer. The place buzzed like a timber saw.

Frank Rizzo sat alone at a corner table. He wore a suit and tie with a red boutonnière. He had a swarthy complexion and a depression in the upper portion of his brow like he'd been hit with a ball peen hammer.

Giuseppe took off his newsboy cap. "*Buon giorno*, Signor Rizzo. This is a friend of mine, Leonardo Robustelli."

Leonardo bowed.

Rizzo frowned. He directed both men to sit.

A greasy-haired waiter put down three small coffees on a tile-top table. The saucers each had a sliver of lemon peel. There was a bottle of anisette.

Rizzo poured a little anisette into his black coffee.

Giuseppe said, "I hope it's okay that I brought Leonardo. He and I traveled on the same steamship to New York."

Rizzo's eyes rose and surveyed Leonardo. "Where are you from?"

"Capodimonte."

Rizzo leaned back. "Are you *carabinieri* or New York police?"

Leonardo's eyes widened. Giuseppe started to speak, but Rizzo held up his hand. "Are you?"

"No, Signor Rizzo."

Rizzo nodded. He leaned forward and stirred his coffee. "Giuseppe, your friend looks nervous. Are you sure he's not a cop?"

"No way. He's just a kid from Naples."

"You understand that you're responsible for him."

Giuseppe's face lost color.

Rizzo looked hard at Leonardo. "If you're a cop, or if you ever talk about me or my business, I'll cut out your liver and feed it to the dogs. *Capisce*?"

Leonardo swallowed. "Signor Rizzo, I won't say anything to anybody. I just need a job."

Rizzo nodded. "So you're a hard worker? That's a nice quality in a young man. Let me see your hands." Leonardo held them palms up. Rizzo grabbed them like a vice. "What happened to your knuckles?"

"Some bastard."

"Good." Rizzo smiled. "These will get dirty. Okay?"

"No problem, Signor Rizzo."

Rizzo released Leonardo. "Are you ready to work on the docks?"

"Absolutely."

"Longshoremen are a rough crowd. You may need to bust heads."

"No problem."

Rizzo leaned back. He stared at Leonardo and sipped his coffee. "Okay. We'll see what we can do." He pointed at Giuseppe. "You'll get $18 per week as a stevedore. You each kick back $5 per week to me. That's $10 every Monday. I don't want to come looking for you."

"Sure. Signor Rizzo."

"Come back Friday morning."

Chapter 15

FRANK RIZZO entered an office with the sign, "International Longshoremen's Association, Local 791." Dust twinkled in the sunlit air, and the room smelled like dirty socks. A half dozen men lounged on benches and eyed him with venomous expressions. Rizzo strode up to a woman with tightly curled brown hair sitting behind a desk.

"Frank Rizzo. Here to see Jimmy Doyle."

"Do you have an appointment?"

"He'll see me."

The woman's mouth puckered like she would throw him a kiss. She rose and went into the closed office behind her. When she emerged, her brow was troubled. "You can go in"

Jimmy Doyle was a florid heavyset man with a burst-capillary nose. He had a mug of coffee on his desk. His brow glistened with sweat. "What do you want?"

Rizzo said, "Do you know who I am?"

"I've heard of you."

"Good. I have two friends who need union cards."

"Are they Italian?"

Rizzo tilted his head. "What do you think?"

"You know the rules. Whites only. No Negroes and no Italians."

Rizzo's forehead scar turned crimson. "You insult me to my face?"

Doyle sputtered. "I didn't mean anything. The union makes the rules. I was just repeating what everybody says."

"You should watch your mouth."

"Okay, sorry."

"Like I was saying, two friends of mine need union cards."

"I can't do it. The membership will hang me if I give jobs to Italians."

Rizzo sat back. "This is a nice office. You must make a decent living." Rizzo picked up a black and white framed photograph from the desk, a smiling woman with two small children. "You have a beautiful family. Do they live in Manhattan?"

Doyle gulped his coffee like a shot of booze. His voice had a nervous quiver. "What are you saying?"

"Come on, a smart guy like you doesn't need me to paint him a watercolor. Give me two union memberships, Giuseppe Fontana and Leonardo Robustelli."

"I don't know."

"You don't want me leaving this office empty-handed. I'll deal with your successor."

Doyle wiped his forehead. "Okay." He opened the top drawer of his desk. He hesitated. "There'll be an avalanche of shit over this."

"I don't have all day."

Doyle took out two blank cards. He signed them and threw them across the desk.

Rizzo stood. "These guys will 'shape' at Pier 59. Make sure they work tonight and every night." He turned on his heel and left the door open on his way out.

Doyle called out to his secretary. "I need to see Kevin Clancy."

Kevin Clancy, the Pier 59 boss, was a gone-to-seed redhead in his fifties. He arrived in Doyle's office and slouched in a chair.

Doyle said, "I gave union cards to Fontana and Robustelli. They'll shape up tonight. Put them to work."

"Are you crazy? Italians? What'd you do that for?"

Doyle huffed. "Frank Rizzo came to see me. He's Camorra. He threatened my family. I don't want that kind of trouble."

"The other guys won't stand for Italians getting their jobs."

"I know."

Clancy said, "Do I at least get a kickback from the dagos?"

"Not these two."

"So you just hand me this bag of crap?"

"Yeah, well, shit flows downstream."

"There'll be trouble."

"I gave Rizzo the cards. You put them to work. After that it's not my problem."

"So if I get them to quit on their own you're off the hook?"

"You're not as dumb as you look."

The waterfront near Pier 59 was a tangle of rail yards, streets jammed with wagons, and dark saloons. Men loitered outside the bars and gave the once over to anyone who passed.

Giuseppe stopped Leonardo. "Do you carry a knife?"

"No."

"You must."

The two men walked up to a weather-beaten wooden shack at the foot of 18th Street. There was a single ship dockside. A group of men with gloves hanging from their back pockets, some with bailing hooks, stood around and talked. When Giuseppe and Leonardo arrived, they were given dour stares.

Giuseppe leaned toward Leonardo. "I worked on the docks in Naples. Follow my lead."

Clancy emerged from the shack with a paper in his hand. Someone said, "Clancy's out," and the men squeezed forward to get into his field of sight.

Clancy peered over the men with a look of disdain. "Kelly, take the forward winch. Connelly, take the aft winch." He called out seven more Irish names and assigned them to the loading dock or to topside hatches. "Fontana and Robustelli, take number five hold."

Someone from the crowd shouted, "What is Clancy doing giving dagos jobs?" There was a collective grumble from the other men. Clancy ignored the protests and reentered his shack.

Leonardo's ears were red. Giuseppe pulled on his sleeve. "Don't listen to these bastards. We have a job. Let's go."

Giuseppe and Leonardo grabbed bailing hooks from a stack on the dock. When they got to the top of the gangplank, the crew boss, Murphy, bald, fat, stood in their path. "Do you dagos know where hold five is?"

Giuseppe glared. Leonardo gave him a cold smile. Murphy moved aside. The two Italians walked aft. The hold was partially loaded. They climbed down the ladder and waited for the winch man to lower cargo. Almost immediately a large crate in a cargo net was winched down to them. They pushed it on top of another crate, rolled it over to partially free the net, then signaled the deck man to have the winch hoist the net away. The net was filled with another crate topside. When the four loops were secure to the winch hook, the deck man raised his arm in a twirling motion and the winch operator lifted the load and lowered it to Giuseppe and Leonardo in the hold. Giuseppe raised his fist to the deck hand when the crate had descended sufficiently. They positioned the crate, freed the net, and the process continued. Hours later, Murphy yelled, "Take a break."

Giuseppe and Leonardo were soaked with sweat. Everyone in the work crew headed to the galley for something to eat.

Murphy went down the hold to check the Italians' work. Afterwards he went dockside and reported to Clancy. Murphy leaned on his desk. "I sent crates down as fast as I could. I used two nets. The dagos didn't complain."

Clancy crossed his arms. "How are they stacking the crates?"

Murphy grimaced. "Boss, them crates wouldn't shift in a hurricane."

"God damn." He puffed out a breath. "Keep the pressure up. We need to get these guys to quit."

* * *

Leonardo and Giuseppe finished their shift and trudged back to the tenement before dawn.

Giuseppe slumped. "They worked my ass off. I need sleep."

Leonardo hesitated at the entrance. "I want to see if there are any leftovers in the restaurant."

Giuseppe made a wry smile. "Hungry for food or Azzura's company? They're closed. She's asleep." He saw the reaction on Leonardo's face. "*Va bene.* I'm going up." Giuseppe's hollow footfalls creaked on the wooden staircase.

Leonardo went to the basement door of the restaurant. It opened.

The restaurant was dark and smelled of stale beer, spilled wine, and cigar smoke. He felt his way like a blind man toward the kitchen area. His foot banged into a table, and he almost tripped on a chair leg. He lit a small kerosene lamp near the stove. Everything was spotlessly clean.

A voice whisper-shouted at him. "What are you doing?"

Leonardo's head came up. "You scared me."

Azzura said, "Quiet. You'll wake my parents. What do you want?"

"I thought I could find something to eat."

"Do you know what time it is? Obviously we're closed."

"Sorry. I'll go." He took a step back.

"Wait. I'm sure we have some bread."

Leonardo raised the lamp. Azzura was robed in pink flannel and barefoot. She had beautiful feet. "Some bread and wine would be great."

Azzura found a crusty loaf and sliced some pieces onto a plate. She poured Leonardo a glass of red wine and sat across from him.

"How much do I owe?"

She waved her hand.

"*Grazie*. No wine for you?"

"I'll have a taste." She poured two fingers into a tumbler. "Where were you?"

"Loading a ship on the late shift." He crunched some bread in his mouth.

"That's hard work."

"I suppose."

"You look strong."

Leonardo shrugged, but the complement filled his chest with oxygen.

"Now that you have work, will you stay in New York?"

"I don't want to leave my mother alone for too long."

"Your father's not alive?"

"Yeah, he's there." Leonardo sipped the wine. "I miss her."

"You're one of those birds of passage who'll go back and forth to Italy." Azzura tasted the wine. She made a face.

"You don't like wine?"

"It's okay. When will you leave?"

"When I've made some money. A man needs to earn, and I want to prove that my coming to America wasn't a mistake."

"So it's all about the money?"

"At first." Leonardo's eyes held Azzura's. "Do you know Italy?"

"Only what my parents told me."

Leonardo said, "Naples has sweet tomatoes and sweeter watermelons. The sea is so blue it sticks in your throat. In the valley below Vesuvius the hills are dotted with bleached-white houses. Evenings are glimmering orange sunsets and clouds with pink-gray bellies."

"It sounds beautiful. You love your home."

"I'd like to show it to you." Leonardo laid his hand near Azzura's. She didn't move hers. "Would you ever leave New York?"

"To live in Italy?" Azzura lifted her hand. "I'm an American. My parents are here. My home is New York." She leaned back. "Do you want more bread?"

"No, thank you."

Azzura rose and picked up the plate.

Leonardo said, "Can I see you tomorrow?"

"I'm going to the market in the morning. It's late. I need to go to bed."

"*Buona notte.*"

"*Buona notte.*"

Leonardo watched Azzura disappear into the shadows. Back at the apartment, Giuseppe was snoring. Leonardo fell asleep with a fantasy of Azzura in his head.

Chapter 16

LEONARDO JUMPED UP, dressed, and ran down the steps. Azzura was half a block ahead. She moved with the grace of a dancer.

She saw him, smiled, and called out. "Walk with me."

Leonardo closed the gap. "I thought your mother never lets you out of her sight?"

"She wouldn't approve of us talking alone."

"But you don't care?"

Azzura shrugged. "I want more independence, but I live in her house. Sometimes it feels like bondage."

"You'll only leave when you're married?"

"I don't know. My parents said that they'll arrange a marriage when it's time." She tilted her head. "To a suitable man."

Leonardo said, "My parents' marriage was arranged. I don't think my mother's happy."

"So were mine. I want to marry for love."

"How will you meet someone while your mother guards the gate?"

Azzura gave Leonardo a small smile. "There are ways. I want a house, some chickens, and a garden in the country. Brooklyn maybe. I'll open a restaurant."

"You're ambitious."

"Aren't you?"

"I suppose. How will you get all that done?"

"I'll sell food from a pushcart. When I have enough money, I'll rent a small place where I can cook and serve."

"Where did you get those ideas?"

"My *comare*. Her name's Natalia Caputo. She's a nurse in the Settlement on Henry Street. That's where I'm going with these." She raised her basket. Loaves of bread were under a cloth. "Afterwards we'll go to the market."

Leonardo stayed on the sidewalk while Natalia greeted Azzura at the door. The women kissed each other on the cheek. Natalia had short dark hair, wore a long white dress and a brimmed hat with a wide black ribbon. She was in her late thirties.

Natalia spotted Leonardo and came down the stoop stairs. She kept her eyes on him. "Who's the curly hair?"

"I'm Leonardo Robustelli."

She turned to Azzura. "Your mother will suffer a conniption fit if she sees the two of you together."

"Leonardo is helping me shop."

Natalia's eyebrows rose. "Since when do you need a man for that?" She took the loaves from the basket, kissed Azzura, and went back inside.

Azzura came down the steps. "Now we can go."

"Is your godmother married?"

"She likes her independence. She's active in politics and women's suffrage."

"Is she an anarchist?"

"Don't be silly." They walked toward Mulberry Street. "Do you know anything about selecting the freshest fruits and vegetables?"

"My mother grew her own."

"That's the best. The trick is to feel the fruit. I'll teach you how to buy tomatoes."

The spoke-wheel pushcarts ran along Mulberry Street like a wooden freight train crammed with slatted baskets loaded with fruits and vegetables. Azzura and Leonardo browsed the wagons. Vendors attracted attention by singing out their merchandise in melodic tones. Children shouted and ran through the maze of carts and people. Men dressed in coats and hats sat on wooden chairs outside storefronts, played cards, and argued politics. Women in shawls handled the wares and dickered over price with vendors who faked outrage. Horse-drawn wagons carelessly packed with loads of furniture and boxes lumbered up the street. A municipal worker in a white coat shoveled manure to the curb like brown snow. Four and five story tenements lined both sides of the street, many with white sheets hung from the fire escapes like flags of surrender.

Azzura took Leonardo's hand. Their faces were close. She smelled like fresh air and lavender. Leonardo looked into her eyes. He leaned forward to kiss her.

Then, she plopped a bright red tomato into his palm. "How does that feel?"

He swallowed. "Firm."

She raised his hand to his nose. "How does it smell?"

"Earthy."

She smiled. "That's a good tomato. Help me pick the best ones."

Leonardo sighed over his missed chance.

The gray-capped vendor had a large mustache. His brow creased as Azzura poured through every basket of tomatoes. "Signorina, you're taking the best I have."

Azzura said, "You should only carry the best."

The vendor clasped his hands together and looked to heaven in mock prayer.

When Azzura's basket was full, she had the contents weighed. She watched to insure that the seller didn't put his thumb on the scale.

Leonardo carried the basket on the way back to the tenement. A brown and white dog with half its left front leg gone limped out of an alley and followed them.

Azzura stopped and brought her hands to her face. "Ooh, aaw."

The dog had huge brown eyes, and he rolled on his back when Azzura approached to pet him. She sat on a stoop and the dog climbed into her lap. Azzura and the dog's eyes locked. She cuddled him.

Azzura and the dog raised their eyes to Leonardo. She said, " Look at that face. He needs a home."

Leonardo said, "I don't suppose your mother wants a dog."

Azzura's mouth pursed.

Leonardo's shoulders sagged. "Okay, he can stay with Giuseppe and me. What shall we call him?"

"Not tripod. He's sensitive about his injury. I can tell."

Leonardo rubbed his chin. "How about Garibaldi? That should help with his self esteem. Also, Garibaldi was famous for attracting women."

The dog smiled.

Azzura beamed. "Perfect."

"What will we feed him?"

"There's always leftover macaroni."

"Do dogs eat pasta?"

"Italian dogs do."

When the three of them neared the tenement, they saw Azzura's mother on the sidewalk. She watched them with arms crossed. Azzura and Leonardo stopped. He said, "When will I see you again?"

"I'm in the restaurant every night."

"You know what I mean."

"I've never been uptown to Macy's."

"I'll take you."

"Tomorrow? We can't leave the tenement together."

"Let's meet at the trolley station at ten." Leonardo moved close to Azzura.

Azzura glanced down the block. "My mother's watching."

Leonardo gave Azzura the basket of tomatoes. He crossed to the other side of the street with Garibaldi and waited.

Isabella stood like a defiant statue until Azzura arrived at the door. She jerked her head for Azzura to go inside.

Isabella peered at Azzura's face. "What's that on your mouth?" She reached for her daughter. Azzura pulled away. "It's lipstick, isn't it? Do you know the type of women who wear lipstick?"

"Oh, Mama, this is America."

"Did you smoke cigarettes? *Madonna mia*, tell me you didn't."

"Mama, stop. Of course not."

"Azzura, a man wants a woman who'll bear him sons, cook, and keep a proper Italian household. Marriage isn't an adventure. If you want a decent man, you must act in the proper manner."

"I did nothing wrong."

"Your reputation is a fragile flower. Ruin it and we're all shamed, and no one will marry you."

Azzura made a face."You don't trust me."

Isabella said, "You're not to be with men whose families haven't been properly introduced. New York is full of immigrant men out of the sight of their families who want to be with a woman and don't think Italian customs apply to them."

"I like Leonardo. We just went to the market."

"What do you know about him? Your father and I don't know anything about his background. Maybe he's a criminal."

"Leonardo's not a criminal. He has a good job. His father is a tenant farmer in Capodimonte."

"When your father and I find the right family, we'll arrange your marriage."

"Maybe I'll pick my own husband."

"That would be an *infamnia*."

"I'm an individual."

Isabella raised her hands. "My God, you've become an American. Marry without parental permission?" Her voice was loud. "I should've sent you back to Italy to be raised by your grandparents so you'd have Italian values. America has corrupted you." Isabella paced the room. "You have no respect. What will your kids be like?" Isabella pointed. "You can't exist outside the family and be a human being. Who are you? I don't recognize you." Isabella put her hands over her face. Where was the respect that Azzura showed her when she was a child?

Azzura turned on her heel and left the room.

Ciro walked in, bleary eyed. "Why all the noise? I'm trying to sleep."

"*Scuzi*, but you should speak with your daughter."

"What now?"

"I caught her with that Leonardo who eats at the restaurant."

"What do you mean, caught?"

"They walked together on the street, close."

"Oh, well."

"You're taking her side? She wore lipstick."

"I'll talk to her."

"She needs a slap. I should've taken my shoe to her. God only knows what she'll do if we don't discipline her. Azzura thinks she runs this household." Isabella held her head. "If my mother were here, she'd know what to do."

"I said that I'd talk with her."

"We should send her back to Italy. She'll be out of this insanity, and my mother would find her a suitable husband."

"We need her to work in the restaurant. I'm going back to bed, and I want quiet."

Isabella watched her husband leave. She shook her head. He didn't understand the danger. She paced and searched her brain. She wondered where she went wrong. Azzura showed no respect for the old ways, and she'd be ruined. Isabella's eyes fell onto the small statue of Saint Anthony of Padua with the baby Jesus in his arms. Saint Anthony was the patron saint of the lost. She'd make a *novena*. She'd be disciplined and attend Saint Anthony's Church every Tuesday for thirteen weeks. She pulled open a drawer and found a small half-burnt candle. She pressed it into a holder at the base of the statue and lit it. This was the way that Azzura would return to her. Saint Anthony wouldn't let her down. She made the sign of the cross. Isabella patted the dampness on her forehead. Her heart calmed. Isabella looked into a mirror. Her face looked strange to her. She put her hand to her cheek. She was no longer young. In Italy she was a girl and happier than she realized. She wondered if her mother would recognize her after all these years in America. She trembled at the thought.

The next day Leonardo was early to the trolley station. Garibaldi followed him. The moment he saw Azzura turn the corner, the street noise went silent in his head. He tried to slow his breathing, but his pulse raced. He wondered if she could hear his heart beat.

She walked up close. "*Ciao.*"

He looked at her painted lips, and his mouth went dry. He wanted to dive into her green eyes. "*Ciao.*"

She petted Garibaldi. His ears flopped and his tongue lolled.

The car arrived. The three of them boarded the trolley, moved past a well-dressed man and woman near the door, and took seats at the rear.

The woman had artificial flowers on her hat. She crinkled up her nose. "Did you get a whiff of that? Italians from down in the boot reek of garlic and body odor. Look at that dog. It must be a carpet of fleas. Why are they allowed on the same street car that other people have to use?"

The gentleman wore gold-frame glasses. "Well, they have to travel in the city."

"Yes, but why not have separate cars or at least segregate them like they do the Negroes in the South?"

"We don't do that in New York."

"Pity."

"It's just for a few minutes. You don't have to *live* with them."

"Thank God. I don't know why the Senate couldn't pass legislation that would've banned illiterates from entry into this country. We excluded the Chinese laborers; why not the Italians?"

The gentleman said, "We need Italian brute labor for construction." He smiled. "Your undergarments were probably sewed by Jews and Italians."

"They're French. And commerce is no excuse for poisoning our society. Everything is changing for the worse."

"Wait until you have an Italian mayor."

The woman stared at him.

He held up a palm. "Okay, not in this century."

Azzura, Leonardo, and Garibaldi exited the trolley at 34th Street and Broadway. The Macy's Department Store was tiered like a wedding cake, and the multi-storied stone structure blotted out the sun. Each section of the building had a different style of pilaster column like the Coliseum in Rome. The "Macy's" sign was proudly displayed along a railing on the top floor. Flags were arrayed at the four corners of the roof and flapped like pennants on a castle tower. Azzura's eyes rose up the side of the building, and her mouth dropped open. "We need to go inside."

Azzura moved quickly. Leonardo and Garibaldi trailed. Inside, she spotted the sign and headed straight for the women's department. On either side of an aisle that stretched to infinity, racks of merchandise were displayed alongside wooden drawers of clothing. Mannequins were decked out in the latest fashions. Sales clerks in white blouses and long skirts stood ready to assist. Women shoppers in elegant dresses and wide-brimmed hats browsed the wares with the solemnity of

Aristotle contemplating the bust of Plato. Azzura picked up silk undergarments and massaged their luxuriousness in her fingers. She looked at the price and her eyes widened. She smiled. She decided that one day she'd wear silk.

There was music, and Leonardo grabbed his head in recognition. Enrico Caruso sang the aria, *The Siciliana*, from *Cavalleria Rusticana*. Leonardo ran toward the sound and discovered a massive display of phonographs and shelves of prerecorded disks. Garibaldi recoiled from the talking machine's gaping sound amplification horns and barked.

A sales manager, snooty, skinny, in a tuxedo, rushed over to him. "Young man, take that stinking mongrel outside at once."

Leonardo called out to Azzura, and she pulled herself away from the merchandise. The manager shooed them into the street.

Leonardo looked embarrassed. "Maybe I should've left Garibaldi home."

"No. That was enough fantasy for one day." She smiled. "Let's walk."

As they strolled past the Waldorf Astoria Hotel and down to the Madison Square Garden tower, Azzura thought about how she should act with Leonardo. If she was too demure, he might lose interest. If she was too forward, he'd think of her as "easy." The argument with her mother left her drained. She knew that her mother wanted the best for her, but this was America, not Italy. Her mother was right on one point. Men controlled a woman's reputation. A man could talk to his friends about a girl, brag, even lie, and she'd be marked indelibly. Could her relationship with Leonardo be different, or was she trapped in the role tradition demanded? She wanted love, not the man her mother would find for her. Garibaldi smiled up at her as he limped along. At least Azzura knew where she stood with him.

Leonardo gazed at Azzura's profile as they walked; a turned up nose and wisps of raven hair behind a cherub's ear. Her lips had a trace of color. When they found Garibaldi, the dog curled up in Azzura's lap and she lavishly stroked him. Leonardo imagined himself in Azzura's arms. His heart swelled.

They were the only passengers waiting at the station for the trolley downtown. Leonardo sounded sheepish. "That wasn't much fun for you, was it?"

Azzura brightened. "Oh no. I loved it." Her green eyes danced.

Leonardo took a deep breath. He stepped forward, took Azzura by the shoulders, and tried to kiss her. His lips pressed a little off center to hers, half on her cheek. When he drew his head back, her eyes widened. Azzura gulped. She put her arms around Leonardo's neck and planted a soft kiss on his lips. So delicious. He never tasted anything better.

Azzura released Leonardo and turned away. Garibaldi jumped up and put his single right paw on her dress. She smiled and petted him. Leonardo didn't move until the trolley arrived and they boarded.

Once seated, Azzura leaned toward Leonardo. "You need to make a good impression on my parents. Otherwise, they won't allow me to talk to you. My parents will host the feast of San Gennaro celebration in the tenement courtyard on Tuesday. Speak to my father. My mother wants to know about your family."

When the trolley dropped them off, Azzura stopped Leonardo. "Wait five minutes before you follow. I don't want my mother to see us together." She gave Leonardo a kiss and playfully tousled his curly hair.

When Azzura left, Garibaldi started after her. Leonardo called him back. Azzura disappeared around the corner. Leonardo put his hand to his lips and smiled.

Chapter 17

THE WALL BEHIND Andrew Tucker's desk was covered with award certificates for meritorious service to the community and a distinguished legal practice, including his being named "Lawyer of the Year" for 1902. These accolades surrounded a framed diploma from the Colonial Academy conferring upon Tucker the degree of Juris Doctor with all the honors and privileges entailed, written in Latin script on parchment, affixed with the gold seal of the university, and dated Anno Domini MDCCCXCV. The law degree was a fake issued by a diploma mill in Syracuse. The documents of praise arrayed around the diploma were ostensibly from reputable organizations, but actually were Tucker's own fanciful or forged creations. Tucker's talent was to fete and grease politicians throughout the city. Every congressman, actual or up and coming star of Tammany Hall that Tucker could reach, was the receiver of his largesse. His political friends reciprocated by applying influence on the judiciary whenever Tucker was brought to court for one of his scams. New York's Society for the Protection of Italian Immigrants had Tucker's picture on their wall as a warning to newcomers if he approached them. Nonetheless, Tucker scored innumerable cons on innocent illiterate victims selling fake railroad tickets or unneeded legal services to release Ellis Island immigrants who merely waited for their relatives to come and claim them.

Tucker met Alberto when Leggiéri attempted to pick his pocket on Park Avenue. Tucker grabbed Alberto's arm and threatened to call the police. Alberto had tears in his eyes as he countered with a long schpiel on his impoverished, orphaned childhood and how it would be injustice piled high if Tucker summoned the cops. Tucker didn't believe a word but was so impressed with Alberto's playacting that he decided that Leggiéri was a young man he could build upon. He enrolled Alberto as a front man for his various legal swindles.

Alberto came down from Tucker's office and met Carlo at the street level. He spoke quickly. "Tucker has a businessman from Philadelphia, Richard Shippen, on the hook. The guy will arrive Tuesday. He wants to buy $20,000 of counterfeit money."

Carlo said, "Twenty thousand. That's the limit."

"Yeah. This will be a big payoff."

"Twenty grand is a lot of capital to come up with."

"It keeps the petty thieves out of the game."

"Where does Tucker get that kind of money?"

"Tucker has a circle of investors that includes some big shot Tammany Hall politicians."

"And I thought Italy was corrupt."

Alberto laughed. "With high level political protection, we call the con the 'sure thing graft.'"

"What's the plan?"

"This time we'll meet the mark at a political club on Grand Jones Street. For this kind of money, we'll have a cop stationed at the bar outside the meeting room in case there's trouble."

The Philadelphia mark, Richard Shippen, was a tall man, in his fifties, with hard to read deep-set eyes. One day he woke up and realized he was an old man and the dreams of his youth would never come to pass. His import/export business was in financial trouble, and his gambling habit had dug a hole for himself as deep as the Mariana Trench.

When he was a boy, Shippen's father played cards at the Philadelphia Club on Walnut Street and introduced Richard to the camaraderie of gamblers. The smell of cigar smoke, the tinkle of silver thrown into a pot, and the drone of adult conversation comforted young Richard as he nodded off to sleep on a padded bench. As an adult, Richard found that he liked to gamble. The thrill of winning gave him the glimpse of control over his life and took his mind away from day to day stress and the relationship with his wife, which amounted to criticism and sharp rebuke whenever he was in her sight. However the drive to maintain the winning high invariably led to loss. The worse his business situation became, the more he gambled. He just needed one big win, but it never came. The only way to break the cycle, he decided, was to pay off his debts by other means.

Alberto met Shippen at Grand Central Station, and they took a carriage to the Lower East Side. Grand Jones Street was a row of brick tenements and storefronts, one of which was converted to the New Brighton Club. Inside was a long wooden bar with mirrors and shelves of booze. A plainclothes cop in a bowler hat and wool suit who was on the Tucker payroll stood with his foot on a rail nursing a glass of dark beer. Next to the bar on the ground floor adjacent to the alley was a meeting room behind a thick oak door where Tucker and Carlo waited. The cop nodded to Alberto just before he and Shippen ducked inside the room.

When Alberto and Shippen entered, Andrew Tucker extended his hand. "Mr. Shippen, I'm Mr. Andrew. That's Mr. Carlo."

Carlo leaned a shoulder against a wall. Shippen nodded.

Shippen insisted that the door be locked. Tucker shrugged and complied; it was three against one.

Tucker removed a stack of bills from his pocket and arrayed them in front of Shippen like playing cards. "May we get down to business?"

Shippen picked up a number of notes and rubbed them between his fingers. His right eye twitched, and his brow glistened. "These are good."

Tucker smiled. "I'm happy to hear you complement our work."

"You have twenty thousand?"

"May I see how you'll pay for the goods?"

Shippen reached into his inside suit pocket and pulled out a wad of bills. He put them on the table.

Tucker picked up the money. He had an embarrassed smile. "Sorry, I need to check for counterfeit."

Shippen nodded.

Tucker rifled through the bills and indicated he was satisfied. He brought out a black leather satchel filled with cash. "I'll organize these into four $5,000 stacks." As Tucker counted, he glanced up. "You understand that if the authorities find you with these bundles, there'll be trouble for both of us? You may want to send them to Philadelphia by Adams Express so they can't be discovered on your person."

Shippen grunted. He wiped a bead of sweat.

Tucker wrapped each stack several times in paper and placed them in the satchel. Tucker picked up Shippen's money. He started an audible count. Alberto nodded to Carlo.

Carlo moved forward. "Mr. Shippen, may I offer you a cigarette?"

Shippen stiffened. He stepped back and pulled out a Smith & Wesson hammerless Lemon Squeezer revolver. "Get back."

Tucker's face turned white. He froze with Shippen's money in his hands. His saucer eyes were riveted on the gun and the black cavern of the barrel.

Alberto put a hand on the knife inside his pocket. He spoke calmly. "Mr. Shippen, what are you doing?"

Shippen's revolver hand trembled. His voice was nervous. "Don't move. I'm taking everything."

Alberto's tone was soft. "There's a policeman just outside the door. Stop now, and we can all remain friends."

Shippen's voice cracked. "I need the money."

Carlo drew his stiletto. "Put down the pistol."

Alberto fingered his knife. His voice was still measured. "You're making a mistake."

Shippen's eyes darted between Carlo and Alberto. "Don't move." He waved the gun toward Tucker. "Give me the money."

Tucker dropped Shippen's cash. It scattered on the floor. He shouted, "Police."

Shippen fired. Tucker grabbed his stomach and sunk to the floor.

Alberto and Carlo lunged. Shippen fired again. Alberto went down. Carlo plunged his stiletto into Shippen's throat. They fell, Carlo on top. Carlo withdrew the knife and dug it into Shippen's chest. Shippen's eyes bulged. He squirmed. Carlo withdrew the knife and raised it to stab again. Shippen made a choking sound. His eyes dulled, and he stopped struggling.

Carlo panted. Blood throbbed in his temples. His body was clammy with sweat. The front of his shirt and coat were smeared with blood. He wiped the knife on Shippen's jacket. He went to Alberto and put his fingers to his cousin's throat. There was no pulse. Carlo blew out a breath. His head felt like it would explode. He wiped the sweat from his face with his sleeve. It left a smudge of red on his cheek.

The door was kicked from the outside and a voice shouted, "Police, open up."

With three dead, the police would surely arrest him. He had no papers. There'd be an investigation. He'd be connected with the Krause murder. Carlo picked up a wooden chair and slammed it against the window. The glass shattered.

Behind him, he heard a shoulder hit the door and the wood start to splinter.

Carlo looked at Alberto and grimaced. He grabbed the satchel with twenty grand inside. Carlo picked up the revolver and shoved it into his pocket. He dove through the window. A jagged edge of glass ripped his hand. He landed hard and went to his knees in the dirt alley. He got to his feet and ran.

Inside the Medina's Spring Street tenement courtyard, the San Gennaro *festa* was lively with people packed together like tinned fish. The smell of burning incense at the foot of the San Gennaro statue mixed with the sizzling sausage and peppers that Ciro cooked on an open grill. Isabella dropped globs of *zeppole* dough into hot oil vats. The treats bubbled up brown. She scooped out the fried dough, dropped them onto paper, and dusted them with powdered white sugar.

Three musicians led by a mandolin player stood on a wooden platform. They plucked out the lively Neapolitan, *Funiculí Funiculá*, about the Vesuvius funicular. The wine and beer flowed, and many of the people were in a mood to sing along. When the music ended, backs were slapped, and for a few minutes the crowd didn't have a care in the world.

An altar had been constructed against a brick wall. At the top was a two-foot, multi-colored statue of San Gennaro. He was dressed as the Bishop of Naples with a purple cassock, a mitre on his head, a jeweled ring on his finger, and a crosier in his hand. Flowers and candles surrounded him. Above, a banner read, *"Congreazione del San Gennaro."* A photograph of the glass and gold ampoules in Naples that contained the Saint's dried blood was at the statue's feet. Every year on San

Gennaro's feast day, the faithful in Italy prayed that the blood would miraculously liquefy. Their prayers were almost always answered. The miracle of the blood confirmed San Gennaro's protection of the city. In a year that the blood remained coagulated, Vesuvius invariably erupted and destroyed part of Naples.

People in the courtyard stepped up to the Saint and mumbled a prayer for intercession. They lit a candle. Some pinned money to the ribbon that hung around the statue. A few held small pictures of the Saint in their clasped hands. Unmarried women prayed that they'd be given a good husband. Mothers came forward with wax figurines representing sick children and placed them at the Saint's feet. A woman prayed that her stillborn baby would reach heaven. Small wax hands, legs, or feet, the body parts that needed healing were placed near the statue. A number of prominent men pushed forward and pinned large denomination bills to the ribbon. Frank Rizzo made a show of attaching a hundred dollar bill.

A couple of Irish cops were stationed on the perimeter. One said, "Pagans." The other nodded.

A priest in his thirties, with dark hair and a ghost's complexion, limped to the altar. He turned toward the people and spread his hands. Everyone knelt on the dirt. "San Gennaro, patron saint and Bishop of Naples, please hear our prayers. Your precious blood miraculously flows again every year and affirms your heavenly intercession for the protection of the people of Naples. Now hear us Neapolitans in America. Just as our families celebrate San Gennaro in Italy so do we in New York. Though we're far from our families and from your church, we remember you and we love you. We ask that you comfort our families in Naples. We know that they're sad because we aren't together. We all mourn the separation. At this little *festa*, we've recreated the smells, tastes and sounds of the world we left behind. San Gennaro, we beg you to intercede with the Blessed Virgin on our behalf. Please take those who immigrated to New York into your bosom. Let us pray. Hail Mary, full of grace ..."

Giuseppe poked Leonardo. "Do you know how the priest got his limp? He was caught in bed with a married woman and tripped down the tenement stairs trying to escape."

Both men laughed.

Giuseppe shrugged. "Priests don't work, and idle hands are the tools of the devil."

"Do they keep the San Gennaro statue in church after the *festa*?"

"Senora Medina stores it in the tenement. The Irish priests control everything, even the Italian parish. She doesn't want them to charge her a fee for the statue's use."

Giuseppe pointed to the people who came forward and placed votive offerings at the Saint's feet. "An Italian feels safer when he pays homage to the hometown Saint. San Gennaro cured my mother's influenza." Giuseppe fingered the red horn that hung around his neck. "Still, I carry this." He made a hand gesture, forefinger and pinky jutting forward from a closed fist. "It wards off *mal occhio*."

Calls rang out for Ciro to sing. Ciro was the best tenor this side of Enrico Caruso, and his performance was a ritual at a *festa*. Caruso was every Neapolitan's favorite singer even though he stopped performing in Naples after he was booed by a claque that demanded payment for applause. Ciro invariably feigned protest, but he never refused. He wiped his hands on a white apron and took a position in front of the musicians. He nodded, and they played the wistful opening to *Torna a Surriento*, a song extoling the beauty of Sorrento and the pain felt over a loved one who left. Every face turned to listen. Ciro's voice resonated off the brick tenement walls like a concert hall. Ciro's voice rose for the final stanza.

"*Ma nun me lassà* (But please don't go away),

Nun darme stu turmiento! (Don't give me this pain).

Torna a Surriento (Return to Sorrento),

Famme campà! (Let me live!)"

Isabella wiped tears from her face, and many men stuck their noses into their drinks to avoid embarrassment.

Azzura went to Leonardo. "Speak to my father."

Ciro had returned to the grill

Leonardo said, "He's back cooking."

She crinkled her face. People wanted to buy food, and she returned to take payments.

Giuseppe put his arm on Leonardo's shoulder. "If you're serious about Azzura, you should tell your mother about her."

"I can't return to Italy until I've made some money. My father would ridicule me."

Carlo Mazzi was sweating and out of breath from running. His eyes darted, and he looked behind. He needed to get off the street. He heard the noise from the *festa*. A crowd would be good cover. He entered the tenement courtyard, saw the two cops, and plunged himself into the throng of people. A man told him that Senora Medina was in charge of the tenement.

Isabella was making *zeppole*. The image of Alberto's bloody body flashed into Carlo's brain. He made an effort to control the emotion in his voice. "Senora Medina?"

Isabella looked into Carlo's steel gray eyes. "*Sì?*"

"I'm Carlo. I'm looking for an apartment, and I was told you were the person to speak with."

"What beautiful Italian. You speak like an aristocrat."

Carlo managed a small smile. His eyes went past Isabella and lit on Azzura.

Azzura frowned.

Carlo focused back on Isabella. "Do you have an apartment I can rent?"

"The only space I have, you must share with two other men."

Carlo glanced at the Irish cops. "Fine."

"The rent's four dollars per week with board and washing."

Carlo took twenty dollars from his pocket. "Here's five weeks rent."

Isabella's eyebrows rose. "You can pay weekly."

"That's okay. Where's the room?"

"Won't you get something to eat first?"

"Thank you, but I'm tired."

"It's on the third floor. The door's always open."

Carlo walked toward the building entrance. He wanted to run.

When Carlo left, Azzura approached her mother. "Who was that?"

Isabella plopped a wad of dough into the oil. It sizzled. She smiled. "Carlo. He's handsome, isn't he?"

"Carlo what?"

Isabella shrugged. "He paid five weeks rent and I forgot to ask."

Azzura's voice rose. "Where did he go?"

"You should've heard him speak. Such melodic Italian. I put him with Robustelli and Fontana. That room could fit a family."

"Mama, didn't you see the bloodstains on his shirt?"

Isabella's eyebrows rose.

Azzura said, "His jacket was reversed. He held the lapels to hide his shirt, but I saw red."

"The light's not good. You're mistaken. I could tell from his intonation that Carlo was an aristocrat, well educated, and well bred. That's the type of man for you." Her eyes flickered upward. "It's the feast day of San Gennaro. I prayed to Saint Anthony and Carlo appeared. It's a sign."

Azzura motioned for Leonardo. He came over. "Senora Medina, we should be properly introduced."

Isabella's eyes didn't rise. "I know you, Signor Robustelli."

Azzura poked Leonardo.

He said, "I'd like to talk to Signor Medina."

Isabella said, "He's busy."

Azzura pulled Leonardo aside. "You have a new man in your room. My mother just said, 'Carlo.' But there was something disturbing about him. He wore his jacket inside out. He tried to keep his shirt covered, but I saw bloodstains. He carried a bag that wasn't large enough for clothes."

"And your mother put him in our room?"

"He spoke like an aristocrat. He gave her five week's rent. That's all she noticed."

The *festa* wound down. Giuseppe left for the apartment. Leonardo lingered.

Azzura nudged Leonardo. "Speak to my father."

"Is this a good time?"

"He's away from my mother."

Leonardo approached Ciro. "May I talk to you on a personal matter?"

Ciro's eyes widened. "Of course."

They moved to a quiet corner of the courtyard and sat on two wooden chairs. While Azzura and Isabella cleaned up, the women shot glances at the two men and each other.

Ciro said, "What's on your mind?"

"Please excuse my directness, but I'm fond of your daughter."

Ciro frowned. "That's blunt. This isn't the way things are done. Your father should be the one to approach me. I understand he's in Italy, but I don't know him or anything about your family."

"Yes, I'm sorry. He's a tenant farmer on a property just north of Naples."

"Farming is honest work. But you just arrived in New York. Isn't your interest in my daughter a little sudden? Do you have a job?"

Leonardo hesitated. "I've worked on the docks a few days."

"I see. Will you stay in New York?"

"I haven't decided. My mother's in Italy."

"You can't decide if you'll stay in New York, and your job prospects are unclear. How do you expect me to talk about Azzura's future?"

"I think I love Azzura."

Ciro gulped. He took a moment to calm himself. "You can't eat love. Speak to me when you have answers to my questions." Ciro returned to the grill.

Azzura went to Leonardo. His face was in shadows. "What did my father say?"

Leonardo shook his head. "Nothing encouraging."

She wrung her hands.

When Leonardo opened the apartment door, Giuseppe was in a chair at the table fighting to stay awake. In the back room, Carlo sat in the dark. He was on a mattress with his back pressed against the wall. He hugged a black satchel between his legs.

Giuseppe's voice was tense. "I found this bastard when I arrived. He won't let me go to bed."

Leonardo faced the man. Carlo pointed a revolver at him.

Leonardo neared a charred-black cook pot and contemplated it as a potential weapon. His mother's words came into his head, "Is New York safe?" He weighed the odds of a saucepan against a pistol and shook his head. "Carlo, I'm Leonardo, this is Giuseppe. We've been up all night and we're exhausted. No one wants to rob you. Put the gun away. We're coming to bed."

Leonardo motioned for Giuseppe to come forward. Carlo kept his eye on them as they both collapsed onto their mattresses. He tucked the satchel under his head for a pillow and lay back. He crossed his arms over his chest, revolver in hand.

Giuseppe was up first. He put sticks of wood inside the iron stove. The kindling crackled when lit. The two men in the back room stirred. Leonardo came to the table. Giuseppe put on a *Napoletana* flip pot of coffee. Carlo smelled the aroma, and came into the light of the window.

Leonardo peered at his face. "I know you."

Carlo turned his gray eyes on Leonardo.

"I've seen you ride a horse on the estate. You're Carlo Mazzi."

Carlo sat back in his chair. "*Sí.*"

"Giuseppe, my father is a tenant farmer working for Don Salvatore Mazzi. Carlo is his son. What are you doing in New York?"

Carlo said, "It's personal. No one is to know I'm here."

Leonardo said, "You're on the run? The bloodstains on your clothes; something happened last night? The police are after you?"

"You ask too many questions."

Giuseppe said, "And the satchel. You robbed someone?"

Carlo put his hand on the revolver.

Leonardo said, "Relax. We know how to keep our mouths shut. I told you last night that we wouldn't rob you. Now that I know that your father is *padrone* to my father, I'll help you. First thing, you need new clothes."

Chapter 18

"SON OF A BITCH." Big Jim O'Neil's face puffed out scarlet against graying sideburns. He sat behind a huge mahogany desk in his Tammany Hall office and slapped an open newspaper with the back of his hand. Teddy Fitzpatrick sat across from Big Jim. Fitzpatrick was gaunt, with short gray hair and a thin nose. "Teddy, look how that bastard editor portrayed me." He turned the caricature for Fitzpatrick to see. "Convict stripes."

Fitzpatrick read the newspaper editorial. "Well, you did screw the publisher out of the mayor's job."

"This sort of personal attack is an abuse of journalistic power."

"The article says you should be arrested for making a fortune from selling the rights to everything from stevedoring to running towboats."

"Everyone knows that the waterfront belongs to the Irish. We protect our interests. What good is power if you don't profit from it?"

Fitzpatrick tilted his head.

Big Jim spread his arms. "Teddy, he portrays me as a criminal. What if my mother sees the cartoon?" Big Jim had moved his eighty-year-old mother into an Upper West Side apartment.

"The newspaper lasts a day. Tonight it'll be used to wrap fish."

Big Jim leaned his elbows on the desk. "Teddy, I disagree. We can't ignore the warning. The Tammany candidate almost lost the last election. This type of propaganda weakens our standing in the Irish community. New York has more Irishmen than Dublin, and we live or die on the support of our people. We can no longer take Irish votes for granted."

Fitzpatrick leaned back. "I sense you've formed a strategy."

Big Jim stood. "You're damn right. Patronage, Teddy boy. Patronage is the answer. It's time to unchain the city budget. Hire Irish. Hire more police, fire, and transport workers. Hire everywhere the city either employs or influences the employment of people. Explode the public payroll. Hire every Irishman who breathes. If you can make the dead vote, empty the cemeteries as well. Meet the Irish when they come off the boats. Give them fake naturalization papers so they can cast their ballots for us. Make sure every Irishman in this city knows Tammany Hall is where his bread is buttered." Big Jim's cheeks shone like Macintosh Apples.

Fitzpatrick nodded. "I like it."

"I'll speak to the archbishop. I'll ask him to mobilize the churches. Priests should give Sunday sermons on humane government. Tammany Hall puts food on the table. No reform politician will threaten us again."

"You're a genius."

Big Jim smiled. He was out of breath. He sat. "Okay, now we can talk about the robbery. What did you learn?"

Fitzpatrick had out his notepad. "The cop who broke through the door said that the mark, Shippen, shot Tucker and Leggiéri, although the police didn't find a pistol at the scene. The guy who got away, Carlo, was a relative of Leggiéri's from Italy. He stabbed Shippen to death. Carlo left with the twenty thousand in a satchel. He also took the gun."

"I had ten thousand in that deal. When do we find this Carlo and get my money back?"

"Jim, we all lost money. I'm sore, too. But ten grand won't pay your bar bill for a month. Shouldn't we just let the cops do their job? You don't want your name mentioned during a scam investigation. A triple murder draws reporters like blowflies."

"It's not the money, it's the principle. No one steals from me."

Fitzpatrick started to protest, but Big Jim held up his hand. "Okay, be careful in your inquiries. We don't need an arrest if this Carlo might squeal about the con and drag our names into it. But make sure the police know we want to see a recovery of the cash."

"The cops have a description of the guy, but it's one Italian dug in like a tick somewhere in lower Manhattan."

"Don't let the cops give you that shit. Tell them to find the dago. Flood the Lower East Side wards with police. Shut down the businesses and the rackets. We'll let the gangs help us find Carlo. The Italians need to learn that Little Italy is run by the Irish."

Chapter 19

DONATO FLORIO relaxed behind his walnut desk as the owner of the Bank of Prisco on Elizabeth Street. Florio was wearing a bowtie, was balding, and sported an elaborate waxed mustache. The vault that framed his back held the savings that Italian immigrant workers sweated blood to compile.

A man with a mustache in a dark suit walked slowly toward the banker. Florio knew the type on sight. This was another Italian who'd failed with a feather shop or a coal basement and now wanted to borrow money to open a saloon. Florio always refused these requests. He received so many similar pleas that he could recite them in his head. As the man neared, Florio anticipated that he'd be subjected to another of these ridiculous petitions. The heat rose to his neck. When the man reached the front of his desk, Florio didn't stand to greet him. He was curt. "Yes?"

Ignazio Terranova didn't remove his hat. He pulled a cloth cap from under his jacket and tossed it at Florio. "Do you recognize this?"

Florio stared at the hat on his desk and gripped the arms of his chair. "It looks like my son's."

"Do as I tell you or I'll bring you his ear."

Florio's voice was hoarse. "Is he all right?"

"At the moment."

"What do you want?"

Terranova's voice had an ominous tone. "Your son will live if you cooperate."

"You want me to pay a ransom?"

"I want $250 thousand."

Florio gulped. "How do I know that I'll get my son back?"

"He's outside in a carriage. Come to the window."

Florio followed Terranova to the front of the bank. He saw his twelve-year-old son in an open carriage. The boy's face was white. His eyes were as wide as dinner plates. Terranova's henchman, Bruno Drago, had his arm wrapped around the kid like a python. Drago's hat was pulled low, revealing only a predator's smile.

Terranova said, "We want the cash, not the kid. But if you go to the police, we know where you live. We can settle with you and your entire family if you cross us as easily as we took your son."

A sheen of sweat surfaced on Florio's face. "If I give you $250 thousand, we'll be bankrupt."

"The money isn't yours."

Florio clutched strands of his thinning hair. "But I'll be ruined. Depositers will hound me."

"Focus on your son."

Florio took out a handkerchief and wiped his brow.

Terranova's eyes looked like a cobra's ready to strike. "Open the vault and give me the money. Now."

Philip Agostini was Ignazio Terranova's attorney and business partner. His Westside ten-room apartment had a view of Central Park. A servant ushered Terranova into Agostini's marble and wood office. A rich blue and silver silk carpet covered the floor. Agostini was tall and wore a green tie and pristine-white shirt under a tailored suit. He was born in Turkey, the son of an Italian minister to that country. When his father held a diplomatic post in New York, Agostini received a law degree from Columbia University. His father returned to Italy, and Agostini made America his home.

Terranova's eyes twinkled. "I needed six olive barrels to carry the money. The wagon's parked on the street. I'm a little nervous. Thieves are everywhere." The two men laughed.

"Good work. Everything is prepared." Agostini removed some papers with official seals from a roll-top desk. "I've formed a real estate corporation with the two of us as sole shareholders."

The servant entered the room with two whiskeys on a tray. The men clinked glasses to toast their partnership.

Agostini said, "The Company will use the money to purchase existing tenements and for new construction in both Harlem and the Bronx."

Terranova pulled his ear. "Are we going legit?"

"We'll have some legal profit. You'll be the proprietor of a wholesale grocery warehouse on Prince Street."

"You think there's good money in groceries?"

Agostini grinned. "Your 'Black Hand' extortion operation will extract protection money from restaurant owners and retail grocers. You'll intimidate them into buying from our high-priced wholesaler. We'll buy back their stock with counterfeit dollars imported from Palermo."

"*Va bene*. What about the cops?"

"Police protection, judicial and political support will all be purchased."

"Now I know why you live in this West Side mansion."

Agostini smiled. "Let's have another drink."

Ciro Medina wiped his hands and removed the paper from the envelope he found slipped under the door of the restaurant. The blood left his face, and he grabbed his forehead.

Isabella hurried over. "What's the matter?"

Ciro showed her the paper.

"*Madonna mia.*"

Azzura heard her mother. "What is it?"

Her father crumpled the letter to his chest.

Isabella crossed herself, "Dear God, no."

Azzura's voice rose. "Show me."

Her father opened his fist, and she took the paper. It read:

> Pay or die.
>
> You are rich. We are poor. Bring $1 thousand to the corner of Mott and Hester, Sunday at ten o'clock in the morning. Otherwise, we'll blow you up with a bomb.
>
> The Black Hand.

At the bottom of the letter was a fist filled in with black ink.

Azzura held her cheek. "We must show this to the police."

Her father took the paper. "Don't be foolish. The police can't protect us from these people."

Isabella hugged her daughter's shoulders. "Ciro, we don't have this kind of money. What are we going to do?"

A short, wiry man walked up to the Medinas. "*Scuzi.*" Six eyes looked at Ignazio Terranova. "I'm sorry to interrupt your family's conversation, but the look on your faces frightened me. The letter you just opened. Is it from Italy? Have you received news of a death in the family?"

Ciro's face was ashen. "No death, but it's a serious matter."

"May I know what's caused you and your family so much obvious distress?"

"Signor Terranova, I'm not sure there's anything you can do."

"You're probably right. I'm sorry to have bothered you." He started to move away.

Ciro looked at his wife. She nodded. "Wait." Terranova turned. Ciro handed him the letter.

Terranova tugged at his black mustache as he read. "This is indeed a serious threat. It's our cross to bear that some Italians prey on others." He shook his head. "These are horrible people. I'm so sorry."

Ciro said, "I don't know what to do. I'm afraid about what will happen if we don't obey."

"Yes, these threats aren't hollow. These bastards bombed a fruit seller's store last week in Harlem." He glanced at Azzura. "They've even slashed the faces of young girls."

Isabella hugged her daughter close. "Mother of God."

"I'm sorry to say these frightening things, but they're true."

Ciro kneaded his forehead. "Everyone talks about these threats. I suppose it was inevitable that we'd face one."

"I understand if you refuse to pay. Someone needs to stand up to these animals no matter the consequence."

Ciro said, "It's not that we don't want to pay. We don't have this kind of money."

Terranova put a forefinger to his chin. "I have an idea. Let me make some inquiries. Perhaps as a neutral party I can negotiate on your behalf for a slightly lower payment. Rely on me not to anger these people."

"You would get involved?"

Terranova bowed his head slightly. "What could you manage?"

Ciro turned to Isabella. "We have about $120 in cash. Maybe we could borrow from friends?"

Isabella said, "Who? Everyone lives hand to mouth."

Ciro shook his head. "I don't know. But $1,000 is impossible." Ciro said to Terranova, "Do you think you could get them to agree to half?"

Terranova's eyes narrowed. "Only $500?"

Isabella blanched. "Ciro, that's too much."

Ciro wiped sweat from his face. "Do we dare offer less?" Ciro faced Terranova.

Terranova gave Ciro a long stare before he said, "Okay. I'll try. I'll take this despicable note with me so they know I speak for you."

Ciro puffed out a breath of relief. "How can we possibly thank you?"

"Please, I've done nothing yet."

"But we so appreciate your help."

"Well, you know that I've opened up a wholesale food supply company on Prince Street. If I could have your restaurant as one of my clients, that would be most appreciated."

"Of course."

The next day, Terranova returned. He huddled with the Medinas in a corner. Ciro and Isabella took each other's hand.

Terranova said, "I have good news. I convinced the bastards to take the $500. I'll deliver the money to protect you from harm. One more thing. A man will come to the restaurant. He'll eat, and offer to purchase some of your liquor. Accept his offer, and don't look closely at the money he uses to pay."

Ciro's eyebrows rose. "The money will be counterfeit?"

Terranova raised his hand. "Pass the money on as you can. Never say where it came from. Do you agree?"

"Yes, all right."

Terranova clasped Ciro on the shoulder. "We've avoided a calamity. I'm pleased. I need to have the $500 on Saturday. I'll be in the saloon on Hester Street."

When Terranova left the restaurant, Isabella's eyes narrowed. "The reason we never purchased from Terranova's wholesale business was that he charges the highest prices in New York."

The couple looked at each other, and their eyebrows rose.

Chapter 20

THE IRISH ROSE SALOON on 16th Street in Manhattan was
cool darkness that smelled like an unwashed beer mug. Crude
dirt-smudged paintings of the "Old Sod" hung crookedly on
the walls. A bar mirror reflected a few dim gaslights that
dangled from the ceiling. Scuffed flooring led to a carved
wooden bar, a metal foot rail, and a row of spittoons. Glasses
and bottles of booze were on a shelf behind the clean-shaven
vested bartender who drew mugs of beer from a barrel under
the bar.

Conversations of the few all-male patrons were interrupted
by the jingle of the bell on the front door. Jarring sunlight
silhouetted Kevin Clancy and Liam Murphy. They strode in,
bellied up to the bar, and the bartender served them dark pints
of beer.

Clancy rubbed his forehead. "Italians in the 'shape' are a
disaster. I'm getting pressure from the men."

Murphy shrugged. "Doyle gave you an order."

"You know that, but the guys blame me. I'm bucking for a
delegate's position in the union hall. If the rank and file turn on
me, I'm sunk."

"What do you want to do?"

"I need the dagos to quit without a stink. There's a bulk
grain carrier to be loaded tomorrow. You'll be the crew boss."

Murphy smiled. "Yeah. I get it. Let's see how they like the
grain hold."

The bulk carrier, *Gorjistan*, was tied to the pier. A grain barge was lashed to its starboard side. Stevedores clustered around the union office shack like bees to the hive. Clancy emerged with a jaunty stride. Without looking at his sheet, he called off Giuseppe and Leonardo's names. "Get to the aft hold. We're loading grain." He gave them a snide smile.

Murphy met them on deck. He thrust his double chin at them. "If the grain shifts on the sail to Turkey, the ship will lilt and capsize in a storm. Get into the aft hold. When the winch operator dumps a load, level out the grain. Shovels are next to the hatch."

Giuseppe's eyes shifted. He made an aside to Leonardo as they walked. "Something's up. They fumigate the hold before loading grain. We could suffocate down there."

A boom hung over the center of the aft hold of the *Gorjistan* like an executioner's axe. Giuseppe and Leonardo stood on the edge of the hatch and watched the process. A half-ton bucket's gaping mouth was buried in a mound of grain on the barge's deck. The operator closed the jaws of the clamshell. Several men on the barge shoveled grain into the top of the bucket to complete the load. Although the dust raised was minimal, the men wore gauze wrapped around their noses and mouths. The winchman lifted the filled bucket and swung it to the ship's hold. He lowered the clamshell ten feet down and opened the jaws. A half-ton of grain rained down, and dust rose like a sandstorm. The next load was dumped before the cloud had completely cleared.

Giuseppe pointed. "Look at that. No one could breathe down there even with masks." The two men laid their shovels down.

In a few minutes, Murphy caught sight of Giuseppe and Leonardo still topside. He waddled up to them. "What the hell are you two doing? Get into the hold." Murphy picked up a shovel and attempted to hand it to Giuseppe.

Giuseppe pushed it away. "Go yourself. It's killing down there."

"Get into the hold or quit. Those are your options."

Giuseppe said, "Go to hell. We're not quitting. I want to talk to Clancy."

Murphy's face became crimson. "I'm the boss on deck. Now get into the hold." He jabbed Giuseppe in the midsection with the blade of the shovel.

Giuseppe gasped and grabbed his belly. Leonardo's eyes widened. His face got hot.

Murphy cocked the shovel for another thrust and shouted, "Move."

Leonardo jumped forward and slammed his hands against Murphy's chest. The crew boss tottered backwards. His heel caught on a cleat, and he toppled over the edge and fell into the hold. He landed on his back in the grain. Murphy screamed, "Help." Only Giuseppe and Leonardo heard his cry over the machinery noise.

Leonardo stepped forward.

Giuseppe grabbed his arm. His head swiveled around. "No one saw him go in."

"Shouldn't we save him?"

Giuseppe's ear to chin scar reddened. "Why? The *sfacim* deserved it."

Leonardo bit his lip as another shovel load moved directly above Murphy's head.

Murphy saw the clamshell hover and screamed, "No." He lifted his arms in self-defense.

The bucket opened and dumped a half-ton of grain on Murphy's head. As the dust cloud dissipated, only Murphy's arm and a black shoe could be seen sticking out of the pile.

Giuseppe sneered. "He's dead. Nobody could survive down there."

Leonardo gulped.

Murphy's body disappeared under the next shovel of grain.

Leonardo wiped the stress sweat from his forehead. "I didn't mean ..."

Giuseppe said, "No one will believe it was an accident. They'll hang us if they can."

Leonardo took a deep breath. "I've never seen a man die."

Giuseppe grabbed Leonardo's arm. "Listen."

"What now?"

"We finish our shift like normal."

"He'll be reported missing."

"When they ask us about him, we play dumb."

Leonardo said, "And when they discover him in Turkey?"

"That's weeks away."

"They know we worked the hold."

"He must have fallen in while we were on break."

"Who'll believe that?"

"There's no proof otherwise."

Leonardo and Giuseppe punched out with the timekeeper after their shift and headed back to Spring Street.

The next day Leonardo's stomach still churned over Murphy's death and he had no appetite, but he joined Giuseppe and Carlo when they went into the restaurant and sat at the last empty table.

Azzura was in the kitchen. Her eyes were down, and she chewed on a knuckle. She saw Leonardo and hurried over. "We need to talk."

"Me, too." Beyond Azzura's shoulder, Leonardo saw Isabella's eye on them. "But where?"

"Wait until it's less crowded."

Carlo smiled at Azzura. "Excuse me. What's your name?"

"Azzura." She didn't return the smile.

"I'm Carlo."

"My mother told me. Do you have a last name?"

Carlo hesitated. "Mazzi."

"I see you have new clothes."

Carlo fingered his lapels. "Yes, not very fancy. My old clothes were soiled."

"I saw bloodstains the night of the *festa*."

Carlo paled. "I cut my hand."

"Really?" Azzura tilted her head.

"See?" He showed her the gash from the jagged window glass.

"That's a bad cut."

A man at another table called Azzura over.

When she left, Leonardo leaned toward Carlo. "Stay away from Azzura. She's with me."

Carlo smirked. "Then why does her mother act like your hand is up Azzura's dress?"

The restaurant door opened and three policemen stormed into the room.

Leonardo saw the blue uniforms and gulped. Giuseppe put a forefinger to his lips.

Carlo spotted the cops and shrunk in his seat. His hand hid his face.

Two patrolmen stood on either side of the door with arms folded. The room went silent. The third cop, a bulldog face with a Rhino body, strode to the center of the room. His voice was a booming Irish brogue. "We're looking for the Italian who murdered Andrew Tucker on Grand Jones Street. Anyone who has information, step forward." His eyes surveyed the restaurant.

Leonardo and Giuseppe looked at each other and breathed a sigh of relief. Carlo turned his back to the cop. Leonardo poked Giuseppe and pointed his head toward Carlo. Giuseppe nodded.

None of the patrons in the restaurant made eye contact with the bulldog. The policeman put his hands on hips. "Okay, play it that way." He pointed toward the *morra* game. "This establishment allows illegal gambling. As of now, the restaurant is closed by order of the police. Everybody out."

Ciro ran to the bulldog. "You can't close us."

"Watch me."

"When can we reopen?"

"When we get Tucker's murderer."

"But I have nothing to do with that."

"Tough." The cop shouted over Ciro's shoulder. "Out, everybody out."

The patrons grumbled. Nobody looked at the cops. The police peered at faces as the men passed but didn't stop anyone. Carlo, Leonardo and Giuseppe cleared dishes from the tables to appear like they worked in the restaurant. When most of the customers had gone, the cops left as well.

Azzura went to Leonardo. "They can't close the restaurant. We need the money."

"What's the matter?"

"My father." She looked toward the kitchen. "Please ask him."

The three men followed Azzura to her parents.

"Papa, please tell Leonardo about the threat."

"Azzura, we've involved enough people."

Leonardo said, "Please, Signor Medina, tell me what's wrong."

Ciro looked at his wife. She shrugged. "We received a 'Black Hand' threat."

Giuseppe stepped forward. "May I see it?"

Ciro frowned. "We gave the letter to Ignazio Terranova. He said that he'd help us, but now we're suspicious."

Giuseppe said, "You're right. Ignazio Terranova is trouble. It's likely he sent the letter. He's clever. You gave him the evidence."

Leonardo asked, "Who is Terranova?"

Giuseppe said, "A Sicilian. He and Rizzo hate each other. What did Terranova say to you?"

Ciro said, "The letter demanded $1,000 or they'd bomb us. Terranova offered to negotiate. He returned and told us he had the extortion reduced to $500. We're trying to figure out how we'll pay."

Giuseppe grimaced. "Terranova is ruthless. He doesn't threaten unless he means to follow through."

Ciro's chin sunk to his chest. "If we don't pay, he'll destroy the restaurant, or worse." His eyes flitted onto Azzura. "He'll harm my family."

Carlo moved into the circle. "Excuse me. I have a solution to your problem. I'll give you the $500 to pay the blackmail."

Ciro's mouth dropped open. Azzura's eyes widened.

Ciro said, "You're kind to offer a loan. But I'd need to repay you, and I'm not sure when I can."

Carlo said, "The money is a gift. I'll deliver the $500 to Terranova myself."

"You'd do that for us? Why?"

Carlo glanced at Azzura. "I like your family."

"I'm not sure I can accept a gift."

Isabella touched her husband's forearm. "Carlo is a gentleman. I knew it as soon as I saw him." She smiled. "*Grazie* Signore."

Azzura's voice was warm. "That's kind of you."

Carlo gave the women a small bow.

Leonardo crossed his arms. He glared at Carlo. "I'll go with Carlo to Terranova."

Ciro said, "The money needs to be with Terranova on Saturday."

Carlo nodded. "That's not a problem."

Ciro gestured. "All of you, please sit. Carlo, you've taken a great weight from my shoulders. You must allow me to reciprocate. I'll make you some *parmigiana di melanzane*."

The three men took a table. Carlo kept his eyes on Azzura. Leonardo's temperature rose. When the food arrived, he just picked.

When the dishes were cleared, Carlo and Giuseppe bid good night. Leonardo lingered.

He went to Azzura. "I don't like the way Carlo looked at you. Your mother likes him."

"The money he's giving us is a godsend. My mother's relieved, and she dreams I'll marry an aristocrat. What did you want to tell me?"

"There was an accident on the docks. A man died."

"Oh my God."

"The police will be involved. I thought that they came for me this evening."

"But if it was an accident?"

"We're Italians working in an Irish union. Everyone will speak against us."

Azzura moved closer to Leonardo. She felt her mother's eyes and pulled back. "I'm glad you told me."

"What if your parents find out?"

"They can't. They'd forbid me to see you."

As Ciro and Isabella prepared for bed, she said, "What did Leonardo say to you after the *festa*?"

Ciro grimaced. "He thinks he loves Azzura. But he just started to work, and he doesn't know if he'll go back to Italy." He shook his head. "Young people."

"What did you tell him?"

"Come back when you have answers to my questions. Were we as confused when we were young?"

"Everything was arranged for me by my parents."

"I'm exhausted. Let's go to sleep."

"Azzura told me that Carlo is a Mazzi. That's the family that owns the estate in Capodimonte. He's interested in

Azzura. He has means and is well born. He's the husband for Azzura."

"I've never met the father. He may have other plans for his son."

"Perhaps we need to reach him. Carlo would be a great match."

"I agree."

In the apartment, Leonardo confronted Carlo. "Did you kill this Tucker the police asked about?"

"No."

"But you were involved?"

"It's none of your business."

"Your actions affected Azzura and her family. That makes it my business."

"You can't help."

Giuseppe said, "We think we can."

Carlo huffed. "I'm going to bed"

Leonardo said, "The police will never stop looking for you. Maybe you can get back to Italy through Canada?"

Carlo said, "Are you trying to get me to leave New York? Maybe you're worried about Azzura? She likes me."

Leonardo stiffened. "She's with me."

Carlo smirked.

Giuseppe nudged Leonardo. "We have the Murphy problem. If the police come here to find Carlo, we'll all be arrested."

Carlo put his hand on the revolver in his pocket. "You're not turning me in."

Leonardo said, "Giuseppe didn't mean that. But we can't just sit. Based on your generosity to the Medinas, I suppose you have cash in that satchel."

Carlo drew the revolver. "That's no concern to you, unless you want real trouble."

Leonardo said, "Put the gun away. You think you can get yourself out of this mess? Sooner or later the cops will grab you. We know someone who could help."

Carlo tilted his head. "Suddenly, you have a powerful friend. Who would that be?"

Leonardo said, "The *guappo* of the Camorra in Little Italy, Frank Rizzo."

Carlo said, "What could he do?"

Leonardo said, "He has connections in Tammany Hall. That's who runs the cops." Leonardo said to Giuseppe. "We need to see Rizzo. You agree?"

Giuseppe nodded.

Carlo put away his pistol. "I'll think about it."

Leonardo and Giuseppe left Carlo outside of the Mulberry Street club.

Rizzo's face looked like a thunderstorm. "The cops have shut down all the gambling joints. No money's coming in. Tell me some good news."

Giuseppe and Leonardo sat. Leonardo fidgeted. No one spoke.

Finally, Rizzo said, "Talk."

Leonardo said, "Last night the crew boss attacked Giuseppe. There was trouble."

Rizzo's eyebrows rose. "What kind of trouble?"

"I pushed the crew boss. He fell into the hold and died."

"That's your good news? I take it there were no witnesses?"

"No. We finished our shift, but maybe we shouldn't return to the docks?"

Rizzo said, "If you don't go back they'll know you're guilty. Go to work. If you get arrested, keep quiet. Where's the body?"

Giuseppe said, "On its way to Turkey."

Rizzo laughed. "How did you manage that?"

Giuseppe grinned. "He was buried in the grain."

"Good. By the time that ship gets to Turkey, the body will be pretty ripe. There'll be no way to determine if he was pushed or fell. The Turks won't bother to return the corpse. But your faces tell me there's something else. What?"

Leonardo pointed. "That's Carlo Mazzi. He's the guy the cops are looking for. He says that he didn't kill Tucker, but we're sure he was there. He has a satchel of money and showed up in our apartment with bloodstains on his clothes."

Rizzo brightened. "Now that's good news. Bring Carlo over."

Carlo sat between Leonardo and Giuseppe and faced Rizzo. Carlo hesitated. Leonardo poked him. "Tell Signor Rizzo what happened on Grand Jones Street."

Carlo said, "I've talked too much already."

Rizzo fingered the hole in his forehead. "Look, Carlo, right now my business is shit because a friend of Tammany Hall was killed and their money was stolen. I don't care what you did, only how I can get the cops off my back."

Carlo said, "How do I know I can trust you?"

"You don't. Did you kill Tucker?"

"No."

"But you witnessed who did?"

"Maybe."

Rizzo huffed. "I don't have time for this game. When the cops grab you, they'll string you up by the balls. You don't have a better option. Talk to me."

Carlo shifted in his seat.

Rizzo looked at the ceiling. "Christ. Tell me what happened or get the hell out of my face."

Carlo kneaded his chin. "Okay. Andrew Tucker, my cousin, Alberto, and I were partners in a con on a mark named

Shippen. The *sfacim* drew a revolver and killed both Tucker and Alberto. I stabbed Shippen and ran."

Rizzo said, "What a about the $20,000 that's missing?"

Carlo's eyes flitted onto the satchel between his knees.

Rizzo mused. "How much of the $20,000 is left in that bag?"

Carlo said, "All of it."

Rizzo said, "My informants told me that Tammany Hall wants the money. That's who unleashed the cops. Give me the bag and maybe I can square things so the police stop looking for you."

Carlo leaned back. "I don't know."

Rizzo said, "There's a lot more at stake for me than $20,000 if we don't get the rackets moving again."

"Maybe you'll keep the money and turn me in?"

"I wouldn't turn you in. I'd kill you and deliver your body."

Carlo stiffened.

Rizzo said, "Relax; like I said, Tammany Hall wants the money, not you."

"I need $500 to keep a promise."

"What promise?"

Giuseppe leaned forward. "The Medinas received a 'Black Hand' extortion threat. Terranova was behind it."

Rizzo said, "I don't have time to deal with Terranova. Okay, keep $500. Ciro makes the best food in Little Italy. I'd hate for his place to get bombed."

Carlo said, "I'll give you the money when you confirm that the cops will call off the search for me."

"Okay, but if you double cross me, there'll be no place safe for you. And let's be clear. I'm doing you a favor. You owe me after this."

Chapter 21

BIG JIM O'NEIL'S parents were part of the mighty wave of Irish immigrants who fled the Great Famine. His father survived the coffin ships of pre-Civil War ocean travel only to be killed in the New York Draft Riots of 1863. His mother raised her son in a West Greenwich Village shanty near Saint Veronica's Church on the meager wages she earned in a garment factory. Jim grew up with the smell of slaughterhouses, soap factories, and waterfront waste in his nostrils. At fourteen he began to "shape" on the Greenwich Village piers. He scraped together enough money to open a saloon on Charles Street, and he turned the second floor into a political social club. The support of various Irish politicos acquired through contributions and get-out-the-vote drives helped Big Jim move up the Tammany Hall chain of command. While Commissioner of Docks, he started a company to lease port space, and a decade later Big Jim became the first longshoreman millionaire. Big Jim was selected as Tammany Hall Boss with the support of the Workingmen's Political League, a group that turned Irish labor unions into an arm of the Democratic Party. A public ceremony honoring his appointment was held, and the "Star Spangled Banner" was played. Afterwards a reporter asked Teddy Fitzpatrick why Big Jim didn't sing. Fitzpatrick replied that Big Jim didn't want to commit himself.

Teddy "Four Votes" Fitzpatrick was one of three children. When his father died of typhus, his mother married an alcoholic laborer and had six children by him. Fitzpatrick was sent to work in the Fulton Fish Market where he learned to size people up. He gravitated to the docks and met Big Jim O'Neil. The two became partners in saloons and real estate. Fitzpatrick developed his political constituency by giving food, coal, and clothing to the needy in his Lower Eastside ward. As he progressed in the Tammany Hall hierarchy, he was assigned the task of providing political protection to various Little Italy street mobs in exchange for get-out-the-vote efforts. That's how he met Frank Rizzo. Fitzpatrick was legendary for the landslide victories he was able to engineer. His "Four Votes" moniker attested to the strategy he advocated for stuffing the ballot box. There were no voter identification papers, so people were passed into the polling stations by sight. Supporters were told to grow full beards before Election Day, then return to the ballot box after trips to the barber shaving down to mutton chops and mustache, just mustache, then clean shaven so they could execute a four vote contribution for Fitzpatrick's candidate.

Rizzo was ushered into Teddy Fitzpatrick's cavernous office. Rizzo wore a black suit and a fedora with a ribbon around the brim. He'd funded some successful congressional races, so the two men had done business before.

Fitzpatrick didn't look up. "Sit."

Rizzo didn't remove his hat. He slouched into a leather armchair in front of a mahogany desk large enough to have deforested a considerable chunk of the Brazilian Amazon. Large windows had a view of the New York skyline and the Chelsea Piers. On the wall was a prominent photo of Big Jim and Fitzpatrick shaking hands. Arrayed around Big Jim's smiling mug like planets orbiting the sun were pictures of Fitzpatrick with various other political cronies and the Archbishop of New York. A portrait of Fitzpatrick's wife and two kids, brightly smiling like they didn't have a care in the world, was on the credenza against the wall. Rizzo took it all in with a look of repose.

Fitzpatrick's eyes rose to Rizzo. "You have information for me?"

"Maybe."

"What does that mean?"

"Maybe I can help you. Maybe you can help me."

"I was told that you had information about the murder of Andrew Tucker at the Grand Jones Street Club."

"Tucker was doing a con. He was a thief."

Fitzpatrick's face flushed. "How dare you besmirch a dead man's reputation?"

Rizzo smiled. "Tucker was killed by his mark, a Philadelphia guy named Shippen. The mark also killed an Italian, Alberto Leggiéri."

"How do you know all this?"

"I get around. I also heard there was twenty thousand dollars missing."

Fitzpatrick sat back.

Rizzo said, "I assume you want the money returned."

"What do you want?"

"Protection from the cops."

"Twenty thousand doesn't buy you a blank check."

"Sure. By the way, it's eighteen thousand. There's a ten percent finders fee."

Fitzpatrick squirmed. "Keep talking."

"First the cops stop the harassment. Everything reopens, especially gambling."

Fitzpatrick stared at Rizzo. He took out a cigarette and lit it. He didn't offer one to Rizzo. "When do I get the money?"

"In a few days."

Fitzpatrick blew a smoke ring. "What's the second thing?"

"The cops forget about the other Italian. He was Tucker's partner, and he did what he had to do."

"Including run off with our money."

"It was a good instinct. He didn't know it was your money. Oh, and as part of our arrangement, if a newspaper reporter ever asks him, he's forgotten it was Tammany Hall cash invested in a con. Anyway, he's forgiven. Do we have a deal?"

Fitzpatrick crushed out his cigarette. "Okay, we have a deal."

Rizzo stood. He shifted on his feet.

Fitzpatrick huffed. "Is there something else?"

"You should allow Italians into the longshoremen's union."

"I'll write that down. Goodbye."

Chapter 22

KEVIN CLANCY knew that his crew boss Liam Murphy hadn't punched out after his shift and was missing. He paced his apartment until his wife shouted he should turn out the lights and come to bed. He was still awake when Murphy's wife arrived at his door.

The woman twisted flame red hair in her fingers. "My husband didn't come home last night."

Clancy tried to sound convincing. "He probably fell asleep on the ship."

"But the *Gorjistan* sailed." Her eyes filled with tears.

Clancy ran his hand through his hair. "Go home and get some rest. I'll make inquiries at the union hall in the morning. As soon as I know something, I'll come to your apartment."

The next day, Clancy was in Jimmy Doyle's office. At the news of Murphy's disappearance, Doyle's face looked like he had food poisoning. He said, "So, where's Murphy?"

Sweat soaked through Clancy's shirt. "Maybe he fell overboard."

Doyle said, "Was he drunk?"

"We'd had a few."

"If he hit the water, someone would've heard. The body would've surfaced."

"Maybe he went to sleep on the ship. It happens."

Doyle shook his head. "He'd awoken by now. We'd have a cable from the *Gorjistan*."

Clancy's eyes darted. "I told Murphy to order the Italians into the grain hold."

Doyle looked at the ceiling.

Clancy said, "I wanted them to quit. Hell, you wanted them to quit."

"I wanted them to be pressured by the other men and leave on their own. But the grain hold? No fool would go down there. You had Murphy push them into a corner."

Clancy spread his hands. "The dagos were hard workers. They'd never quit. The men were on me for having Italians in the 'shape.' I'm up for a delegate's job. The vote would've gone against me."

"Sure. You were pressured by Goddamn politics. I understand." Doyle shook his head. "Could Murphy have tripped and fallen into the grain?"

"Or been pushed."

"Murder?"

"No one saw anything. But where is he?"

"Yeah. You're right. Whether he was tripped or shoved, he's probably dead."

Clancy's face glistened. "God damn. What do you want me to do?"

"We have no choice; get the cops involved."

The scene at the 18th Street Pier was murmured conversation. The men milled around with hands in pockets. A gaggle of uniformed police huddled with Clancy and squinted into the evening light. Leonardo and Giuseppe saw the cops and paused at the gate.

Leonardo said, "Oh, no."

Giuseppe said, "Remember, stay calm and tell them nothing."

"Azzura's parents will find out I'm in jail."

Giuseppe shrugged. "There's nothing we can do about that."

Clancy spotted Leonardo and Giuseppe and pointed. The cops rushed forward and placed them under arrest.

A police carriage brought them to the Tombs. The Tombs was a brutal fortress of concrete, block stone, and a turret worthy of a medieval prison located on Centre Street. The "Bridge of Sighs" connected the Tombs to the Criminal Court Building. The span's name was taken from the Venetian bridge that connected the torture chambers with the Doge's Palace across the canal. Criminals were said to sigh at their last sight of sunshine before being condemned.

The Tombs prison was overseen by Killian "Third Degree" Byrne, Chief of Detectives. Byrne's "Third Degree" interrogation technique of accused murderers often extracted confessions before their attorneys arrived.

Leonardo's mug shot was snapped and he was thrown into a six by eight-foot cell. He sat on a narrow cot. The shadow of cell bars slashed across his face. The space smelled of urine and vomit. Outside the iron door appeared Killian Byrne.

Byrne's smile looked like a jack-o-lantern's with wide spaced teeth the size of Chiclets. He was a burly man with sausage-like fingers. He clanged open the door, walked into the cell, and loomed over Leonardo. His back blocked the light, and Leonardo's face darkened like an eclipsed sun.

"Mr. Robustelli." Byrne enunciated every syllable. "I'm investigating the disappearance and suspected death of Liam Murphy. Do you know Mr. Murphy?"

Leonardo's eyes averted Byrne's. He nodded.

"He was your crew boss the night he disappeared?"

Another nod.

"I know you killed Murphy. You and Fontana worked the grain hold where Murphy disappeared. He had a reputation for being a son of a bitch. Did you kill him because he gave the two of you a hard time?"

Leonardo's sweat smelled like cheap vinegar.

Byrne said, "Yeah, Murphy was tough on you and Fontana because you're Italians. So you killed him. You were too smart to throw him overboard. Someone would've heard the splash. So you buried him in the grain. Right?"

Leonardo's face flushed.

Byrne frowned. He put his hand on Leonardo's shoulder. Leonardo flinched. "But maybe you weren't the one who killed Murphy? Fontana did it. Yeah, Fontana's the criminal. He has a record in Italy, doesn't he? You were there when Fontana killed Murphy, right? You want to tell me, but you're afraid of Fontana?"

"No."

"Don't tell me you're innocent. It was either you or Fontana who killed Murphy."

Leonardo's throat closed up. He needed to urinate.

Byrne softened his tone. "Your mother is in Italy? How will she feel when she hears that her son is on trial for murder? Do you want her to come to America and watch you be tried for your life?"

Leonardo saw the image of his mother's face. Tears began to form. Leonardo covered his eyes.

"Fontana killed Murphy, didn't he? Tell me. Save yourself."

Leonardo remembered his mother alone on the Naples pier. He'd abandoned her. This ordeal was his punishment.

Byrne saw the dampness in Leonardo's eyes. "Good. You feel remorse for what you did. I'll tell that to the judge. Come on, son, tell the truth. You'll feel better."

A guard argued with someone down the line of cells. A rotund bearded man in a vested suit and tie appeared at the black iron bars. "I'm William Schuster. I represent Leonardo Robustelli and Giuseppe Fontana." He waved a paper in his hand. "I've filed a writ of habeas corpus. This man will have his day in court. The interrogation stops now."

Leonardo breathed a sigh of relief.

Byrne put his hands on hips. "How the hell did you get here so fast?" He touched his chin. "Son of a bitch. You knew Robustelli and Fontana would be placed under arrest." Byrne turned to Leonardo. "Tell me Fontana killed Murphy or you'll be executed for murder. This is your last chance."

Leonardo shook his head.

Byrne left in a huff. Schuster entered the cage and sat next to Leonardo. "Mr. Rizzo sent me. Tomorrow you'll be brought across the bridge to a courtroom and a judge. Let me do the talking."

"Will I get out of here?"

"Let's take it one step at a time."

When Schuster was gone, Leonardo was served an evening meal; a stew of beef intestines and potatoes. The smell brought his stomach up to his throat, and he pushed the dish back through the iron bars. Leonardo's cell was two strides wide. He paced for an hour. His mind whirred. He knew nothing about the criminal court system in America. In Italy everything was possible. He might be tortured. He had to hold out. If he confessed, his mother would be devastated. He had to keep this horrible incident from her. Knowledge of his arrest would break her heart. He could be kept inside the Tombs for years waiting to make bail. Rizzo sent the lawyer, but would he put up cash for his release? Sooner or later his mother would find out. His stomach churned with acid.

Leonardo heard the squeak of the cell block door open and the patter of rushing feet on the cement floor. Azzura appeared. She had a basket under her arm. "Leonardo?"

"I'm here." He pressed his face to the bars and they kissed. "Oh God, it's so good to see you." They kissed again. "How did you get in?"

"Detective Byrne. He came to Spring Street. He told me I could bring you dinner." She unpacked her basket. "It's macaroni. It's cold." She handed the plate to Leonardo through the bars. "They wouldn't let me bring a fork into prison."

"Did Byrne speak to your parents?"

"Yes."

"Oh, no. What did they say?"

"They're shocked. They've forbidden me to see you. I snuck away. Byrne told me that he doesn't think you're guilty. He says you're shielding Giuseppe."

Leonardo slumped against the bars. "This is such a mess."

"Byrne told me that if you say it was Giuseppe, he'll let you out of jail."

"I can't."

"But if Giuseppe killed the man."

"He didn't."

"Oh my God."

"It was an accident. I only wanted to earn some money."

Azzura's tears flowed. Leonardo reached for her through the bars. "Please don't cry."

Azzura wiped her face.

The night guard's shadow appeared. "You need to leave."

Azzura and Leonardo reached for each other. They kissed.

The guard pulled her away. Leonardo's arms extended through the bars. "Please come tomorrow."

While Leonardo and Giuseppe were in the Tombs, Carlo set out to deliver the $500 blackmail money to Ignazio Terranova. Carlo stepped into a Hester Street saloon. The air was heavy with the gray haze of cigar smoke. The bar was crowded. The room droned with men in conversation punctured by the occasional burst of argument. Carlo heard a shout of triumph. His eyes were drawn to a corner table where Terranova was seated playing cards with four other men, including Bruno Drago. Terranova had the Italian deck of forty cards in his hand. Terranova peeled off four five-dollar bills. Each of his playing opponents placed their own fiver on the table to cover his bet. Terranova turned a card face up. It was the six of clubs. Terranova took his time turning over the next card. If it would be a second six, he'd win. He turned over a deuce of hearts. Drago smacked his hand onto the table and called for a second deuce to appear. Terranova put his hand on the next card. "*Sei, sei, sei.*" He turned over the two of spades.

Drago shouted, "*Sì.*"

"*Figlio di puttana.*" Terranova threw the cards across the table. Some splattered onto the floor. Terranova passed the "bank" to Drago.

Carlo stood at his shoulder. "Signor Terranova."

Terranova's brow was furrowed. "Not now."

"I'm here on behalf of the Medinas."

Terranova took a deep breath. He looked up at Carlo. "Do you play *zecchinetta*?"

"Sometimes."

Terranova told Drago to save his seat. He huddled with Carlo in a corner.

"My name is Carlo. I have the $500 for the Medinas."

Terranova smiled. "Do you have a last name?"

"Not for you."

"Your accent is Neapolitan. Are you with Rizzo?"

Carlo stared.

Terranova said, "So how do you know the Medinas?"

"They're friends." Carlo extended an envelope. Terranova put his hand on the cash, but Carlo didn't release it. "This is the end of it."

Terranova lifted his chin. "What do you mean?"

"No more 'Black Hand' threats to the Medinas."

"You misunderstand. I acted on behalf of the Medinas with the blackmailers."

"Sure. But don't bother them anymore."

Terranova smiled. "It must be affection for the daughter, Azzura, that's caused you to be confused. She is lovely."

"I assume we have an understanding. Leave the Medinas alone." Carlo released the envelope.

Terranova motioned for Drago to come over. The legs on Drago's chair squeaked on the linoleum when he pushed it back.

"Drago this is Carlo the Neapolitan. He won't tell me his last name."

Drago and Carlo looked at each other like rutting stags.

Terranova said, "Carlo is playing hero for the princess, Azzura Medina." He laughed.

Drago held the lapels of his jacket. His hands were meaty and stubby; they looked almost webbed.

Terranova said, "So we need to make some inquiries about him."

"Just leave the Medinas alone." Carlo spun on his heel and walked toward the door.

Terranova's voice rose. "You may find that hero is a dangerous occupation."

Terranova told Drago to follow Carlo. When Drago stepped outside the saloon, Detective Byrne and another policeman grabbed him. The cop raised a pistol. Byrne grabbed Drago's arm. "We need to talk to you about a murder in Brooklyn. You're coming with us." They hustled him into a carriage and took him to the Tombs.

In the morning Leonardo and Giuseppe were hauled across the Bridge of Sighs to the Criminal Court Building. Judge Rufus Crawford, with mutton chop sideburns, sat behind a raised bench. The room was small and wood-paneled. Leonardo and Giuseppe were behind a chicken wire screen and railing along a side wall. Byrne and Schuster stood before the judge.

Crawford looked at his court docket, then at Leonardo and Giuseppe. He frowned at Byrne. "More Italians?"

Byrne shrugged.

Crawford said, "I don't suppose they speak decent English. Why do we allow these crooks and murderers into this country?"

Schuster cleared his throat. "If Your Honor pleases."

Crawford sounded weary. "Yes, Counsel?"

"I'll speak for the defendants."

"All right. This hearing is to determine if there's sufficient evidence to hold Leonardo Robustelli and Giuseppe Fontana in detention. Detective Byrne, let's hear from you."

"Your Honor, Liam Murphy, a crew boss on the docks from the International Longshoremen's Association Local 791, is missing. He was last seen with Robustelli and Fontana on the ship, *Gorjistan*, while it loaded grain at the Chelsea Piers. Murphy never punched out at the end of the shift, which indicates that he didn't leave the ship. Murphy wasn't pleased that the two Italians were assigned to work under him. I believe they argued, and the Italians threw Murphy into the grain hold where he suffocated."

"I see. Mr. Schuster, your response?"

"Your Honor, as Detective Byrne said, Liam Murphy is missing. He could be in Hoboken for all we know. He wouldn't be the first man to run away from his wife. Men do forget to sign out after their shift. If Murphy was hurt, he could have fallen overboard, or as Detective Byrne suggests, into the grain hold by accident. If there was foul play, there were at least a dozen other men on the ship and working the docks, any of whom could have caused Murphy harm. There's not one shred of evidence that my clients hurt Murphy. There's no evidence that Murphy is even injured. In short, Your Honor, Detective Byrne alleges murder, but there's no body. I respectfully request that Robustelli and Fontana be released."

The judge looked at Byrne.

"Your Honor, despite what Mr. Schuster said, there's a high likelihood that harm came to Liam Murphy, and the Italians were the only men with a motive."

Crawford leaned on his hand. "But you don't have a body?"

"No."

"I'm sorry, Detective; no body, no murder."

"Your Honor, these men are material witnesses to the events surrounding Murphy's disappearance. I believe that when the *Gorjistan* reaches Turkey and empties its grain cargo, Murphy's body will be found. I ask that you detain these men until that time."

Crawford looked relieved. "Yes, that's reasonable."

Schuster raised his hand. "Your Honor, I request that bail be set."

"All right, bail is set at $1,000 each. We're done here." Crawford banged down his gavel. "Next case."

Leonardo looked at Giuseppe. "A thousand dollars?"

Giuseppe grabbed his head. "We'll never get out of here."

The men's shoulders sagged. They were led back to their cells by a guard.

When Bruno Drago was eight, a loose roof tile fell and cracked his head. From then on his hair was parted along a diagonal scar. Soon after the accident Drago had his first epileptic seizure. As a teenager Drago gained a reputation for violent reaction to authority. The *Picciotteria*, the criminal element in Reggio Calabria, recruited him for theft and murder for hire. When Drago was twenty his romantic interest in a young married woman was rebuffed, so he murdered her husband, hoping to clear the way. Drago was caught and sentenced to life. He served ten years before he escaped and was smuggled by the *Picciotteria* to New York.

Drago was a man who craved bloodshed. He walked into Terranova's saloon on Hester Street and asked for work. Terranova checked Drago's record in Italy and learned, like he, Drago was on the run from the Italian police. Terranova also knew that the Calabrian *Picciotteria* prided themselves on a code of silence. Terranova first used Drago in the Florio kidnapping. He had confidence that Drago would have no qualms about slitting the Florio boy's throat if Terranova gave the order.

Drago became Terranova's 'Black Hand' enforcer. A businessman who owned five butcher shops in Brooklyn, went to the police for protection after receiving an extortion threat. Drago and three others from Terranova's gang rowed a boat to Brooklyn and assassinated the man as he was closing one of his shops. Detective Byrne arrested Drago on suspicion outside the Hester Street saloon after Drago's confrontation with Carlo and took him to the Tombs for questioning.

There was a man in Leonardo's cell when he arrived. "Bruno Drago," said the guard. "He's a 'Black Hander' we picked up for questioning." Drago had the face of a Pit Bull. "We think he murdered a butcher." The guard unlocked the door. "Enjoy yourselves."

Drago's simian eyes watched Leonardo as he stepped inside. The guard left.

Drago spoke in a Calabrian accent. "This cot's mine." He folded his arms.

Leonardo didn't know how long he'd be locked up in the Tombs, but with Drago trying to dominate him, the time would be unbearable. He sized the man up. Drago was big and solidly built. It would be a tough fight, but Leonardo was in no mood to have Drago walk over him. Leonardo's ears got hot. He gave Drago an evil smile.

Drago saw the storm building in Leonardo. He unfolded his arms. The knuckles on his fists were clenched white.

Leonardo saw concern on Drago's face. Leonardo's heart pounded. A bead of sweat dripped down the small of his back. His body tensed. A sequence played in Leonardo's brain where he leapt on Drago and beat him to a bloody pulp. His smile widened.

There were footsteps, and the guard appeared. "Robustelli, you made bail." Leonardo heard the key in the lock, and his tension deflated.

As Leonardo left the cell, Drago sneered. "Hope to see you again."

In an hour Leonardo and Giuseppe were on the street with Schuster.

Leonardo said, "Mr. Rizzo posted bond?"

Schuster gave Leonardo a wry smile. "In a way. We used a bogus bail bondsman. He put up a building on Mott Street as collateral."

"Mr. Rizzo owns the building?"

"No, you two do."

Leonardo and Giuseppe looked at each other quizzically.

Schuster said, "You owned the building when it was put up to guarantee your bail. The bail bondsman gave you title to the property for today."

Leonardo said, "What do you mean?"

Schuster smiled. "Tomorrow he'll transfer title to another prisoner as collateral for his bail."

Giuseppe said, "I don't get it."

Schuster said, "If you two don't show up when called the collateral is forfeited, but there'll be no property to confiscate. So nobody loses money."

Leonardo said, "But, we'll be on the run."

Schuster said, "You'll need to talk to Mr. Rizzo about that. He paid my fee and the bail bondsman for his service. Enjoy your freedom."

Chapter 23

CARLO RETURNED to the restaurant after paying Terranova. His face was troubled. Ciro and Isabella rushed to him. Azzura followed.

"I gave Terranova the $500. He denied that he was the blackmailer, but he lied. You're safe for now."

Ciro grabbed Carlo's hand with both of his. "*Grazie.*"

Isabella kissed his cheeks.

Azzura smiled. "Thank you for helping us."

Carlo's face softened. "I won't let anything happen to you."

Azzura blushed.

Isabella held a chair. "Sit. Have a plate of pasta. Azzura, serve Carlo some wine."

Ciro said, "I'll make a veal roast."

Leonardo and Giuseppe dragged into Ciro's after their release from the Tombs. Their clothes were disheveled and they smelled like sewers. Their three-day beards gave them the look of escapees from Devil's Island.

Carlo sat at a table like a Roman Emperor. Before him was a stuffed veal roast and three types of pasta. Azzura was at his shoulder, pouring wine. Giuseppe rushed for the food. Azzura handed the bottle to her mother and ran to Leonardo. She hugged him. Ciro and Isabella looked at each other like a turd was dropped into the ravioli.

Azzura pulled Leonardo into a quiet corner. "How did you get out?"

"We made bail."

"So Detective Byrne thinks you're innocent?"

"The judge ordered our release. Byrne is relentless. He'll come after us again."

Azzura cupped her forehead. "Why won't he leave you alone?"

"He thinks we're murderers, but without a body he couldn't charge us."

"I don't understand."

"Murphy's buried in the grain hold on a ship to Turkey. When they uncover him, Byrne will arrest us again."

"This is crazy."

Leonardo said, "I need to speak to Rizzo."

Azzura said, "Isn't he the reason you're in trouble?"

"He just got us a job."

Azzura frowned. "A job in the Irish union. Your presence antagonized the other men."

"What would you have had me do? Quit? Show fear? We have a right to work."

Azzura turned her head. "Why didn't you stay with Gentile?"

"I was treated like dirt under the boss's fingernails. I'll never go back." Leonardo took Azzura's hand. "I'll need to leave New York."

"You'll return to Italy?"

"I don't want to be arrested again. You were in the Tombs. It smells like death. We'll go to Naples together."

Azzura took back her hand. "America's my home."

"It's not safe for me here. How can you ask me to stay?"

Azzura bit her lip.

Isabella called out for her daughter.

Giuseppe was alongside Carlo. He stuffed gobs of food into his face. "What's this feast for?"

Carlo said, "I paid off Terranova. Leonardo, have some of this delicious food. There's far more than I can eat." He smiled at Isabella. "And the *vino* is fabulous."

Isabella beamed. She handed the bottle to Azzura. "Here, pour for Carlo."

Azzura shifted on her feet. Isabella returned to the kitchen.

Leonardo sat. "I assume the payoff went smoothly?"

"Yes and no. Terranova is a slimy bastard. He has an ogre, Drago, who works for him. They're ruthless *cafones*."

"They put Drago in my cell at the Tombs. We almost fought. Ugly, vicious bastard."

Giuseppe forked some veal onto his plate. "If you tangle with Terranova or any of his gang, it's a fight to the death. There are no half measures with them. Best we avoid them."

Carlo said, "I told Terranova to stay away from the Medinas, but I just made him mad."

Giuseppe frowned. "Watch your ass is all I can say."

"I can take care of myself."

"Sure." Giuseppe gobbled some rigatoni.

Carlo said, "So how were the Tombs?"

Leonardo scowled. "Like its name. A crypt for the half-alive with guards. Rizzo arranged our bail or they'd have buried us in that prison."

Isabella came to the table with an opened newspaper. "The Hippodrome has a circus spectacular going on. It sounds like a magnificent show." She showed the article to her daughter.

Azzura nodded.

Isabella said, "Carlo, why don't you take Azzura?"

Leonardo halted a fork-full of food at his mouth.

Azzura said, "Mama."

Carlo brightened. "That's a terrific idea." His smile was a row of perfect white teeth. "Azzura, how about tomorrow?"

Isabella beamed. "Wonderful."

Azzura's eyes flitted past Leonardo. "I don't know."

Isabella said, "The show sounds grand. You must go."

Azzura shrugged.

Carlo said, "We'll continue this celebration."

Azzura avoided Leonardo's eyes.

Isabella said, "That settles it."

Leonardo glared at Carlo.

After dinner the three men went up to their apartment. Giuseppe saw the sick smile on Leonardo's face and stepped between him and Carlo.

Leonardo's voice was loud. "I told you to stay away from Azzura."

Carlo was calm. "Isabella suggested the date and I accepted. Face it, the Medinas don't want you for Azzura. Ask Giuseppe."

Leonardo's ears were red. "Azzura doesn't like you."

"I think she does. An Italian girl needs to follow her parents' wishes. They'll settle her future, and Isabella will never accept you."

Leonardo pointed his finger. "Touch her, and I'll cut your throat."

Carlo stiffened. "Don't threaten me."

Giuseppe held the men apart. "Carlo, tomorrow you should get yourself a different apartment."

"Yeah. Okay. But now I'm going to bed." He turned his back on them.

The featured show at the Hippodrome Theater was an extravaganza, "A Yankee Circus on Mars." The Theater was a red brick and terra-cotta Moorish Palace with four corner towers topped with huge globes covered in electric bulbs. The expanse filled a city block. The stage inside was as large as a boardwalk pier and flooded with light. "Yankee Circus" featured a cast of hundreds with space ships, elephants, a baboon, clowns, and an orchestra that played non-stop.

Halfway into the production the lights were dimmed, and the sound of oboes rose for a ballet, the "Dance of the Hours," from Amilcare Ponchielli's Opera, *La Gioconda*. One by one dancers appeared atop an elevated stepped platform like the notes on sheet music. Each woman was dressed in a different color gossamer skirt. They pirouetted, arms floating in the air like pulsating waves. Suddenly the dancers streamed down both sides of the platform stairs like tumbling leaves and formed a line across the lower stage. A single woman in white emerged at the top of the stairs. She stepped across the platform with a series of athletic pirouettes, *pas jeté*, and arabesques to the sound of stringed instruments while the women below moved like flowers stirred in a spring breeze.

Azzura watched the dance routine on the edge of her seat. Her hands were clasped at her chin and her eyes followed every step.

Carlo leaned toward Azzura and his arm touched hers. While she stared ahead, Carlo focused on her. Her shoulder was close to his, and he felt a tingle as if an electric pulse had jumped the gap. His eyes outlined the silhouette of her body. He breathed in her form on a floating carpet of lavender. His heart pounded. He felt a curious sense of lightness.

After the show the crowd flooded onto the street. They buzzed with talk of what they'd seen. Azzura and Carlo emerged from the milling people at the theater's entrance and strolled downtown.

Azzura bubbled. "I couldn't have imagined anything like that. What a spectacle. Hundreds of people on stage. I'd only seen pictures of elephants before. They're gigantic. And the lights were dazzling."

Carlo said, "Yeah. It was great."

"The best thing was the ballet. The women's costumes, the colors, the athletic leaps, the music." Azzura fanned her flushed face. "I feel like I can't catch my breath." She stopped. "Thank you for taking me."

Carlo looked into Azzura's green eyes. He took her by the shoulders and kissed her.

Azzura stepped back and put a hand to her mouth. "Carlo, you shouldn't."

"Why?" He moved close.

She turned her face. "You shouldn't take advantage. I appreciate what you did for my family. I don't know how my parents would've paid the 'Black Hand' money without you."

"Are you telling me you didn't like the kiss?"

"I have feelings for Leonardo."

"Maybe you like me more?"

"I'm not a village girl flattered by your attention."

"But you enjoyed the kiss."

"I'm not a conquest. You're not serious about me."

"I am."

"I don't believe you."

"But you believe this." Carlo kissed her again.

She pulled away from him. "You're trying to confuse me."

"You're not confused. You know you want me."

"You're playing with me." Azzura walked away.

Carlo caught up. "I'm not. It's true, I hadn't taken women seriously. But tonight when I looked at you in the theater, how excited you were, how beautiful, something clicked in my head. You're different." He moved close. "I love you."

"Don't say that. You don't mean it."

"I do."

Azzura stopped. "Take me home please." She walked ahead.

Carlo lifted his arms. "Azzura." She didn't stop. He caught up, and they arrived at the station. She wouldn't look at him while they waited. When the trolley arrived, they took their seats in silence.

Azzura wrung her hands in her lap. Carlo was handsome and charming, but he was too sure of himself. Everything was so easy for him. She'd be a challenge until she gave in to him, then he'd decide she was just another boring girl and move on. Carlo's forehead was troubled. His gray eyes were on her. They were soft. He sounded sincere when he said that he loved her. She didn't know if she should believe him. Leonardo also said that he loved her, but he wanted to live in Italy. Her mother rejected Leonardo and doted on Carlo. Azzura didn't want to fight with her mother. Might Carlo really love her? Azzura sighed. She needed to sleep. She'd think about this in the morning.

When they exited the trolley, Carlo took Azzura's arm. "My feelings for you are genuine."

"You hardly know me."

"I know you well enough." He kissed her and held her in his arms.

"I can't think."

"Feel, don't think."

"Please let me go."

"All right."

Azzura's face was still flushed when they walked into Ciro's. Isabella asked brightly, "How was the show?"

Azzura's eyes averted Leonardo's. His face was stone. "It was nice. Goodnight." She left for her parents' apartment.

Isabella called out, "Azzura." Her daughter didn't stop. Isabella turned toward Carlo.

"It was a great show." He shot a glance at Leonardo. "The best I've ever seen. I'm glad you suggested I take Azzura."

Isabella's face relaxed.

Carlo whistled as he left the restaurant. Leonardo scowled at him, and the heat rose up his neck.

Chapter 24

THE NEXT DAY Leonardo and Garibaldi caught up with Azzura on her way to market.

She stooped to pet the dog.

Leonardo said, "What happened with Carlo?"

Azzura didn't look up. "Nothing."

"Did he try to take advantage of you?"

She stood and walked. "I don't want to talk about it."

"If he tried anything I'll kill him."

Azzura stopped short. "Is that your answer? Violence? Hasn't violence caused you enough trouble? Didn't that night in jail teach you anything?"

"I can't stand the thought of him touching you."

"I'm not your property." She turned away. "And you're going back to Italy."

"I didn't say I was definitely going back. Did Carlo try anything?"

"If I tell you, you must promise not to fight with him."

"Damn." Leonardo clenched his fists.

"I'm not going to tell you anything if you can't control yourself."

"Okay. I'm calm. Tell me."

"He kissed me."

Leonardo grabbed his head. "Son of a bitch."

"Stop."

"What did you do?"

"I told him he shouldn't take advantage of me because he helped my family."

"That's right. There's more. What else?"

"He kissed me and told me that he loved me."

"God damn. What did you say?"

"I told him that I had feelings for you."

"Do you have feelings for him?"

Azzura looked away.

"Azzura, he lied. He doesn't love you. He just wants, you know, to be with you."

"And you don't want to be with me?"

"I love you. Of course I do."

"You and Carlo are the same."

"I want to marry you."

Azzura sighed. "But I want to stay in America."

"Do you want to see me in jail again?"

"Of course not. But the man's death was an accident. That's not murder."

"You're being naive."

"If I went to Italy with you, I'd be a stranger in a foreign country. What would I do there? Spin all day while you go to work? Be a traditional Italian wife? That's not a life for me." Azzura held her head. "Everything is so difficult."

"I need to tell you something about Carlo. Remember the night he first came to the tenement?"

"He had blood on him. He said that he cut his hand. He showed me the gash."

"That wasn't his blood on his clothes. He killed a man."

Azzura's eyes widened. "How do you know?"

"He told me. The police who came and closed the restaurant were after him. I know you suspected him at first, but your mother didn't."

"So why wasn't Carlo arrested?"

"Political corruption. He stole Tammany Hall money that was used in a scam. The money was returned to the politicians in exchange for the police leaving Carlo alone. That's not all.

I'm sure Carlo murdered someone in Italy. That's why he's in New York. He's on the run from the Italian *carabinieri*."

"Are you telling me this because you're concerned I have feelings for Carlo?"

"So you do care for him?"

"Leonardo, stop. I don't like it when you act this way."

"I want to open your eyes."

"Thank you, but I see clearly what you're doing."

"Don't be mad. If your parents know the truth, they won't think Carlo's the one for you."

"I'll make my own decisions about the men in my life. You can't make my parents prefer you by having them turn against Carlo."

"I don't want you to see Carlo anymore."

"Stop trying to control me. That's what my parents do and I hate it." She shook her head. "I need time to think." She walked away.

"Azzura."

Garibaldi whined as she quickened her pace.

Chapter 25

NATALIA CAPUTO was a young nurse and midwife on the Lower East Side when she was called to a Spring Street tenement. The baby had turned in the womb and the mother was suffering back labor. Natalia sent a boy with a dollar to fetch the Lodge Doctor, a shiny-faced man with an impatient air. The doctor used forceps and the baby girl finally emerged, but she wasn't breathing. The child was pronounced stillborn and the doctor handed her to Natalia. The mother shrieked. Natalia ran to a tub and plunged the baby into a cold bath. The child cried. The mother, Isabella Medina, heard the sound and smiled through her pain. The baby was Azzura. Natalia became her godmother.

Azzura arrived at the Henry Street house just as Natalia flew out the door. "There are two sick children on Elizabeth Street. Come, you can help."

Azzura and Natalia entered a lower level tenement apartment. A woman in her late twenties who looked forty was at a coal stove boiling garments. Two emaciated babies were on the floor, their skin blooming with the rose spots of typhoid fever. Natalia and Azzura each picked up a child. Their bodies were racked with fever.

The haggard mother grasped her face in her hands.

Natalia said in Italian, "Have you called a doctor?"

The woman's eyes filled with tears. "No money."

"Where's your husband?"

"He needs to work."

Natalia and Azzura each sat with a child in their lap. Natalia took a milk bottle from her kit. She and Azzura fed them in turn.

Natalia said, "We need to take them to the hospital."

The mother sobbed, "Carriages cost money."

Natalia said, "I'll pay."

Once the children were in the hands of the hospital doctor, the two women walked back toward Henry Street.

Azzura said, "That was frightening. Will the babies be okay?"

"I think so. But in another week, those children would've died."

"Dear God."

"What did you come to see me about?"

"Men. I need advice."

"Plural?"

Azzura gave Natalia a little smile.

Natalia said, "One of them must be that curly-headed Leonardo I met going with you to market. He's about your age."

"He's sweet when he's not acting jealous."

"Sweet. Okay. What's the other boy's name?"

"Carlo. He's older."

"Is he also sweet?"

"No. He's an Adonis and confident."

"You're in love?"

"I don't know. They both said that they love me."

Natalia smiled. "Men profess love as often as their loins move them. You know what men want?"

"I haven't crossed that line."

"That's wise."

"Can you love two men at once?"

Natalia sighed. "Perhaps. But they won't accept it."

"You're right. They're both jealous."

"I understand. What's your mother say about all this?"

"She likes Carlo. He's an aristocrat; for her the perfect match. She thinks Leonardo is unworthy. It's infuriating."

"It's early for you to be taking such a serious interest in men. I thought you had ambitions for yourself?"

"I feel ensnared by tradition. I don't want to live my mother's life."

"So shouldn't you be wary of falling in love too quickly? Plus, you know your parents will want to control the husband you choose. That's a conflict that could break your heart."

"If I don't find someone on my own, I'm afraid that my mother will force the issue."

"You feel constrained by your parents. But marriage isn't emancipation. Once you marry, you give up your independence to a huge degree. You'll be at the mercy and whim of the man you choose. You won't have a life of your own. You'll be filled with your husband's motivations and with children, keeping house. Look around you. How many married women do you know who pursue anything but their husband's ambitions?"

"Is that why you're alone?"

Natalia sighed. "There was a doctor. He ministered to the poor, that's how we met. He also helped women in trouble, those who needed abortions and prostitutes who'd contracted venereal disease. I saw him as a pioneer and admired him for it."

"So what happened?"

"He appealed to a lot of women. I suppose I should've been more open-minded, but I wanted him for myself. He tired of our arguments and left."

"And no one since?"

Natalia shrugged. "I have my work." She paused. "And no regrets."

"I'm not sure I could be a single woman."

"I understand. But what are you doing about your goals? You have more options than opening a restaurant. Have you read the pamphlets I gave you? Come to one of our suffrage rallies."

"I will. I promise."

"Azzura, about Leonardo and Carlo. You'll want to know the depths of each man before you decide. Think about what you gain, but also think about what you lose. I understand that you want to make your own selection based on love, but that seemingly independent decision will limit the rest of your life's choices."

Chapter 26

PAULO INNOCENTI had manicured nails and a waxed mustache. He wore a tidy vested suit with a scented handkerchief in the pocket and a flower in his lapel. Innocenti was an etcher, engraver, and master printer. Alfred Stieglitz saw Innocenti's work and awarded his shop a contract. Innocenti perfected a delicate and detailed photogravure technique to replicate Stieglitz's photos onto metal plates. The renderings were so exact that on one occasion when Stieglitz's original photographs failed to arrive at an exhibition, Innocenti's magazine reproductions were placed on display.

Every Sunday morning Innocenti walked to the baker on St. James Street. His wife loved *cornetti* at breakfast, the crescent-shaped pastries stuffed with jam, lemon curd, or chocolate. The bell jingled on the bakery's door, and Innocenti was greeted with the smell of fresh baked bread and rum cake. The bakery was crowded. Innocenti's mouth watered over the *sfogliatella, canoli,* and *bocconotti* while he waited for his turn. The baker's daughter, a buxom girl in black pigtails, scurried behind the counter as patrons sang out their choices, which she picked and placed in a cardboard box. Innocenti felt a presence at his shoulder.

"*Buon giorno,* Don Innocenti."

Innocenti looked at the man and gulped. The wealthy Italians who'd felt the bite of the "Black Hand" had talked about Ignazio Terranova in hushed tones.

"*Buon giorno,* Don Terranova."

The girl asked and Innocenti selected a variety of *cornetti.*

Terranova said, "Ah, my wife prefers the *canoli*. She says they remind her of Sicily. Your wife is well, I hope?"

"Err, yes. I hope your family is also well?"

Terranova beamed. "They're quite well, *grazie*." Terranova lowered his voice. "Don Innocenti, I must ask you for a favor."

Innocenti's stomach sank.

"Your engraving skill is well known. In fact your artistry is the talk of the Italian community. They say that if you created the image of grapes, birds would flock to peck at them."

Innocenti managed a tight lipped smile. "You're too kind."

Terranova moved close enough for Innocenti to feel his acrid breath on his cheek. "I need you to do a job for me."

Sweat rose on Innocenti's forehead. "What can I possibly do for you?"

The baker's daughter had placed Innocenti's order in a white box. She drew string from a large roll of twine hung on a spike and tied the package. Innocenti took some bills from his pocket to pay.

Terranova stopped him. "Allow me." Terranova gave the girl a five-dollar bill and received change. From it he extended a two-dollar bill toward Innocenti.

Innocenti hesitated and took the note. "I don't understand."

Terranova locked arms with Innocenti and walked him out to the street. He pointed at the two-dollar bill. "I want you to make those for me."

Innocenti stopped short. "Counterfeit?"

Terranova pulled him closer. "That word hurts my ears. The problem I have, Don Innocenti, is that the notes that come from Sicily are of poor quality. The only places they can be passed are busy saloons and oyster bars where the light is dim. Unfortunately, bar owners have become wary and are refusing to accept my currency. I need bills that allow me to do my business in the bright light of day where I can pass thousands not just a pittance."

Innocenti absent-mindedly wiped his forehead with the two-dollar bill. His voice quivered. "Counterfeiting is illegal. I could go to jail."

Terranova's tone had an edge to it. "Do this favor for me, and you'll be under my personal protection."

Innocenti almost cried. "Do I need protection?"

Terranova smiled. "Don't worry. No one will touch your wife. *Capisce*?"

Innocenti swallowed hard. "But what if I'm caught?"

Terranova snickered. "Don't worry. Your signature won't be on the bills. We pay for political protection, and I have the best attorney in New York to help me. We're a huge organization that stretches from Palermo to New York."

Innocenti gnawed his lip.

"When you're with us, you'll have all the money you need to treat your wife to every extravagance, not just a few pastries."

"If I make the plates, where will you print the notes?"

"I have a location nearby. You'll be my consultant for purchasing the best press."

Innocenti's eyes darted. "I'm very busy."

Terranova pressed a finger into Innocenti's chest. "Signore, you must make time. For me."

Innocenti nodded. "Yes. Of course."

"Excellent. When you've completed your task and begin to receive your share of the riches that flow to us, you'll be glad you made this decision."

Chapter 27

A WOMAN LEANED OUT of a tenement window, stretched her mouth with her fingers, and whistled. The sharp sound was like a siren over the squeak of wagon wheels and children's shouts as they ran in the street. A dark curly haired boy of ten looked up. His mother called out, and waved him home. She ducked back inside. The boy's shoulders slumped with inevitability and he trudged toward the tenement door. For a moment Leonardo saw the image of his mother calling him to dinner. He was with Giuseppe outside the Mulberry Street social club.

When Rizzo saw them enter, he raised his arms. "My gladiators."

Leonardo sat. "*Grazie*, Signore, for arranging bail."

Rizzo nodded. "I have plans for you."

"We can't return to the docks."

"Not yet anyway."

"You have something else in mind?"

"The Irish must allow Italian longshoremen." Rizzo smiled. "And I need to get my fingers into the freight handling money machine. You guys will help when the time is right. In the meantime, you both need to earn some money. Leonardo, you like to hang around Ciro's. Take the *morra* game and the lottery. You won't make a fortune, but you can keep an eye on that lovely Azzura. Giuseppe, I have some cash that needs to be put to work. Solicit the businesses and gamblers who hang out around Houston Street. They always need loans. The vigorish is twenty percent per week. Can you handle that?"

Giuseppe said, "Sure, boss."

Rizzo looked over their shoulders. "Where's Carlo?"

Leonardo glowered. "We had words."

"Over what?

Leonardo said, "Azzura."

"That figures." He turned to Giuseppe. "How did Carlo's payoff go with Terranova?"

Giuseppe said, "He told Terranova to stay away from the Medinas."

Rizzo smiled. "That Carlo has balls. No wonder Azzura is attracted to him."

Leonardo's ears got red. "She doesn't like him."

"Yeah, sure. Just don't kill each other over her. Giuseppe, tell Carlo he owes me, and he shouldn't be a stranger. One of these days I'll need to settle with Terranova."

Giuseppe said, "The time couldn't come too soon. Leonardo had a run-in with Bruno Drago at the Tombs."

Rizzo said, "Ugly pig. Lives to kill. He's Terranova's enforcer and counterfeit passer. You guys should carry pistols."

Leonardo said, "I have a stiletto. I don't want Azzura to see me carrying a gun."

Rizzo frowned. "Silly. So where's Carlo living?"

Giuseppe jerked his thumb. "At the tenement. Isabella Medina rented an apartment for just him."

Leonardo had a dour expression. "She'd bring him breakfast in bed if he asked."

Rizzo laughed. "That's a tempting image. If I didn't like Ciro so much I might grab a little of Isabella for myself. *Madonna mia*, that woman is a force."

Leonardo sat back.

Rizzo said, "Don't give me that look. When you get older, mature women ripen in your eye."

"If you say so."

"You'll see. The mother is a preview of the daughter. Look at Isabella and see Azzura in twenty years. Think about that the next time you're with them."

Bruno Drago strode into Ciro's like Alexander entered Persepolis. Carlo and Leonardo were both in the restaurant, but they hadn't spoken since Carlo moved into his own apartment. Leonardo ran the *morra* game. Carlo ate dinner at a table nearer the door. Drago's orangutan eyes panned the room. He spotted the two men, and his lips curled into a smile. He straddled a chair and called Azzura over for his order. Drago leered at her. After she left, he grinned at Leonardo and Carlo in turn. They glared back at him. Drago finished eating and approached Ciro. "Signor Terranova wants to purchase four cases of your booze."

Ciro wiped sweat off his lip. He shot a look at Carlo but received a deadpan stare in return. "Yes, I'll sell."

Drago pressed some notes into Ciro's hand. "The goods will be picked up tomorrow."

When Drago was out the door, Carlo ran after him. Leonardo was in the middle of a game and didn't follow.

Carlo called out.

Drago rotated like a heavy vessel at sea. "Carlo the Neapolitan. What do you want?"

"I warned Terranova to stay away from the Medinas."

"I guess he didn't listen." Drago pulled out a revolver.

Carlo recoiled.

Drago said, "Terranova told you that being a hero was a dangerous occupation. Get into the alley."

Carlo raised his hands. He stepped backwards. His pistol and stiletto were in his pocket, but Drago would kill him if he tried to draw a weapon. Carlo's heel caught on a garbage can and he stumbled. The noise sent screaming cats scurrying. Carlo's eyes focused on the black tunnel of the gun barrel. A brick canyon of walls surrounded him. "You don't need to do this."

Drago grinned. "I do this for pleasure." Drago's face looked like a wolf about to pounce on prey.

From the shadows, Leonardo rushed forward. Drago turned his pistol too late. Leonardo jammed his stiletto into Drago's side. Drago grasped his rib cage. Leonardo pushed. Drago's shoulder slammed into a wall. He tried to force the gun toward Leonardo's body. Carlo lunged forward with his knife and stabbed Drago in the throat. The three men fell to the ground. Drago opened his mouth to scream. He gurgled. He struggled until the light dimmed in his eyes.

Leonardo and Carlo rose, sweating and panting. There was blood on their hands. The alley was deserted. No one inside Ciro's had heard the fight. They wiped their hands on discarded rags.

Leonardo's eyes darted. "What are we going to do with him?"

"Stuff the *merda* into a garbage can."

"He can't be found at Ciro's. Terranova will come after the Medinas."

Carlo said, "We can't drag a dead body around New York."

They heard a cowbell's clang on the street.

Leonardo's head went up. "Wait."

He ran to the end of the alley. Guido Basso was passing with his rickety rag cart piled high with burlap bags.

Leonardo called out, "Guido, wait." He ran over.

Basso smiled. "Young Leonardo, good to see you." Basso saw Leonardo's face and frowned. "What's wrong?"

"I need your cart to haul something away."

Basso tilted his head. "I stay with the cart. What kind of something?"

"You need to keep this secret."

"Why? Now I'm scared."

"Come." Leonardo grabbed Basso's sleeve.

In the alley, Basso saw Drago's body and stopped. "What have you done?"

Leonardo said, "He's a criminal. He tried to kill me. It was self defense."

"So go to the police."

"They won't believe me."

"Why not?"

"I was in jail."

"Sweet Jesus." Basso gestured toward Carlo. "And who is this?"

Carlo said, "You don't need to know."

Leonardo said, "Are you going to help us?"

Basso said, "You've gone crazy."

Leonardo picked up the pistol. "Look. He had a revolver."

Basso stepped back. "Are you going to kill me?"

Carlo shook his head. "Why did you bring him here? Now he's a witness."

Basso said, "Please don't hurt me."

Leonardo said, "Don't worry. Let us use your cart."

Basso saw Carlo's bloody knife. "After I help you, what happens?"

"Just don't tell anyone."

Carlo said, "Maybe we should just take his cart?"

Leonardo said, "And do what with him?"

"I didn't bring him here."

"No way. Guido, don't worry about him. Help us."

Basso gulped. "I don't have a choice."

Leonardo said, "Do you have something to put the body in?"

"A burlap bag."

"Bring the cart into the alley."

The three men positioned the cart. Basso handed Leonardo the bag. "What have you gotten yourself into? You should've come to work with me." He shook his head.

"I had no choice."

"You can never undo this."

Carlo said, "The three of us will take the cart."

Basso said, "Are you planning to kill me?"

Leonardo said, "You can stay here. We'll bring the cart back when we're finished."

"This cart puts bread on my table. I don't trust it to anyone."

Leonardo said, "We need to get rid of the body."

Basso said, "Where?"

"The East River." Leonardo rifled through Drago's pockets. He took a wad of counterfeit bills and stuffed them into his jacket.

Carlo found a couple of loose bricks. "Weigh him down with these so he sinks."

Leonardo shoved the weights into Drago's clothes. He grabbed Drago's revolver and stuck it under his belt. They maneuvered the body into the bag.

Leonardo said, "Guido, where's the best place to dump him into the river?"

Basso hesitated. "Near the Williamsburg Bridge."

The two young men hoisted Drago's body atop the pile of rags on the wagon. Basso pulled.

Carlo scanned the street. "Three men alongside a rag cart will raise suspicion. We'll follow you. Don't try to run away."

Basso jutted his chin at Carlo. "Do you think these old legs would get me far?" He grabbed the cart handles. Leonardo and Carlo trailed a half-block behind.

Leonardo was dank with sweat. "When you followed Drago outside, I knew there'd be trouble."

"Good thing."

"He would've shot you."

"Why did you stop him?"

"He was a threat to Azzura." Leonardo shuddered. "Still, his dead-eye face is in my head."

"Death stays with you."

"And I don't even like you."

Carlo shrugged. "I know."

They walked a couple of blocks.

Leonardo said, "You told Azzura that you love her?"

"She's easy to love."

"You lied."

"I didn't."

"She doesn't want you. Leave her alone."

"Why don't you let her decide?"

Leonardo pointed at Carlo. "Just because I saved your life doesn't mean I won't kill you."

"I get it."

They walked on.

Carlo said, "What are we going to do with Basso?"

"Leave him alone."

"He could go to the police."

"He's illegal. He'd get into trouble."

"Not if he turns in two murderers."

Leonardo said, "I won't kill an innocent man."

Carlo and Leonardo passed under a tenement window. A heavily rouged woman leaned out. She was all cleavage. "Hey, boys."

Leonardo jumped back. Carlo looked up.

The woman smiled broadly. She had bad teeth. "Got a dollar? Let's have a good time."

Basso continued down the street. A couple of policemen with domed hats and a double line of brass buttons down their chests heard the cowbell and stepped out of a saloon. They approached Basso. Carlo and Leonardo stiffened.

Leonardo felt the revolver in his belt. "The weapons. We need to stash them."

Carlo swiveled his head around. "Where?"

The tall cop peered down the street.

Leonardo said, "Too late. Let's go inside."

Carlo and Leonardo rushed up the tenement stoop. The woman opened the front door, and they stepped inside to a living room gas-lit in a gauzy red hue.

"I'm Rosie." She had on a low-cut green billowy dress. Face powder crumbled in the spider web cracks that framed her eyes. She smelled of sex and sweat.

Three young women smiled at the men. They lounged on two flower-patterned chairs and a couch with a Turkish rug draped over it. A blonde in a chair leaned on her elbow. She had on a white negligee with black stockings pulled over her knees. A brunette on the couch wore a strapped chemise that barely covered her nipples. She sat on one leg. Her thighs were parted. She tilted her head at Leonardo and mimed a rouged kiss. The third woman, a freckle-faced redhead, sat sideways with her bare legs hung over the arm of the chair. She swung her feet slowly while she twirled henna-dyed hair with a forefinger.

Leonardo's mouth got dry.

Carlo swallowed.

Rosie said, "Want a drink while you look at the merchandise?"

The men stared. They shook their heads.

Leonardo poked Carlo. His voice was hoarse. "See what the cops are doing."

The policemen were still with Basso. Carlo said, "What if he gives us up? Rosie, is there a back door to this place?"

"A back window. But don't worry about the police. We service them, too."

Leonardo saw a large jar with what looked like *orrecchiette* pasta floating inside.

Rosie noticed his gaze. "Those are ears. If a john was rough with me, I chewed one off. When I had good teeth."

Leonardo's eyes widened.

"Don't fret, dear. The girls don't bite anything off."

The tall cop with orange hair tilted his head. "What are you doing out so late?"

Basso steadied his voice. "I'm headed for the Williamsburg Bridge. I'm working in Brooklyn tomorrow."

The shorter cop, black hair and mustache, poked at one of the burlap bags with his club. "What are you carrying?"

"Rags."

The tall cop looked closer. He pointed with his billy. "Is that red?" He leaned forward. "That could be blood."

Basso's smile disappeared.

The short cop's eyes narrowed. "Rags don't bleed."

"I picked up some dead cats. Maybe your wife has a coat with a cat fur collar?"

Orange hair looked at the shorter cop. "Do cats bleed?"

The other man shrugged.

"If the cat's fresh, I use the meat in a stew. Have you ever eaten cat?" Basso smacked his lips.

The short cop looked nauseous. "Ugh."

The tall cop raised his palm. "No way. Okay, old man. Keep walking."

"Goodnight Officers."

The cops walked in the direction of the brothel. The short one shook his head. "Cat stew? Jesus."

"If you threw red sauce on shit, the Italians would eat it.

"Rosie said, "Well, gents, show us some money."

Carlo was at the window.

Leonardo said, "We're not buying tonight."

Rosie stepped closer. "Shy?" She ran her hand along Leonardo's leg. He blushed. "You are shy. Maybe you want to try something more mature?"

Her breasts were close to his face. Skin tags ran up her neck like an archipelago. He reeled at her body odor. "Carlo, where are the cops?"

"Passing now."

Leonardo said, "We need to go."

Rosie said, "It's not polite just to shop."

Leonardo pulled out a handful of counterfeit money he'd taken from Drago. "Here."

Rosie took the crumpled bills with both hands.

Carlo said, "They've turned the corner."

The men hot tailed it out of the house and ran down the street toward Basso.

Leonardo wiped his face. "Jesus. Did you see how those women were dressed?"

"They were vultures in doves' feathers." Carlo stopped short. "My God, are you a virgin?"

Leonardo's face turned scarlet. "Hell no. I've had plenty of women." His voice was loud.

"Yeah. Sure."

They neared Basso; the old man glowered at them. They held back.

Carlo said, "What if Basso goes to Terranova?"

"He won't betray us."

"How do you know?"

"He doesn't know Terranova. He doesn't know Drago's connection with him. Plus, he's Neapolitan. He wouldn't rat us out to a Sicilian."

Basso rolled the cart to the north side of the Williamsburg Bridge where the ground sloped steeply down to the water. Carlo and Leonardo unloaded the body and half-stumbled down to the river's edge. They took both ends and swung the bag three times before they flung Drago into the water. The bag drifted on the slow current. They watched it float away until it was too dark to see.

Leonardo craned his neck. "Did it sink?"

"I couldn't tell."

They climbed back up.

Basso said, "Okay. What now?"

Carlo took some money from his pocket.

"I don't want anything from you."

"Everybody has to eat." Carlo stuffed the bills into Basso's jacket.

"May God forgive you." Basso pulled his cart away, and the jangle of the cowbell faded into the darkness.

When Carlo and Leonardo returned to the tenement, Ciro's was closed.

Carlo started up the stoop. "Do we tell Rizzo about this tomorrow?"

"We need his help against Terranova."

Carlo shrugged and went upstairs.

Leonardo waited and stepped down into the dark restaurant. He felt his way past the tables and chairs to the kitchen. He shout-whispered, "Azzura." In a few moments he saw the flicker of a candle.

Azzura was in her long pink nightgown. "Where did you go?" She held the candle up. "Your face. What happened?"

"We handled some business."

Azzura put down the candle. "What did you do?"

Leonardo leaned forward and kissed her. He put his arms around her and pressed her close. He ran his hands down her back.

"Leonardo."

"I love you. Come up to my room."

"What's got into you?"

"I want to make love to you."

"We can't."

"Strangers make love. Why shouldn't two people who care for each other?" Leonardo enveloped her and kissed her hard.

Azzura pushed him away. "Stop."

Leonardo dropped his arms. His shoulders sagged.

Azzura put her hands on her hips. "Is this about Carlo? You need to prove I'm yours?" She kissed him lightly on the cheek. "Go to bed."

When Leonardo entered the apartment, Garibaldi jumped up. He petted the dog absently. Garibaldi clutched Leonardo's leg with his good paw and rubbed his belly against his calf.

"No, Garibaldi." Leonardo shoved the dog away with his foot. "Go find yourself a tramp."

The dog's head shrank down. Leonardo collapsed into bed.

Chapter 28

THE NEXT DAY patrons in the restaurant were abuzz, talking about the ugly "Black Hander" who confronted Ciro the night before. Leonardo and Carlo huddled with Ciro in the kitchen.

Ciro said, "What happened? Were you able to warn off the Black Hander?"

Leonardo grimaced. "His name was Drago. The threat's not over."

"*Mama mia.* He gave me counterfeit currency to purchase liquor." He handed Leonardo the bills. "What should I do?"

"Follow Drago's orders. When Terranova's men show up, give them the booze. If they ask about Drago, tell him he ate, paid for the alcohol, and left. That's all you know."

"Here comes trouble." Rizzo sipped a whiskey as Leonardo and Carlo approached his table at the club. "Tell me."

Leonardo said, "I killed Drago last night."

Carlo said, "He pulled a pistol. He would've killed me. We both stabbed him."

Rizzo said, "So you two are friends now?"

Leonardo and Carlo grimaced.

Rizzo sat back. "I guess not. What did you do with the body?"

Leonardo said, "We dumped him into the East River."

Rizzo said, "How did you move the corpse?"

Leonardo hesitated. "We used the cart of a rag picker I know."

Rizzo rubbed his chin. "Can he be trusted not to squeal?"

"I think so. But it's my problem."

Carlo frowned. "It's my problem, too."

Rizzo said, "You know my philosophy. When there's a doubt, kill it."

Carlo said, "The rag picker's name is Basso."

Leonardo glared at Carlo. "Basso won't betray us."

Rizzo shook his head. "It's an unnecessary risk."

Leonardo kneaded his chin. "Terranova knows that Drago went to Ciro's. I worry that he'll hurt the Medinas when Drago doesn't show up."

Rizzo tilted his head. "All roads lead to Azzura with you. Drago's absence won't be missed for a couple of days. Terranova will assume he's with a whore. But when the body's discovered, the stab wounds will prove Drago was murdered. We should kill Terranova." Rizzo's eyes locked on Leonardo. "He knows Carlo and Giuseppe, but not you. You could get close."

"I don't know."

"Don't you want to protect Azzura? As you said, Terranova could take revenge. A bomb could kill anyone."

"Maybe Drago's body won't be found."

"I'd make it worth your while."

Leonardo squirmed.

Rizzo said, "If Drago's body turns up, there'll be no time for indecision."

Carlo sat back. "I can take Terranova out."

"No. He'll kill you on sight. Where's the money Drago passed to Ciro?"

Leonardo handed the counterfeit notes to Rizzo.

Rizzo fingered the bills and held them up to a light. "These are good. Not like the *merda* Terranova used to pass. He didn't get these from Sicily. He has a press in New York." Rizzo leaned forward. "Find out where Terranova prints these things."

Carlo said, "What do you have in mind?"

Rizzo smiled. "Just locate the press."

Chapter 29

TEDDY FITZPATRICK strode into Big Jim's office and sat across the desk from him. "We have a problem with the shipping companies."

Big Jim put down his newspaper. "Tell me."

"You remember Rizzo?"

"Nauseatingly."

Fitzpatrick smiled. "He's informed me that the steamship companies are negotiating with some of the Great Lakes' unions to come to New York and compete with our International Longshoreman's Association. I confirmed his story."

"I don't like the sound of that."

"Yeah, Great Lakes translates into not Irish. Plus, they'd bring people in from out of state. Non-voters."

Big Jim sat up. "What do you propose we do?"

"Call a strike. We negotiate for a closed shop. The steamship companies can hire ILA members only. If you drop out of the union, you lose your job. We force everyone to be a member to work. No independent stevedoring companies allowed."

"Will the rank and file go along?"

"We'll advertise that the strike is for higher wages. We negotiate for another dime per hour. That way everybody gets something. The steamship companies will fold. If they don't, fresh produce will rot on the docks. Ship sailings will be delayed. There's millions in cost for the companies to fight us."

Big Jim smiled. "Go forth, my son."

* * *

Jimmy Doyle and Kevin Clancy bellied up to the bar in the Irish Rose Saloon.

Clancy chugged his dark beer. "Can you believe the cops let Robustelli and Fontana go?"

Doyle said, "The way I heard it, the judge said, 'no body, no murder,' so they got bail."

"Yeah, but shit, I had to tell Murphy's wife that the Italians were freed. She's convinced that Murphy is dead."

"That can't have been fun."

"My shoes were soaked by the torrent of tears. Plus the guys on the dock blame me for allowing the Italians to work. I lost the delegate vote."

"I'll find a way to make it up to you."

"The *Gorjistan* still hasn't arrived in Istanbul."

"Jesus, Murphy's body festering in that hold could be a black-green blob of jelly by now."

"Bloody hell." Clancy signaled for another beer. "Would the union pay to return Murphy's body to the States?"

"Absolutely. We'll pressure the cops to nail those two dagos. This isn't over. I have something to take your mind off Murphy for a while. Tammany Hall wants us to call a strike. We'll demand higher wages and a closed shop contract with the steamship companies. White Star Lines has been threatening to bring in outside unions. Tell the men. We walk out Friday."

Rizzo summoned Leonardo and Giuseppe to the social club. They'd never seen him so ebullient. "The steamship companies hate the International Longshoremen's Association. They've wanted to break the union's stranglehold on the New York docks for years. So they've schemed with some of the

Great Lakes longshoremen unions to bring them in and compete with the ILA. I informed Tammany Hall about the conspiracy and, just as I thought, the ILA won't stand still for it. Friday they're going out on strike." He rubbed his hands together. "We're in business. The steamship companies stand to lose millions in a strike. Rail cars will be backed up to Connecticut trying to unload for overseas shipment. The stench of rotting bananas will engulf lower Manhattan. The companies can't afford a strike, so they need people to work."

Giuseppe shrugged. "They'll bring in the other unions?"

"No. The ILA strike screws that option. The Great Lakes unions won't cross a picket line. The companies can't hire union workers."

Giuseppe said, "So the companies will settle the strike. How does that help us?"

Rizzo laughed. "That's where we come in. The companies won't need to settle. I'm recruiting Italians to break the ILA strike. We thwart the Irish union and make a pot load of money in the process." Rizzo hit the table. "The steamship companies will pay top dollar for strikebreakers. I'm using Leonardo's old *padrone*, Gentile, to recruit men. Part of the deal is that he forgives your steamship ticket debt. I'm always looking out for you. Right?"

Leonardo smirked. "Sure."

Rizzo said, "You two will be crew bosses. We work until the ILA folds."

Giuseppe scratched his cheek. "The ILA won't take this lying down."

"Of course. We need to arm our people."

Leonardo raised his palms. "What if the ILA settles quickly? They get their jobs back, the steamship companies go on with life, and we don't make much money."

Rizzo said, "If Tammany Hall won't allow Italians into the unions, we'll break strikes all over New York. This is the wedge Italians will use to join the rank and file."

"And you get more influence with Tammany Hall?"

Rizzo grinned. "I love sticking it to those Irish *cafones*. Get to the Bank Street pier for the Friday night shift. It's the White Star Steamship Line."

Azzura took an order from a man with a walrus-mustache.

"I need to talk to you." Carlo, behind her, watched as she scribbled

"I'm working."

She headed toward the kitchen. Carlo followed. She called out, "Mama, spaghetti Bolognese for the gentleman."

Isabella kneaded dough. "Okay." She beamed at Carlo. "*Buona sera.*"

"*Buona sera*, Signora." Carlo turned to Azzura. "You've been avoiding me since the Hippodrome."

"I'm not avoiding you. I'm busy."

Azzura grabbed a bottle of wine and a tumbler. She returned to the man's table.

Carlo snatched the bottle from her hand. "Is it because I said I love you?"

Azzura looked away.

The man grinned at them. "A little wine, please."

Carlo filled the man's glass and put the bottle on the table. He called out to Isabella. "I'd like to speak with Azzura. May we go outside?"

"Of course." Isabella wiped her hands on her apron. "Azzura, go with Carlo. I'll look after the tables."

Carlo took Azzura by the wrist and led her out the door onto the sidewalk.

Azzura said, "You're hurting me."

"Why won't you talk to me?"

"Let go."

"If you promise not to walk away."

"All right." She rubbed her wrist.

"I didn't mean to hurt you."

"What do you want to say to me?"

"I can't stop thinking about you. You're my first thought when I wake up and my last before I fall asleep."

"Carlo, please."

"When I see you smile, my chest hurts."

"You can't get everything you want."

"I don't want everything. Just you."

"Do you?"

"Let's get married. We'll live in Italy. I'll put Naples at your feet."

"At my feet? You would have me wear Naples as boots? How would that work, me wearing Naples? I would surely scuff up the whole of it."

"You know what I mean. I have money. You'll be able to wear any city on your feet. I'll have Rome fashioned into silk slippers if you like."

"I'm an American. Anyway, you don't want an independent wife."

"I love you." Carlo took Azzura by the shoulders and kissed her.

"Carlo, you shouldn't."

"You like it when I kiss you."

"We're in the middle of the street. Everyone can see."

"Come to my room."

"Stop it. Do you love me, or do you just want to possess me?"

"Both." He kissed her again.

"Leonardo told me you murdered a man. Probably two men."

Carlo released her. "Whatever I did was necessary. I acted either in self-defense or for honor."

"And the Italian *carabinieri* are after you."

"My father has a plan for me to return to Naples soon."

"Neither you nor Leonardo understands. America is my home."

"Did Leonardo tell you that he killed a man?"

"There was an accident on the docks."

"I'm not talking about that. He stabbed the thug who accosted your father in the restaurant."

"I don't believe you. Are you trying to change my feelings for Leonardo?"

"It's true. I'm not blaming him. It was necessary."

"What if I tell you that I love Leonardo?"

Carlo stiffened. "I don't accept it, and your parents would never allow you to marry him."

"You're so sure of yourself."

"If I approached your father, he'd give you to me. You'd need to obey his wishes."

"Don't try to force me."

"I'll make you forget Leonardo."

"I want to marry the man I choose."

"Why not me?"

"You want me as long as you can't have me."

"Not true."

"You want a china doll, a trophy, another conquest."

"No."

"You want to beat Leonardo. Maybe I'll marry him."

Carlo smiled sardonically. "Azzura, grow up. If not me, your parents will arrange another marriage. Your mother thinks that you've become wild. The only reason you're not married off already is because I'm interested. But if I leave, they'll act immediately."

Azzura turned away.

"They'll give you to some old businessman who has enough money to buy a young wife. Some man who smells like garlic and sweats vinegar when he makes love."

"Stop it."

"He'll have you pump out a baby every year. You'll be condemned to a life of drudgery. If you survive childbirth, physical labor will be etched into your face."

Azzura's eyes welled. "You're being mean."

Carlo softened his tone. "I love you. I want to save you from that life. But you must face the reality of your choices."

Azzura wiped her eyes. "If you loved me, you wouldn't say these things to me."

"I want you to see that I'm the man for you."

"I'd leave home before I'd marry a man against my will. I'm going inside now."

Carlo followed her into the restaurant.

Azzura strode past her mother toward their apartment in the rear. Isabella saw the shadow across Azzura's face. She pulled Carlo aside. His face was flushed. "What happened?"

"She throws Leonardo at me."

"What about him?"

Carlo puffed out a breath. "Maybe she loves him."

"Did you tell her of your feelings?"

"It seemed to make no difference."

Isabella frowned. A customer called out to her. "*Uno momento.*" She turned to Carlo. "Ask my husband for Azzura's hand. He'll agree."

"But if she loves Leonardo?"

"You'll make her love you. We'll talk to her. She'll respect our wishes."

"She'll resent me."

"She'll get over it."

Carlo crossed his arms. "Azzura has her mother's resolve."

"If you want her, this is the way."

"If Leonardo were gone."

"What are you saying?"

"Never mind."

"Go to my husband."

"Not yet."

* * *

Leonardo and Giuseppe stopped at Ciro's before heading for the Battery to join up with the other strikebreakers. Carlo was feted by the Medinas. Isabella was all smiles. Azzura stood at Carlo's table with her arms folded.

Leonardo pulled Azzura aside. "We're headed for the docks. We're going to break a longshoremen's strike."

"That sounds dangerous."

Leonardo shrugged.

Azzura said, "Are you working for Rizzo again? That man has been nothing but trouble for you."

"I make money with him."

Azzura said, "Money can turn a gentle man to meanness."

"What are you talking about?"

"The man who accosted my father the other night. Carlo said that you killed him."

Leonardo raised his chin. "Did he tell you why?"

"He said it was necessary."

"I saved Carlo's life."

"Leonardo, you killed a man, and you have no qualms of conscience?"

He took in a deep breath. "Of course I do."

"Then get away from a life that drags you into violence."

"I made a commitment."

"Don't my feelings count?"

"I can't back away."

"Then go."

Giuseppe called out to Leonardo. "We need to get going. Carlo, want to join us?"

Carlo twirled spaghetti. "I'm busy."

Azzura was curt. "Don't exert yourself."

Carlo smirked. "Okay, I'll come along."

Leonardo said, "Giuseppe and I are the crew bosses. You work for us."

Carlo laughed. "Sure."

Leonardo turned to Azzura. "I'll see you tomorrow." Leonardo bent to kiss her. She gave him her cheek.

Isabella saw the kiss and made the sign of the cross.

Chapter 30

ISABELLA ENTERED St. Anthony of Padua's Church on Sullivan Street and read the parchment posted in the narthex, "To all those who are discouraged and need hope." Isabella nodded. The church was deserted. She padded up the stone nave to the red-glass encased candles arrayed in a wrought iron stand along the west aisle. Her eyes rose to the statue of St. Anthony in his Franciscan brown cloak. Isabella made the sign of the cross. She lit a candle with a long ember.

She prayed silently. "St. Anthony, my daughter's honor is in danger. She's too friendly with an unsuitable man. I'm afraid that she'll stray into sin. I want her to marry Carlo Mazzi. Please give Carlo the courage to go to my husband and seek Azzura's hand." She made the sign of the cross.

Isabella moved toward the base of the transept and the steps of the sanctuary. She took a handful of rice from her pocket and sprinkled it onto the marble step. She raised the bottom of her skirt so that her bare knees came in contact with the rice when she knelt. As her weight pressed down on the stone, the coarse grains cut into her skin like thorns. Tears formed. She covered her mouth not to cry out. Jesus was tortured and died on the cross. Her sacrifice was small compared to His. Her eyes rose. The apse was a columned niche framed by octagonal walls of green marble. At the top of the altar was a statue of the Virgin Mary dressed in blue with the baby Jesus in her arms.

"Holy Mother, hear my prayer." Isabella took out her black beads. Her lips moved as she silently fingered and recited the rosary. After an hour she stood. Blood oozed from the wounds in her knees.

Mauro Gentile checked off names from his clipboard. There were several hundred Italians spread out in Battery Park. Leonardo approached him.

Gentile's basset hound eyes flickered. "Signor Robustelli, we meet again."

"Yes, under better circumstances for me."

"You've cultivated an interesting friend, Signor Rizzo."

"He told me that you forgave my steamship ticket debt."

"It's part of my arrangement with him. Besides strikebreaking, what sort of work does Signor Rizzo have you do?"

"This and that."

"I see." Gentile waved the back of his hand at Leonardo. "I need to make sure everyone is accounted for. *Ciao*."

Leonardo wandered among the men. They stood or sat in small groups. He scanned for familiar faces. He saw Beppo Lucchese and stopped short. He shouted, "Beppo," and ran over.

Beppo spread his arms wide and they embraced. "I thought you were back in Italy."

"I was in quarantine a few days, and they let me go."

"*Bravo*."

"I thought you were in a Pennsylvania coal mine."

"I was. The pay's good."

"So what are you doing in New York?"

Beppo looked sheepish. "I had to get away from my American wife. An Italian woman born in the States doesn't know her place." And her mother ..." Beppo waved his fingers. "*Madonna mia*, I think that woman has testicles."

Leonardo smiled. "Do you have a place to stay?"

"I found another woman in New York." He shrugged. "I'm incurable."

They laughed.

Gentile called everyone together. He led the men out of the Battery and headed north on West Street. They skirted the Irish neighborhood near the Greenwich Village docks. The looks from the saloon patrons they passed could've turned them to stone. The Italians walked with eyes straight ahead.

At the Bank Street pier, Jimmy Doyle talked to a knot of longshoremen. "Boys, we don't want any violence. Stay out of the saloons. I don't want any drunken riots. The Italians are scabs. They have no experience as longshoremen, and soon the companies will be begging for us to return to work."

Someone shouted, "I hear they're armed with pistols."

"If that's the case, I'll petition the New York District Attorney to file criminal charges against the White Star Line for supplying the weapons."

Someone said, "What if we're attacked?"

"Defend yourselves. But don't start anything. We want to use moral suasion on these people to get them to quit."

Somebody shouted. "A club across the skull is my idea of moral suasion." The crowd laughed.

"This is a serious matter, boys. The steamship companies want to exterminate the ILA, and we're not going to let that happen."

The Italians filed past Doyle and the longshoremen. Taunts rang out.

"Scabs."

"Dagos."

"Bastards."

Two weeks into the International Longshoreman's Association strike, Teddy Fitzpatrick walked into Big Jim O'Neil's office.

Fitzpatrick plopped into a chair. "The strike's a disaster. The cargo companies won't negotiate. They say that they're happy with the Italians on the job."

"Give it more time. The shipping companies always give in."

"I don't think so. Plus the longshoremen are putting pressure on us. We're hearing grumbled worries that the cargo companies will make the Italians permanent."

Big Jim said, "The longshoremen won't accept the Italians getting their jobs. There'll be riots."

"Exactly. We don't want the docks to go up in flames. It's bad for business and terrible publicity."

Big Jim slapped his desk. "Who's leading the Italians?"

"Oh, you'll love this. The rumor is that Frank Rizzo is involved."

"The guy who extorted ten percent to get the Tucker money back?"

"The same."

"The guy who warned us about the Great Lakes unions?"

"Uh-huh."

"Son of a bitch. He's a gangster. Why the hell is he involved breaking strikes?"

"He knows the piers sweat money. He wants to rake wages from Italian workers. He wants to get leverage on cargo shippers so he can get paid for strike protection. In short, he wants in on our rackets."

Big Jim's face reddened. "That bloody Rizzo suckered us. He told us about the Great Lakes unions to draw us into a strike."

"The threat from the Great Lakes was real. But I didn't imagine Rizzo sending Italians in to break the strike."

"What do you suggest we do?"

Fitzpatrick puffed out a breath. "There are no good options."

Big Jim grimaced. "What's the least worst?"

"Call off the strike."

Big Jim's eyebrows rose. "Give in to the steamship companies? Agree for the longshoremen to go back to work with no increase in wages?"

Fitzpatrick shrugged. "We should be happy if the cargo companies don't counter and ask for a reduction in pay."

Big Jim shook his head. "The rank and file won't be happy."

"It's our best choice."

Big Jim leaned back. "And how do we stop a repeat of this fiasco?"

Fitzpatrick spread his palms. "Union busting pays better than the other jobs open to Italians. If there's a strike, they'll be back."

Big Jim nodded. "That's my point."

Fitzpatrick continued. "We need to take away their incentive to give us trouble. We allow Italians into the union."

Big Jim gasped. "The longshoremen will hate that."

"Jim, there's plenty of work. When we eliminate the Italian strikebreakers all longshoremen's wages will go up. That's what we tell our people."

"And what about Rizzo? What stops him from finding another bunch of out of work Italians or even Negroes to break future strikes?"

"Give Rizzo a seat at the table. Make him one of the vice presidents in the ILA"

Big Jim slumped in his chair. "Oh, Christ."

"It's a title. We put him on our team. We take credit for opening up the union, and the Italian votes come to us."

"I'll have to rub up against a grease ball on the union board?"

Fitzpatrick shrugged. "Wear old clothes."

"Go to hell."

Kevin Clancy slouched in Jimmy Doyle's office. Clancy shook his head. "The longshoremen are going nuts. They think the Italians will take their jobs."

"No way."

"When there's no money coming in, people have time to think the worst."

Doyle said, "I have the word from Tammany Hall. We're to capitulate. We order the men back to work for the same pay."

"They'll go crazy. We get them to go on strike, and all they wind up with is their dicks in their hands?" Clancy shook his head.

"Tell the men we have a plan to neutralize the strikebreakers."

"How?"

"We allow Italians into the ILA."

Clancy's eyes widened. "You're joking."

"It's the only way."

"This will go down like swallowing glass. Expect trouble at the docks."

The word went out that the longshoremen had capitulated and the strike was over. The Italians worked their last shift. As quitting time approached, longshoremen gathered at the docks. Giuseppe and Leonardo could see the crowd gather from the deck of the ship. The Irishmen were armed with bailing hooks and clubs. Carlo and Beppo came up behind them.

Giuseppe took out his knife. "Let's stay together."

The Italians left the ship as a group. Near Bank Street gate, the longshoremen confronted them.

"Scabs."

"Dagos."

The Irishmen blocked escape. The Italians faced them. There wasn't a cop in sight.

A volley of paving stones flew at the Italians. A number of missiles hit their targets and first blood was drawn. The Italians had stilettos or grasped bailing hooks. Before a second volley could be launched, the Italians rushed the longshoremen. The two groups clashed amidst shouts and curses. The pier was a maelstrom of clubbing and stabbing. A score of men fell bleeding with cracked skulls or stab wounds. Leonardo and Giuseppe were shoulder to shoulder. Carlo and Beppo stood behind. The four men protected each other's backs. A rush of Irishmen surged forward. Leonardo and Carlo drew revolvers, and the longshoremen backed off. Around the four men, bodies littered Bank Street like the aftermath of a bayonet charge. The copper smell of blood filled the air. A small squad of police appeared at the perimeter of the riot.

Leonardo spotted the cops. He shouted over moans and screams. "Let's get the hell out of here."

The four men took off east, down Bank Street. Their path was a gauntlet of Irish saloons.

Behind them, the cops pushed themselves into the fight with billy clubs held high. More police arrived, a number on horseback. The remaining Italians broke off and made for the Sixth and Ninth Avenue elevated railroad stations at Christopher and Fourteenth Streets. The longshoremen retreated from the cops and melted into the Irish neighborhood.

As Leonardo, Giuseppe, Carlo, and Beppo ran, shouts echoed down from the tenements.

"Get the Italians."

"Kill the dagos."

Women leaned from windows or stood on fire escapes and threw bottles, stones, anything that was handy down at the four men. One dropped a flowerpot that struck Beppo a glancing blow to his forehead. The gash streamed blood down his nose and chin. Another pot missed Leonardo's head by a foot, hit the concrete, and exploded into shards. A couple of men stepped from a bar, grabbed Giuseppe, and tried to drag him into the saloon. Carlo aimed his Lemon Squeezer revolver and the Irish released Giuseppe. Men and women flew from doorways at street level swinging iron pokers, baseball bats, and broken bottles.

A heavy man in a black derby burst from an alley and charged at Leonardo's back with a length of pipe. Giuseppe yelled, but Leonardo didn't hear. Carlo saw the impending attack. He raised his pistol, but hesitated. Black derby closed to smash Leonardo's skull. At the last moment, Carlo pulled the trigger. The man went down. Leonardo heard the shot and saw his attacker bleeding out on the pavement. He nodded to Carlo and moved ahead. Giuseppe glared at Carlo, and the two men followed.

The Italians dodged blows for blocks until more police showed up. Some of the neighborhood people attacked the cops, which drew fire away from the four men. The police tried to cordon off the area, but in the confusion, the Italians slipped through the net and made their way back to the Spring Street tenement.

A number of Ciro's patrons had fought in the riot, and they straggled into the restaurant. Natalia Caputo and a few nurses from Henry Street attended to the victims. Isabella and Azzura assisted. Men sprawled on the tables and floor; the inside of Ciro's looked like a hospital triage center.

Natalia administered to the gash in Beppo's head.

He gave her a dopey smile. "*Bella*, are you married?" He touched her waist.

She pressed cotton soaked in iodine and alcohol against the wound.

"Ouch." Beppo grabbed his forehead.

Natalia said, "Hold this. That will occupy your hand. I have other patients." She moved on.

Giuseppe grabbed Carlo's shoulder and spun him around. "Why did you hesitate to fire?"

Carlo's eyes flitted onto Azzura.

Giuseppe was in Carlo's face. "You thought you'd eliminate a rival?"

Carlo stared back. "If I wanted to kill Leonardo, I'd do it myself."

Giuseppe's scar reddened. "If anything happens to him, you'll answer to me."

Leonardo came over.

Giuseppe said, "Carlo hesitated before shooting the man who attacked you."

"Is that true?"

"Yeah. For a moment I thought I'd rather you be gone."

Leonardo said, "But you fired. Why?"

Carlo said, "I want Azzura to choose me, but it has to be her decision. If you were dead, she'd mourn you and wonder what might have been. You'd become a martyr. She'd learn I could've saved your life and never forgive me. The act to win her would push her away."

Chapter 31

ON THE DAY of the strikebreaker riots in New York, Nunzio Robustelli in Naples walked slowly toward the Mazzi home. A passing cloud darkened Nunzio's face and cast a shadow under his almond shaped eyes.

Salvatore Mazzi tended to a black stallion that he was no longer healthy enough to ride. He sighed and passed the reins to a worker. He turned to Nunzio.

Nunzio's eyes averted Salvatore's. He wrung his cap in his hands. "My wife is very ill."

Salvatore stiffened. "What's wrong?"

"She stopped eating when her son left. Now she has a high fever, and can't get out of bed."

"Has a doctor seen her?"

"No."

"I'll have Doctor Sprandio go to your house immediately. You need help caring for her. I'll contact Father Paulo. I'll ask him to send two nuns."

Nunzio nodded. "She's asking for her son. I don't know how to reach him in New York."

Salvatore said, "Has she asked to see anyone else?"

Nunzio looked Salvatore in the eye. "Who would Anna ask for?"

Salvatore's eyes averted. "I don't know. I was just wondering."

"She's asked for no one else."

Salvatore scratched his cheek. "I know how to contact Leonardo. I'll buy him a steamship ticket on the fastest boat back to Naples."

"*Grazie*, Don Mazzi." Nunzio left.

The next day, Carlo withdrew some cash from the Bank of Napoli. The clerk handed him an urgent cable from his father. The first paragraph of the wire closed with the sentence, "Final preparations for your return are being made." The second paragraph had a message for Leonardo.

Back at Ciro's, Carlo pulled Leonardo aside. Azzura came over. Carlo showed them the cable. "I'm sorry. Your mother has taken ill."

Leonardo's face lost color. Azzura touched his arm.

"My mother asked for me." Leonardo had tears. "I must return to Italy immediately. Don Mazzi purchased a first class ticket for me. It's waiting at the steamship line office. The boat sails tomorrow."

Azzura turned toward Carlo. "That's generous of your father."

Carlo said, "The Robustellis have worked for us many years. My father treats them like family."

Ignazio Terranova looked at the gray bloated body on a slab in the morgue. His face flushed. He clenched his fists.

Detective Killian Byrne pointed. "Is that Bruno Drago?"

Terranova nodded. "How did you identify him?"

"The scar across his skull and the mug shot. We weren't certain. As you can see, his face is distorted."

"Where did you find him?"

"In a bag floating in the East River. A couple of kids discovered him while they were fishing."

Terranova pointed at the purple puncture marks in Drago's neck and side. "He was murdered."

"Yes. The coroner found no water in the lungs. He was killed before being dumped into the river." Byrne tilted his head at Terranova. "Did you kill him?"

Terranova smirked. "Is that your best detective work?"

"Who do you think killed him?"

"New York is a dangerous city."

"Could it have been a rival gang? One of Rizzo's crew?"

Terranova's jaw tightened. "Is there anything else, Detective?"

"You should cooperate with the investigation."

Terranova fidgeted. "Can I go?"

"Yes. But if you're thinking about revenge, I won't stand for a gang war in my city."

Back in his Hester Street saloon, Terranova slammed his fist on the bar. "Whiskey."

The bartender had greasy hair parted in the middle and a poorly trimmed mustache. His hand trembled when he poured.

Terranova slugged down the shot and smacked the glass down on the bar. He'd sent Drago to the Medinas and hadn't seen him since. Carlo the Neapolitan must have killed him. He made a fist. "Son of a bitch."

The bartender almost dropped the bottle.

It was well past midnight. Garibaldi barked furiously.

Giuseppe sat up in bed. "God damn. Shut up."

Garibaldi howled.

"Shit."

Leonardo stood. "Garibaldi. What's the matter?"

The dog scratched the door.

Leonardo approached him. Garibaldi withdrew and whined. "He's never shied away from me."

Giuseppe put the pillow over his head. "Take him out to piss."

Leonardo cracked open the door. The dog's nails scraped the floor as he sped out and down the stairs as fast as three legs would take him. Leonardo followed him outside. The moon was full. Leonardo spotted a man crouching in the shadows near Ciro's entrance. Garibaldi barked and scampered down the stoop steps. The man took off down the street. Leonardo was barefooted and couldn't give chase. He called Garibaldi back.

"Good boy." He petted the dog. The noise had awoken Ciro, Isabella, and Azzura. Leonardo picked up a bundle the size of a gorilla's fist off the doorstep. The unlit bomb was wrapped securely with twine with a foot-long fuse stuck out from the top.

Giuseppe came up behind him. "*Merda*. That's dynamite. It would've blown open a hole big enough to drive a garbage wagon through. It must have been Terranova. Revenge for Drago."

Ciro's eyes widened like moons. "Should we go to the police?"

Giuseppe grimaced. "The Irish cops won't solve the problem."

Leonardo pulled Giuseppe aside. "I'm leaving for Italy tomorrow. You need to protect Azzura."

Giuseppe squeezed Leonardo's shoulder. "Brother, don't worry."

Leonardo said, "Signor Medina, keep Garibaldi while I'm gone."

"But what if they try to bomb us again?"

Leonardo handed Giuseppe a revolver. "Giuseppe will sleep in the restaurant."

Azzura's chin rose. "Where did you get that pistol?"

"I took it off a man who'd kill for enjoyment."

Azzura hugged herself. "I'm scared. These are bad people."

Leonardo said, "I can't leave you here in this danger."

Azzura said, "But your mother. You must go to her."

Leonardo grabbed his forehead.

Azzura touched his arm. "I want to ask Carlo for help."

Leonardo frowned. "I'll talk to him tomorrow."

In the morning Carlo entered Ciro's. Leonardo approached him. "A bomb was placed at the restaurant's door last night. Garibaldi woke me or it would've exploded."

"Jesus Christ. It was Terranova. They found Drago's body."

"I should've killed him like Rizzo said."

"Doesn't your ship leave today?"

Leonardo gnawed his lip.

Azzura came over. "Leonardo told you what happened last night? I'm terrified."

Carlo said, "I told you that I wouldn't let anything happen to you. I'll take care of Terranova."

Azzura said, "You'll kill him? No."

"It's the only way to be certain that you won't be harmed."

"I won't sanction murder."

Carlo huffed.

Leonardo said, "Giuseppe will guard the restaurant. Maybe you can help him."

"I'll guard Azzura."

Leonardo said, "What does that mean?"

"I'll stay as close to her as she'll allow. Maybe that's the way to make her love me." He turned to Azzura. "I do love you."

Azzura blushed.

Leonardo said, "Goddamn you, Carlo."

Carlo said, "I'll keep telling her until she's convinced."

Leonardo's ears were crimson. His lips formed an eerie smile. He clenched his fists. The two men stood quickly. The backs of their chairs hit the floor with a crack.

Azzura pushed between them. "Stop it." They backed off. "Neither of you understands that you can't fight for me. You can't kill for me. My family is in danger, and I'm tired of your childish jealousy." She put her hands on hips. "Both of you, calm down. Leonardo, go see your mother; she needs you. Right now, my family and I need Carlo's protection."

Carlo said, "You have it."

Leonardo looked sheepish. "I'm sorry. It's just."

"Enough." Azzura walked away.

Leonardo pointed at Carlo. "We'll settle this when I return."

Carlo smirked at Leonardo's back as he left the restaurant.

Chapter 32

LIKE A RUBY in a jar of honey, the sun sank on the Naples horizon. Clouds gathered in bulbous masses, and patches of rain in the distance smeared the sky. The air smelled earthy. Captain Baldassare Ceruti of the *carabinieri* walked his chestnut stallion up to the Mazzi home. He took note of the men armed with shotguns stationed at the gate and around the house and barn. They looked like the city types he arrested for robbing apartments in Naples. Salvatore Mazzi met him on the portico, and they sat in the shade.

"Don Mazzi, to which Camorra gang do these ruffians belong?"

Mazzi halted his coffee cup at his lips. "Captain, I don't know what you're talking about."

"Don't you?" Ceruti took out a notepad. "I've questioned Captain Diehl of the *Dinnamare*. He concurred with the sailor, Erik Lund, on Di Stefano's description. He said that he didn't know if Di Stefano was his real name. I pressed Diehl, but he said he wasn't paid to allow Di Stefano on board." Ceruti put down his pad. "I don't believe him."

Mazzi's face was expressionless.

Ceruti picked up his coffee. "I've been in touch with the New York Police. Don Mazzi, your wife's maiden name was Leggiéri, wasn't it?"

Mazzi sat back. "Yes."

"That's interesting. According to police reports, an Alberto Leggiéri was killed in lower Manhattan recently."

Mazzi blanched

"There was a triple murder, and the main suspect was a man named Carlo. Witnesses said Carlo claimed to be a relative of Leggiéri. That's an amazing coincidence, don't you think?"

Mazzi squirmed.

"The police conducted an intense search for Carlo, but for some reason the manhunt was suspended. I suspect politics was involve."

Mazzi's eyes were on the horizon.

Ceruti's voice grew stern. "Don Mazzi, the games are over. I know that Carlo is in New York, and he's a suspect in three murders. The Silvestris' investigation has undoubtedly turned up the same information as mine. If Carlo is arrested in New York, he'll not be safe even in a jail cell. He'll be targeted for assassination."

Mazzi leaned back.

"On the other hand, if Carlo returns to Italy, I promise that he'll live to stand trial. The evidence against him in the Silvestri murder is circumstantial. Carlo will need to take his chances in an Italian court."

"I understand." Mazzi stood. "Thank you, Captain, for your visit. I'll let you know when Carlo returns home."

Mazzi walked Ceruti to his horse. Before Ceruti mounted, he surveyed the men around the property. "Don Mazzi, you may find that these types of people are easier to acquire than to shed."

Mazzi shifted on his feet.

Ceruti said, "*Arrivederci.*"

Vincenzo Mazzi was summoned to the estate. When he arrived, the two men sat in the loggia.

Salvatore said, "Carlo cabled and confirmed the information Ceruti gave me. Alberto Leggiéri was murdered. But Carlo says it's unrelated to the Silvestris and that a New York *guappo* with political connections arranged it so that the police won't pursue the matter."

"That's good news."

"Yes." Salvatore took a sip of blood orange juice. "Have you made the preparations that will allow Carlo to return?"

"Yes."

Salvatore said, "It's a dangerous plan. Are you sure you want to proceed?"

"What choice do we have? The Silvestris know Carlo is in New York."

Salvatore said, "If your strategy works, there won't be anyone who would testify against Carlo."

"Exactly."

"But if it doesn't."

Vincenzo said, "You worry too much."

Salvatore's mouth tugged into a smile. He put down his juice. "I don't think I mentioned that Carlo met Leonardo Robustelli in New York."

Vincenzo said, "Has Carlo a hint that Leonardo is his half-brother?"

"No."

Vincenzo nodded.

Salvatore said, "Nunzio was here this morning. Anna has taken sick. I sent Doctor Sprandio to her. She asked for her son. I've sent him a steamship ticket."

"Will you go to see her?"

Salvatore looked away. "She didn't ask for me. No."

Vincenzo shrugged. "Maybe that's for the best." He consulted his pocket watch. "It's time to go."

The brothers rose, embraced, and kissed each other on the cheek.

Salvatore said, "*Buona fortuna.*"

Vincenzo got into his mule cart. "*Ciao.*"

Bartolomeo and Domenico Silvestri saw Vincenzo Mazzi leave the estate from a nearby hillside. Two henchmen from the Russomanno gang were alongside. Domenico said, "Let's go. We'll use his boat and dump him into the Mediterranean."

Vincenzo arrived at his house in a couple of hours and parked his cart near the barn. The sun hung low. A fiery orange glow lit the undersides of the clouds, and they draped like blue-gray shrouds on the horizon. Vincenzo hastened to get the animals put away before dark. He unhitched each mule in turn and walked them to the barn and into their stall. As he worked, he looked around. He sniffed the air. He listened to the birds. Everything seemed normal. He gave the mules pails of feed and water and walked to the front of his house. He gathered fishing nets from a wooden storage box outside his door, slung them over his shoulder, and walked toward his dock.

The Silvestri brothers and the two Russomanno Camorra members followed Vincenzo's cart. They kept their distance and moved slowly in order that they not create a dust cloud. They parked their carriage about a half-mile from his house and walked the remaining distance. Each man carried a shotgun. They paused about two hundred yards from his house. They saw Vincenzo emerge from the barn and gather his nets. As he walked to the boat, Domenico made a hand signal, and the four men closed the distance.

On the dock, Vincenzo heaved the nets off his shoulder and onto the deck. The Silvestris quickened their pace so as not to give Vincenzo time to cast off. They crept along and used cover as they neared him. Vincenzo stepped onto his boat. He bent down for something on deck. His stalkers closed to within ten yards. They brought their weapons to their shoulders anticipating Vincenzo would rise. At that moment five members of the Zangara Torre Annunziata clan stood from behind nearby bushes with shotguns ready and fired. With the first volley Domenico was cut in half and Bartolomeo went down. The two Russomanno henchmen dropped their weapons and ran. Vincenzo and the five men jumped after them. The two gang members hadn't gone twenty yards before they were shot dead.

Tazio Zangara, nephew to *La* Senora, was in his twenties, handsome, with a black mustache and a deep cleft in his chin. He walked over to Bartolomeo Silvestri as he tried to crawl away. Tazio put his shotgun into Bartolomeo's mouth and fired. Tazio surveyed the bloody scene with a satisfied look. "Vincenzo, get your axe. We'll make some chum. It's good you have your nets. These *strunz* will help us catch some big fish tonight."

Vincenzo looked at the bodies of Domenico and Bartolomeo and nodded. Now Carlo could come home.

Tourist visitors to *Castel Nuovo*, the medieval stronghold of the Kingdom of Naples, didn't notice the simply dressed woman and hunched over man with the three-day beard. Their eyes were on the triumphal white arch that commemorated a Spanish King's entrance into the city.

The heads of the Santa Lucia and Torre Annunziata Camorra clans sat at an open table. Giulietta Zangara sipped a small coffee. Ciccio Russomanno had a face like an angry turtle. He had no drink in front of him, and his arms were folded. Two separate knots of rough-looking men stood out of earshot behind their respective *guappos*. Tazio Zangara stood with his clan and watched the Russonmannos for a sign that violence was imminent.

Ciccio Russomanno was first to speak. "Donna Zangara, you asked for this meeting. What do you want?"

Zangara drained her cup and sighed. "Last night I had a dream." She shuddered. "Actually, I should say it was a nightmare."

Russomanno squirmed.

"It was a terrible scene. Women cried and ripped at their clothes. Children were in tears and babies bawled. I asked one of the women what was the matter. She said that every wife was a widow, and the children had lost their fathers. All the men in the Russomanno clan were dead."

Russomanno straightened.

Zangara had a concerned look. "We must work together, Don Ciccio, that this terrible portent never comes to pass."

Russomanno's face was granite. "Your nephew, Tazio, killed two of my people."

"A tragedy. But, Don Ciccio, the Mazzis contacted us for protection. Vincenzo was at his home when the Silvestri brothers snuck up to ambush him. Tazio intended to defend Vincenzo and himself. How was he to know that two of your clan came to commit murder?"

"Blood must be answered with blood. That's the way as you well know."

"Yes. I revenged the murder of my father and brother, Tazio's father, by members of your family." Zangara swept the cup and saucer off the table with the back of her hand. The china hit the ground with a crack and smashed into pieces. Both knots of men jumped forward and tensed in anticipation of a command to strike. Zangara held up her hand, and everyone stopped as if frozen. "Don Ciccio, I apologize. When the images of my martyred father and brother come into my head, I think that too few Russomanno throats were cut to balance the scale. Perhaps I made peace too soon."

Russomanno tensed.

"If Tazio were killed, even if he were run over by a trolley, my desire for revenge would be insatiable." Zangara's stone eyes skewered Russomanno.

Russomanno raised his voice. "There will be no peace until the dead members of my family are avenged. The Mazzis started this war. They must pay."

Zangara ran her finger along the edge of the table. "The Mazzis in Italy are under my protection."

Russomanno sat back. He blinked a few times. He stood. "Donna Zangara, I understand." He motioned for his men to follow as he strode away.

Tazio approached his aunt. "Is it war?"

Giulietta Zangara stood. She patted her nephew's cheek and smiled. *Caro*, sometimes it's best to cook your enemies in warm water."

Killian Byrne's office at the Lower East Side police station was a small oasis amidst a desert of gray desks and swirl of hulking, handcuffed men and prostitutes in skimpy garish outfits. At least five foreign languages could be heard interspersed with broken English. The air in the room smelled of bad alibis. Jimmy Doyle sat in a metal chair across from the detective at his desk.

Byrne consulted some papers. "According to my counterpart's cable from Istanbul, Liam Murphy's body is in a decrepit state. There are no stab wounds. It's difficult to determine if Murphy was struck, but there are no broken bones. His skull shows no sign of trauma."

Doyle said, "The International Longshoremen's Association will bring the body back."

"We'll have the coroner take a look when it arrives."

"When will you arrest Fontana and Robustelli?"

"It'll be tough to prove murder."

Doyle's face reddened, "We demand justice."

"I've already tried to crack these two nuts. They've had time to speak to each other and perfect their stories."

"Are you telling me you won't arrest them?"

"Without evidence, I don't like to waste time."

"Detective, I have connections with Tammany Hall. Do I need to ask Big Jim O'Neil to get you to act?"

Byrne leaned back. "No. I'll arrest Fontana and Robustelli when the body's in our custody."

Doyle stood. "I'll be in touch."

Detective Byrne and a couple of cops walked into Ciro's. Giuseppe spotted them and slunk into the kitchen. Ciro directed him to the exit in the back.

Ciro approached Byrne. "Can I help you?"

"You have Leonardo Robustelli and Giuseppe Fontana staying in this tenement. I've already been up to their apartment. Do you know their whereabouts?"

Ciro wiped his hands on a towel. "I don't."

Byrne gave Ciro a long look. "They can't disappear forever."

Ciro put his hand on his hip. "Why don't you pursue some real gangsters like the bastards who run the 'Black Hand' extortion?"

"You've been threatened?"

Ciro bit his lip. "I didn't say that. But every Italian businessman lives in fear he will."

"The police commissioner will organize a new squad of Italian police to go after the 'Black Hand.' They'll have their own lieutenant."

Ciro shrugged. "I suppose that's something."

"I'll be back."

Byrne and his cops strode into the social club on Mulberry Street and confronted Frank Rizzo.

Byrne said, "Robustelli and Fontana are part of your crew."

Rizzo said, "I don't recall those names."

"Sure you do. You arranged bail for them."

"What do you want them for?"

"Liam Murphy's body has been found in Istanbul. I want to question them about his death."

"Murphy? How long has he been dead? His body's probably ready for the glue factory. The New York Police have money in their budget to import gelatin? If you had proof of murder, you wouldn't be making social calls. What gives?"

"The ILA is paying for Murphy's return."

"Ah, you don't want an ass chewing from Tammany Hall. I get it."

"When you see Fontana and Robustelli, tell them to surrender. It'll go easier on them."

Chapter 33

THE ANCHOR LINE'S STEAMSHIP *Perugia* was smaller than the *Prinzessin Irene*, but first-class passage was as different from steerage as Dante's spheres of *Paradiso* were from his circles of the *Inferno*. Gleaming bronze, soft wood paneling, cushioned chairs, and pristine tablecloths were highlights. First class had its own orchestra. Leonardo wondered over Quaker Oats, Kippered Herring, and Zwiebacks on The Bill of Fare. Leonardo's fellow travelers were mostly uptown Manhattanites. He hoped they couldn't see his threadbare sleeves or big toe bulging through his shoe. They gave him disapproving looks and whispered snide remarks as if the letter "P" for peasant was emblazoned on his forehead. Americans skirted him like Italian was contagious. Fortunately, luxury accommodations and ample ventilation kept seasickness away.

A red bearded *editorre* from a New York Italian news publication, befriended him. The periodical raised funds to commission the Garibaldi statue in Washington Square Park. The King of Italy had awarded the editor an honorary title of *Chevalier*.

The editor slapped the arm of his chair. "America itself is named after the Italian, Amerigo Vespucci."

Leonardo gave him a wry smile. "I don't think the Americans like to be reminded."

When Leonardo's ship arrived in Naples, a carriage was waiting for him, and he was driven to his home. Leonardo entered his house; Nunzio stood and left without a greeting.

Two nuns in black habits and white-framed faces were in attendance. The younger one stirred soup for Anna. The other sat at the wooden kitchen table and sewed. The fireplace mantle held a slew of holy pictures and saint statues Leonardo didn't remember.

Anna was on Leonardo's bed near the fireplace. She looked shrunken. She wheezed from labored breathing. Leonardo's heart sank. "Mama." He went to her.

Anna's blue eyes blinked open and brightened at the sight of him. Leonardo knelt beside her. Anna tried to rise, but she fell back. Leonardo grasped her shoulders. She cradled Leonardo's face in her hands. "My son. My son." He gave her a kiss on the cheek and got a wet one in return. She was covered with sweat and had the sour smell of pain. Anna clutched Leonardo. He was shocked how little strength she had in her hands. After a time, she drifted off to sleep.

The younger nun pulled Leonardo aside. "I'm so happy she recognized you; she started to hallucinate yesterday." She motioned Leonardo closer. "She's in and out of consciousness. Doctor Sprandio said that it's near the end."

Leonardo swallowed.

"But she waited for you." She made the sign of the cross. "Thank God you're here."

Leonardo sat on a chair beside his mother and listened to her breathe. He put his hand to her forehead. Her brow was fevered. The nuns asked Leonardo to step away so they could change and sponge-bathe her. Leonardo went outside. Nunzio had parked himself in a wooden chair on the porch. He'd carved some peaches into a tall glass and filled it with red wine from a jug. He forked out the sliced peaches and drank the wine while he looked over the fields.

Leonardo stood at Nunzio's shoulder.

Nunzio said, "Did you make any money in New York?"

"Not much."

"Humph." Nunzio looked up at Leonardo. "Don Mazzi bought your ticket?"

"Yes."

"I know."

Leonardo's face flushed. "You need to gloat?"

Nunzio ate a chunk of peach.

Leonardo said, "How did she get sick?"

"She became depressed when you weren't here. She lost weight. She had pain." Nunzio sighed. "I don't know."

"I shouldn't have left."

Nunzio shrugged. "She lived for you, not for me." Nunzio drank some wine. "She married me, but she never loved me. I thought it was because of another man. I was patient. She'll come around, I thought. She'll see that he's moved on with his life, and I'll be there for her." Nunzio laughed sardonically. "I was a fool." He looked up at Leonardo. "The other man was you. You were my rival for her affection."

"What are you saying?"

"It wasn't a battle. I wasn't a contestant." He shook his head.

"How can you speak to me that way when my mother's on her death bed? What kind of father says these things to his son?"

Nunzio drank the last of the wine and put down the glass. He looked up at Leonardo. "You still think I'm your father?" His Chinese eyes crinkled in a smile. He turned to look out at the fields.

Leonardo stiffened. He paled. His brain whirred, and he brought his hand to his face. Sweat broke out on his forehead. Leonardo backed through the doorway into the house. Emotion had risen into his throat. His mother stirred. Her arms stretched for him. He went to her.

Anna said, "*Che é successo?* What's going on? Your face is sad. Did you eat? I'll make you something nice." She smiled. "I like this bed. This is my bed." Anna closed her eyes. Leonardo felt his mother's last breath on his face.

"Mama?" Leonardo's eyes welled.

The younger nun put her hand on Anna and felt for a pulse. "She's gone. I'm sorry."

Leonardo couldn't fight the flow of tears.

Leonardo went through the small metal box by Anna's bed. There were the coral earrings, his cloth baby slippers, and a group photograph from her wedding day. His mother's face was young and beautiful. Her eyes sparkled like the sea with a smile as bright as a mirror in the sunlight. Nunzio's arm was on his mother's shoulder. Leonardo looked at his face. It was the happiest Leonardo had ever seen him. He studied Nunzio's features and saw nothing of himself. The couple's parents and the Mazzis also stood in the group photo. The young Salvatore Mazzi's eyes were on Anna. There was something familiar in his sculpted features.

The only unforgivable sin in Naples was not to attend a family funeral. The wake was at the house. Relatives from both Nunzio and Anna's side of the family, many older and unrecognizable since Leonardo last saw them, came to pay their respects. Vincenzo and Salvatore Mazzi attended. Salvatore's face was gray, and he leaned on his brother. Leonardo nodded to them. Salvatore wanted to say something, but Leonardo's thoughts were elsewhere. His mind was on memories of his mother; the child's games she'd create, her pet chickens, walking through the wildflowers in the rain, her hands stroking his face when he was ill. Pressure built in his head and pounded out his forehead. He thought about the day he announced he'd leave for New York and their last day on the Naples pier. He bit his cheek to keep from crying.

Leonardo went to his mother's coffin. Her face looked like alabaster. Flowers were pressed around her; their sickly sweet smell masked the odor of death. A thought came into Leonardo's head. Had he smelled a single flower in America? He couldn't remember. He bent and kissed his mother. Leonardo brought his hands to his face. He'd shredded his cheek with his teeth, but the tears flowed.

The day of the funeral was stormy. The steel-gray sea churned up white foam waves. Junipers shook their branches in violent denial that the sun would shine again. Flowers threw their petals to the ground like folded hands of playing cards. Leonardo's face was pummeled by windblown rain. He struggled for breath in the billowy fog. He walked alongside Nunzio. They trailed his mother's casket carried on a cart pulled by two black horses. Aunts, uncles, cousins, and villagers, including the Mazzi brothers, followed in the procession with faces as somber as the granite crypts that stood like gray Greek temples in the cemetery. Men wore their best suits, and women dressed in black.

Bearers came forward and removed the coffin from the cart. Leonardo waited as the pallbearers placed his mother in the simple mausoleum. His eyes blurred. Everyone, men and women, came to him, hugged him, and kissed him on the cheek. Salvatore Mazzi squeezed his shoulder. Nunzio walked away, and Leonardo was alone.

The next day Leonardo approached a black-draped widow. She was the midwife to his mother when he was born. The woman saw him and twisted a handkerchief in arthritic fingers.

Leonardo said, "Signora, please tell me who my father is."

Her mouth opened. She looked away. "I knew this day would come."

"My mother is gone. There's no need for secrecy anymore."

She put her hand to Leonardo's face. "You were such a cute baby. Your mother loved you so much."

Leonardo caught a sob in his throat. He whispered, "I know."

She sighed. "I remember how ecstatic she was when she saw you were a boy. You were her whole world."

Leonardo bit his cheek to control himself.

"She wouldn't have a child with Nunzio."

Leonardo caught a breath. "There were pregnancies?"

The old midwife shrugged. "They were terminated. I helped. Her love was all for you."

Leonardo swallowed. "Who is my father?"

"Salvatore Mazzi."

Leonardo nodded. *Grazie.*

Azzura scrambled some eggs and poured them into a frying pan with sizzling onions and sliced potatoes. She plated the food and added a chunk of crusty bread. She brought the *colazione* and a cappuccino to Carlo's table. The aroma was mouth-watering.

Carlo said, "You're spoiling me."

"I appreciate what you've done for my family. With you and Giuseppe watching over us, my parents are able to sleep. I feel safe with you around."

Carlo laughed. "Women have expressed a variety of emotions to me, but never that I made them feel safe."

Azzura said, "You have an infectious laugh. I'm fond of you, Carlo."

"Fond. That's not enough."

"I'm not sure what I want, except that I can't become a kept woman in Italy. And you're leaving soon."

"Next week. I'm even looking forward to farm work. Home draws me, but I'll miss you. Can't I convince you to come?"

"New York is my home."

Carlo put his hand on Azzura's. "I'd do everything I could to make you love it there."

Azzura's eyes went down to the table.

Carlo said. "I've decided that your happiness is most important. If you're not happy with yourself, you won't be happy with me. Now that I have a reason, I'll return often to New York. I won't stop pursuing you until we're together."

Azzura said, "Where are you off to today?"

"Frank Rizzo."

Azzura made a face.

"This will be my last meeting with him."

Giuseppe cracked the tenement door and watched Carlo as he left the restaurant. He fingered the scar that ran down his cheek.

* * *

Carlo sat across from Frank Rizzo at a table in the Italian social club.

Rizzo said, "Giuseppe's sick. I need you to do a job for me."

"I don't work for you."

"What, you forgot how I squared it for you with the cops? This will be a small down payment for what you owe."

Carlo huffed. "Okay, what do you want?"

"There's a *figlio di puttana* who calls himself Titus Papanika-some-shit. Greek *sfacim* who thinks he's smarter than everybody. I'd be just as happy to see his brains on the concrete as receive the money he owes. So do what you gotta do."

Titus Papanikolaou hung out at a new pizza joint on Houston Street. He was a nervous, skinny guy with curly black hair and a red garnet pinkie ring. He had on a gray suit and a black fedora. He sat at an inside table and looked at the *Atlantis* newspaper. When the front door jingled, Papanikolaou appeared not to notice Carlo walk in.

Carlo stood over Papanikolaou. "You have the money you owe Frank Rizzo?"

Papanikolaou spoke in a staccato meter. "Hey, hello. Whoa, I didn't see you. What's your name?"

Carlo stared at him.

"You're Italian? I'm Greek. *Una faccia una razza.* Greeks and Italians are the same, right? Hey look, you want a slice of pizza? Jesus Christ, relax."

Papanikolaou waved to get the attention of the guy behind the counter, but the owner had ducked into the back room when he saw Carlo confront Papanikolaou.

Papanikolaou tried to smile.

Carlo's voice rose. "Frank Rizzo's money?"

"Whatever your name is, *paisan*, loosen up. Cool off. Goddamn, what a face. You look like you want to kill somebody."

"Mr. Rizzo told me that if you don't pay what you owe, I should splatter your brains on the pavement."

One of Papanikolaou's eyes twitched. He had a nine-inch stiletto in his newspaper. With a single movement he rose and plunged the knife into Carlo's solar plexus. Carlo gasped like he'd been hit with a punch. He grabbed for Papanikolaou's neck. Papanikolaou pushed him backwards, pulled out the knife, and stuck Carlo in the throat. Blood sprayed the wall. Carlo went to the floor, Papanikolaou on top.

Papanikolaou's face was close. He spit the words at Carlo, "Greetings from the Silvestri brothers."

Carlo bled out on the floor.

The Naples sky was smeared by distant rain. Leonardo approached the gate of the Mazzi estate.

Tazio Zangara leaned on a fence post with a shotgun cradled in his arms like a baby. "What's your business here?"

"I came to see Don Mazzi."

"He just learned that his son Carlo was killed. He's not seeing anyone."

"I'm his son."

Zangara stiffened.

Salvatore Mazzi sat on his portico, head in hands. He looked up when he heard their conversation. He called out to Zangara to allow Leonardo inside.

Zangara frowned and waved Leonardo through.

Salvatore Mazzi's riding boots trampled down the stone stairs, and he walked up to Leonardo. His face was furrowed. "Carlo is dead."

"I know. I'm sorry."

"What do you want to say to me?"

"Are you my father?"

Mazzi sighed. "It's like I'm looking into a mirror."

"Why didn't you tell me?"

"Your mother forbade me to have any contact with you."

"Is that why you wouldn't give me land to work?"

"You're my son. I wouldn't make you a tenant slave to me."

"You didn't love my mother?"

Mazzi shook his head. "You know nothing."

"You allowed her to marry Nunzio?"

Mazzi blew out a breath. "You came to hear the truth?"

"Yes."

"Let's go to the portico."

They sat and Mazzi gathered himself. "I'd ride the countryside on a black stallion. Once in a while I'd spot a willing peasant girl. But your mother was different." Mazzi looked into the distance. "She had long black hair and blue eyes that swallowed me. There was a deep intelligence in her face. When I rode up to her, her eyes evaluated me." Mazzi's gaze met Leonardo's. "I didn't force myself on her. Quite the contrary." Mazzi pointed. "We'd meet in the valley beyond the trees; golden afternoons, gurgling streams, and calling birds. I fell in love. We were together for a few months, then she broke it off." Mazzi sighed.

"And when you learned she was pregnant?"

Mazzi's eyes dropped. "My marriage had been arranged. My parents were aristocrats, and a divorce for them was out of the question. Plus, in their minds your mother was just a village girl." Mazzi took a deep breath. "Even so, I offered to leave Carlo's mother. My father would've disowned me. But your mother refused. She didn't want me, she wanted you. Somehow she knew you were a boy, and I was a means to an end. You were the only one in her heart. The question you should've asked was, did she ever love me?"

"I don't know."

Mazzi nodded. "My father made arrangements with Nunzio's family. Nunzio was given a house and guaranteed a position on the farm for life. When my father died and I took over, I gave Nunzio an additional monthly stipend. You were taken care of, but your mother didn't want me in your life."

"Did you think about us?"

"Often."

"But you had no contact with her?"

"Rarely. When you decided to go to America she came to me for money. As soon as I saw her, the memories flooded back. I almost asked her to marry me then. But her tone, her manner stopped me. I preferred my fantasy to another rejection. I had a few American dollars. I gave them to her."

"I wondered how she came by them."

"So now you know that Carlo was your brother." Mazzi sat back. "When the Silvestris were killed, I thought Carlo would be safe." Mazzi shook his head. "They struck at him from inside the grave." He raised a fist. "Carlo must be avenged. You'll do it."

Leonardo recoiled.

"You're my son. He was your blood. Blood is all. It's a matter of honor. You must avenge his death." Mazzi leaned forward. "I'll give you my name. We'll have a formal adoption. You'll be my heir. You went to America for money. You'll have money and property. You'll inherit everything when I die."

Leonardo said, "And what about this scum who's on the estate?"

"They're Torre Annunziata. We must negotiate with Senora Zangara."

"The Camorra will hollow you out like a cantaloupe."

Mazzi stiffened. "Not if you're here."

"I'm leaving for America tomorrow."

Mazzi had rheumy eyes. "Your mother will be placed in my family's crypt. In a place of honor."

"She didn't want you when she was alive." Leonardo stood.

Mazzi shouted to Leonardo's back. "Think about it. Everything will be yours."

Chapter 34

CIRO RUSHED into the apartment out of breath. "Carlo was stabbed in a restaurant on Houston Street."

Isabella pulled her hair and screamed.

Azzura's hands framed her face. "What happened?"

"A Greek killed him. The man was arrested, but he's claimed self-defense. Carlo had a stiletto on him."

Isabella wiped her eyes. "I don't believe Carlo would hurt anyone."

"Mama, Carlo led a violent life. Now this." Azzura sobbed.

Isabella said, "He helped us and Terranova had him killed."

Ciro shook his head. "I'm not sure. He was on a job for Frank Rizzo."

Azzura gasped. "Rizzo? That man is a plague."

Isabella pointed at Azzura. "Carlo loved you, and you had feelings for him."

"Mama, not now."

"Carlo would've been the husband for you. It was only a matter of time before he approached your father. He was a Mazzi. An aristocrat. Now he's gone. Saint Anthony failed me."

"Why don't you like Leonardo?"

"*Madonna mia.* He's just a peasant."

"That's so unfair."

Ciro raised his hands. "He's been in jail."

Azzura said, "He didn't do anything wrong."

Ciro said, "He works with Rizzo. You don't think Rizzo has corrupted him?"

Isabella was stone-faced. "We forbid you to see him."

"I'll see who I want."

Ciro straightened. "Don't defy us."

"What will you have me do? Marry someone I don't love?"

Ciro said, "You know that our marriage was arranged. That's the way it's done. Love comes with time."

"I don't want to live your life."

Ciro said, "You're young. You desire a young man. It's natural. But lust fades and marriage is forever. You can't marry based on an infatuation. The man we select will have a solid foundation. You'll have children. Your life will be fulfilled."

"What about happiness?"

Isabella said, "Happiness is elusive."

"I'd be happy with Leonardo."

Ciro said, "That's what you think today."

"You don't care about my feelings."

Ciro said, "That's not true. It's because we love you. We don't want you to make a terrible mistake."

"If it's a mistake, it's my mistake."

Isabella crossed her arms. "We'll disown you if you disobey us."

Azzura threw up her hands. "How can you say that to me?"

Isabella said, "We're your parents."

Azzura raised her chin. "I'll make my own decision." She stormed out the door.

Isabella turned to Ciro. "Azzura's life is ruined. It's a disaster."

The corners of Ciro's mouth turned down.

Isabella grabbed Ciro's shirt. "Our daughter is lost, and it's your fault. You took us out of Italy into this," she spit out the word, "corruption. In Italy Azzura never would've disobeyed us." She turned away.

Ciro said, "We came to America to make a living."

Isabella said, "You ruined my life chasing money. Scrounging for pennies in this country has turned the cream of our lives sour." Isabella pointed. "If we lose her, I'll never forgive you."

Isabella strode into their bedroom and changed into a black dress.

The weather was chilly on Leonardo's return voyage. The ship slapped the waves on a slate gray sea. The wind whipped off the water and sliced across Leonardo's cheeks. He sat on a deck chair. He tightened the blanket around him like a chrysalis. His mind weighed Salvatore Mazzi's offer to adopt him.

The months that passed since he first arrived in New York seemed like years. Gentile had told him that he could return to Italy with a hundred dollars. He winced at the memory of Mazzali's deception and the sting of his dismissal by Carson. When you're the dregs of the labor force, any bastard above you has the power to crush you in his palm. You claw your fingernails to the nubs trying to make a living. It's a life lived in desperation; and what would he and Azzura live on? The only honest work he could get paid him a pittance. He'd seen how families existed without money. Wife and children conscripted into fourteen-hour-a-day labor clinging onto the singular dream to buy a home and leave the stinking tenement. He didn't want that for Azzura or himself.

He'd entered Rizzo's sphere with his eyes wide shut. Better pay and a union job, as Guido Basso told him, were unattainable for Italians, then Rizzo laid opportunity at his feet. He couldn't have imagined it would lead to Murphy's death and jail for him. Thank God his mother never knew, but now she was gone. There was an odd sort of freedom in her passing. Her approval didn't hang over his head. He was his own man.

Rizzo's rackets offered good money, but at great risk. Rizzo was a violent and clever man. Leonardo knew he'd been manipulated at every turn, yet he admired Rizzo for it. But Rizzo's criminal lifestyle had a fuse attached. Jesus said, "All who draw the sword will die by the sword." It could happen in a gang fight, a strikebreaker riot, or while eating in a restaurant. The call would come. Carlo didn't know when. He wouldn't either.

Were Frank Rizzo and Salvatore Mazzi really any different? Mazzi was an aristocrat, but his son committed murder. He and his brother killed the Silvestris to protect Carlo. Rizzo was born with few options, but he wouldn't accept poverty as his lot. Violence paid off for Rizzo from an early age. Brutality was the tariff he paid for success. The difference between Rizzo and Mazzi was the circumstances of their birth.

Azzura would be disowned if she married him against her parents' wishes. He couldn't be the reason she lost her family. Eventually she'd resent him. If he became Mazzi's adopted son, he'd be rich. Azzura's parents would see him in a different light. He'd be accepted, even welcomed. They ignored Carlo's violent past. They'd forget his. Salvatore Mazzi's demand echoed in his ears. He'd need to commit another murder, this time premeditated. Could he tell Azzura? Would the act win her, or push her away? Would he lie to her? Had he changed in the last few months, become hard-hearted as Azzura implied? No, he'd just grown up.

Leonardo saw Azzura on the pier and his heart lightened. Azzura threw herself into his arms, and they kissed. She'd brought Garibaldi. The dog jumped up and shook Leonardo's hand with his right paw. They found a quiet table in a small café.

Azzura said, "I'm sorry about your mother's passing."

"I had a few moments with her before she died."

"Thank God." Azzura put her hand on his.

Leonardo said, "A mother's love is unique. With her gone, it's as if the sun was extinguished and I'm naked in a frozen world. A part of my heart was ripped out with a claw hammer."

Azzura said, "You're not alone."

Leonardo squeezed her hand. They kissed. "I need to tell you something."

Azzura's eyes widened.

"I learned that my biological father was Salvatore Mazzi. My mother's parents forced her to marry Nunzio to cover their shame."

Azzura straightened. "Carlo's father was your father?"

"Yes. Everyone lied to me my whole life. Now I know why Nunzio was so cold to me."

"He knew you weren't his child."

"And even so, he stayed married to my mother. But she never loved him."

"It must have been difficult for him. To love and not be loved. That's so sad. And to learn that Carlo was your brother must have been a shock."

"I had two fathers and no father. I had a brother and no brother."

Azzura squeezed his hand.

"Mazzi offered to adopt me. To make me part of his family."

Azzura's eyebrows rose. "Because Carlo is dead?"

"Partly. He wants his name to live on. And he needs help to expel the Camorra gang that's infected his estate. He wants me to avenge Carlo."

"You mean kill someone? You refused?"

"I walked away. But I had time to think. Carlo was my brother."

"The police and the courts will handle the matter."

"The Greek who killed Carlo has claimed self-defense. What if he's set free?"

"Leonardo, think about what you're saying. Murder?"

"In Italy blood is everything. People understand the need to revenge the killing of a family member, and vendetta crimes rarely lead to conviction."

"Vendetta? When does the cycle stop? That's why the courts punish murderers. So families can have justice without resorting to killing."

"But sometimes justice isn't done."

"In America the police would come after you. You'd go to jail, perhaps be executed."

"If I were a Mazzi, your parents would welcome me."

"My mother mourns Carlo like he was her son."

"If your parents didn't accept me, you'd lose them."

"I don't want you to commit murder. You can't rationalize and say it's for us."

Leonardo understood that Papanikolaou was a hired killer, and Carlo was fingered in New York. Only a few people knew Carlo was a Mazzi. Who had betrayed him?

Leonardo strode into the Italian social club. Rizzo was at his normal table. Leonardo sat across from him, and Rizzo ordered two coffees.

"My sympathies on the loss of your mother."

"*Grazie.*"

The coffees arrived. Rizzo poured a drop of anisette into his and offered some to Leonardo.

He gave a slight negative shake of his head. "In Italy I learned that Salvatore Mazzi is my father, and Carlo was my brother."

Rizzo leaned back. "Really?"

"You sent Carlo to Papanikolaou and he was murdered."

Rizzo's forehead scar flushed crimson. "I sent Carlo on a job to collect money."

"You never used Carlo before."

Rizzo's face changed from red to shadow. "You think I fingered Carlo?"

"The Silvestris paid for Carlo to be killed. I know you love money."

"Carlo was part of my crew, like you."

"So who informed the Silvestris that Carlo was in New York? Only a few people knew he was a Mazzi."

"Okay. I'll explain myself to you just this one time. I don't take orders; I give them." Rizzo leaned forward. "Even if Carlo wasn't my man, I wouldn't kill him for a few bucks from some aristocratic bastards."

Leonardo took a sip of coffee. "Did Terranova have Carlo killed?"

"Much as I'd like to send you against Terranova, it wasn't him. The Silvestris were aligned with a Neapolitan Camorra gang, the Russomannos. That's who arranged the killing. They fulfilled their obligation to the Silvestris even after the brothers were dead. The Neapolitan mob hired a Greek to do the job. They'd never hire a Sicilian."

"Terranova could've learned Carlo's last name."

"Terranova would have his own reasons to kill Carlo. But he'd never help a Neapolitan gang."

"So who then?"

"I'm supposed to solve puzzles for you?" Rizzo took a sip of coffee. "I'm not sure I want to tell you."

"You're not suggesting Ciro Medina informed on Carlo?"

Rizzo waved his hand. "Ciro's an innocent."

Leonardo frowned. "So who's left?"

Rizzo pulled on his ear. "You know someone who ran with the Camorra in Naples before he was put on a steamship to New York."

Leonardo's eyes widened. "Only Giuseppe."

Rizzo drained his coffee.

Leonardo's mouth dropped open. "No."

Leonardo stood at Giuseppe's shoulder in the apartment. "Why did you do it?"

Giuseppe gazed out the window. He ran his finger along the wooden frame. "I owed a debt in Naples." Giuseppe's eyes were like a penitent's. "Isabella preferred Carlo for Azzura. He might've murdered you for her." Giuseppe sighed. "I didn't know he was your brother."

Leonardo slumped into a chair. "I didn't either."

Giuseppe straightened. "Regardless how you felt toward Carlo, you must avenge a brother. You're a man. It's a matter of honor."

"I have no desire to hurt you. You've been more brother to me than Carlo could've been."

"The Greek was released from the Tombs. The judge bought the self-defense nonsense."

"That's outrageous."

"I'll atone for my act. Leave the Greek to me."

"I must be there."

Giuseppe took out Drago's revolver and Carlo's Lemon Squeezer. "Carlo left this with me when I guarded Ciro's."

"The Greek will be wary."

Giuseppe handed Drago's revolver to Leonardo. "Perhaps not. He thinks all his enemies are in Italy."

The snub-nosed 38 lay heavy in Leonardo's hand. He sat across the table from Giuseppe, each checking his pistol. Leonardo peered through the grimy window to the sky filled with clouds and light flakes of snow dropping over the tenement like volcanic ash.

The bartender tipped Giuseppe that Papanikolaou would be at Mike's Bar on Pell Street that evening. Leonardo cracked open the cylinder of the pistol. He ejected the bullets into his palm, examined them like they were gems, and slowly slipped the cartridges back into the chambers. He snapped the cylinder shut. Giuseppe's face had gone slate like the weather. The scar that ran from ear to chin turned a bright shade of purple, an angry color. Giuseppe nodded, and they rose. They clomped down the creaky wooden stairs and opened the heavy door to the street. The manure piled against the curbs was dusted with snow. Leonardo sniffed at the acrid smell. He and Giuseppe stepped onto the stoop and a gust of wind blew through his clothes. He shivered and hugged himself. The two men pulled down their newsboy caps and turned up their collars. On the street, men headed home from their labors. Leonardo bent his face down as if not making eye contact would shield his identity. He bumped into a few shoulders. Some men turned and protested, but he kept moving all the way to Pell Street.

Mike's Saloon was a red brick front across the street from an alley crammed with overfilled steel trash cans with loose lids. The odor was rotted fish. Cats hissed at each other for first dibs. Leonardo and Giuseppe ducked into the shadows and watched the saloon's front door.

The day darkened into twilight. Leonardo's mind toiled with Mazzi's price for adoption. What would he tell Azzura? He shook his head. He shivered and fingered the revolver under his belt.

Papanikolaou was rail thin and fidgety. He dressed in black. He sauntered up to Mike's, gave the alley a cursory look, and stepped inside the bar. Leonardo followed Giuseppe to the door. He took a deep breath. His heart pounded. The men pulled their pistols and entered. The bar had a large mirror crowded with bottles of booze on a shelf. Papanikolaou had his heel on a foot rail next to a row of spittoons. They saw Papanikolaou suck down a whiskey. They crossed the floor. Papanikolaou called down in his staccato cadence to the bartender for another shot. He saw the guns too late. Giuseppe fired. Papanikolaou stiffened. Leonardo's hand sweated. He could hear the rush of blood in his ears. His finger wrapped around the trigger, but his hand wouldn't squeeze. Giuseppe fired again. The sound in Leonardo's ears was like an echo in a distant canyon. Papanikolaou doubled over like he'd been punched in the belly. Leonardo watched him crumple to the floor in slow motion. Leonardo stepped forward, put his pistol close to Papanikolaou's ear and pulled the trigger. Brain and blood painted the spittoons.

Leonardo was frozen. The image of Papanikolaou's gaping skull was burned into his brain.

Giuseppe yanked his arm. "Let's go."

The other men in the bar sat and stood like posed statues. Giuseppe dragged Leonardo to the street. No cops were around. They ran down the alley. They tossed their pistols into the trash. They climbed a backyard fence, hurried through a tenement's back door, and emerged on the next street. They melted into the neighborhood and made their way back to Spring Street.

The November day threatened rain or snow. Rizzo, in the social club, had the *Il Progresso* newspaper opened. His finger was on a story. He read, "Police reported that a man named Titus Papanikolaou was shot three times in Mike's Saloon on Pell Street."

Rizzo's eyes glanced over the paper. Leonardo was expressionless.

Rizzo continued. "Papanikolaou was pronounced dead at the scene. Witnesses said that two perpetrators walked up to Papanikolaou and shot him three times. They couldn't identify the killers. Police say that two weapons were found in a trash can across from the saloon. One was a Smith & Wesson Lemon Squeezer revolver. A subsequent investigation determined that Richard Shippen of Philadelphia owned the pistol. Shippen was murdered on Grand Jones Street in September. The man sought for that murder, Carlo Mazzi, was killed a few weeks ago. The police have no suspects in the Papanikolaou shooting."

Rizzo had a twinkle in his eye. "How neat. You've been busy since you returned from Italy. Are you ready to come to work?"

"Not now."

"I'll be here." Rizzo raised the newspaper.

Leonardo and Azzura sat at a quiet table at Ciro's. Azzura averted her eyes. "That man who shot Carlo was murdered."

Leonardo said, "I didn't kill him."

Azzura examined Leonardo's face. "Do you swear?"

"I do."

She threw her arms around him. "Thank God."

"Salvatore Mazzi sent me a cable. He's asked me to return to Naples."

"You won't go?"

"Azzura, the body of the crew boss was found when the *Gorjistan* arrived in Turkey. The police still suspect me. Detective Byrne can arrest me at any time."

"Why won't he stop harassing you? It was an accident."

"It doesn't matter. It's political. You were in the Tombs. I don't want to go back."

"I'm sure the courts would find you innocent."

"Okay. Let's say you're right. But then what? I've decided that working for Frank Rizzo means jail or winding up dead on the street gunned down in a gang dispute."

"That's been my fear."

"But it was Frank Rizzo who got me out of the Tombs the last time. Without him I have no money for bail. I could rot in jail awaiting trial. And what other options do I have for making a living in New York? Work as a beast of burden? The Mazzi name is my chance for a title, money, and land."

"In New York we can be together, maybe start a restaurant."

"What do I know about running a restaurant? Azzura, don't you see? If I'm a Mazzi your parents will accept me. I'll have a new name and money to defend myself against Byrne."

Azzura wrung her hands.

"I'm going back to Italy to claim what's mine. I love you and I don't want to lose you."

Chapter 35

LADY JANE AYNSLEY was in her thirties with auburn hair, bright eyes, and a pouting mouth. She lounged with Terranova's attorney, Philip Agostini in his Upper Westside apartment living room. They'd met at the 1900 Paris Olympics. Lady Jane was an equestrian and competed in the hack and hunter combined. Agostini was in Paris supporting his friend, Giovanni Giorgio Trissino, who won two medals. Lady Aynsley lived in London. She and Agostini conducted their affair on two continents.

Agostini said, "Four o'clock. Time for tea."

Lady Jane smiled. "Lovely."

Agostini's butler brought in the bone china tea set, two pots, one with tea, the other with hot water.

"I hope Darjeeling is all right?"

"Delightful."

The two-level serving tray had bite sized scones above and cucumber sandwiches below.

Agostini held a cup. "Some milk?" Agostini poured in a dollop and filled the cup with tea. "One or two lumps of sugar?"

"Two, please." Lady Jane placed her teaspoon at the six o'clock position in the cup and moved it gently to the twelve o'clock position and back again. She placed the spoon on the right side of the saucer without a click.

Agostini said, "Would you care for a cucumber sandwich or a scone?"

"A scone please."

When both of them were served, Agostini sat back. "I've never understood a cucumber sandwich. It's so insubstantial."

"Why, my dear Philip, that's exactly the point."

Agostini's eyebrows rose.

"We English make some effort to discriminate between social classes. What could be a more arrogant way to distinguish nobility from working people than to consume food without nutritional value while the poor struggle to earn enough money for a decent meal?"

"And I was trying to avoid making a political statement."

"Italians have their nobles. 'Rule by the best.' That's the Greek meaning of the word aristocracy."

"I'm afraid that's not always true."

"Of course. In England noble birth is the highest honor. A marquis might be as thick as a Dodo. No matter. And in Italy, the *chevalieri* are knights without horses. Laughable."

"What's brought this on?"

"Don't you find the American system more honest? Aren't the 'Robber Barons,' those who are ruthless enough to make the most money, the real American aristocracy?"

"I suppose."

Lady Jane gave him a sly smile. "People like you, Philip."

Frank Rizzo strode into Terranova's Hester Street Saloon. He wore his gray fedora at a jaunty angle. He stood in the middle of the room and looked around. Faces locked onto him in recognition. Someone poked Terranova at the card table. He saw Rizzo and leaned back.

Rizzo went to the bar. Terranova rose and joined him along with four of his thugs.

Terranova said, "Frank 'hole in the head,' that injury must have finally warped your brain for you to walk in here alone."

Rizzo fingered his scar. "If you like it, I can arrange for you to have one that would go clear through your scull"

"Not today I think." The four men surrounded Rizzo.

Rizzo smirked. He reached toward his vest. The men flinched, and he hesitated. A bill protruded from a pocket. He took it out with two fingers, waved it in the air, and threw it onto the bar. The bartender had moved as far away as he could from the drama. Rizzo called down to him. "Whiskey."

Terranova nodded. The bartender grabbed a bottle and a shot glass from the shelf. The shaky pour overflowed into a puddle.

Rizzo said, "Join me? I'm paying."

Terranova chuckled. "No thanks."

Rizzo downed the whiskey in a gulp.

Terranova picked up the two-dollar bill. He recognized it as his counterfeit. "You like my work?"

"Excellent quality. I came over to see the press, and the show."

Terranova smiled. "You've developed a death wish."

"My death wish is for you."

Terranova's face darkened. He drew his stiletto. Two men grabbed Rizzo's arms and held him. "The only show today will be when I slit your throat." Terranova nodded to the thug with a pockmarked face.

Pockmarks gave Rizzo a quick frisk. He looked at Terranova and shrugged.

Terranova said, "Alone and unarmed?"

Rizzo said, "I didn't want the police to arrest me for carrying a weapon."

At that moment Detective Killian Byrne and a brace of police armed with pistols stormed through the front and rear entrances of the saloon.

Byrne shouted, "This is a raid. Everybody, hands up." He pointed his pistol. Terranova dropped the knife.

Cops had everyone line up against the bar and they were searched. All manner of cudgel, knife, and pistol were confiscated. Police with sledges broke through the back room door. A printing press and a significant inventory of counterfeit bills were discovered.

Byrne smiled. "Terranova, it seems I have you by the bills. You're under arrest."

Rizzo laughed.

Terranova sneered. "My lawyer will have me back on the street in a day."

Byrne said, "Philip Agostini? I think you'll be disappointed." He told a burly cop, "Get this piece of shit out of here."

Terranova was dragged away.

Byrne faced Rizzo. "What the hell are you doing in Terranova's saloon?"

"Drinking. What else?"

"You wouldn't happen to know anything about a tip we received concerning a counterfeit press?"

Rizzo smiled. "Not a thing."

Byrne said, "Just the same. Come to the station and let's have a chat."

Rizzo said, "I'm always cooperative with the police."

When the butler opened the door to Philip Agostini's apartment, Detective Byrne and a pack of cops burst through the door. "Where is he?"

The butler stammered. "In the master bedroom, sir."

Byrne threw open the door. Agostini's boudoir was featherbed and silk. Lady Jane screamed and pulled the sheets up to her chin.

Agostini jumped out of bed naked. "What the hell is this?"

Byrne said, "Apparently, it's *coptus interruptus*. Get dressed, Agostini. You're under arrest."

Agostini put his hands on hips. "What for?"

Lady Jane gasped. "Phillip, what's going on?"

Byrne said, "We have records that show you and Ignazio Terranova are partners in a real estate company that owns a Hester Street saloon where counterfeiting has been conducted. We raided the place an hour ago."

Agostini's mouth dropped open.

"Like I said, get dressed."

A couple of cops entered the room. They looked at Lady Jane with wide eyes.

Agostini stepped into his pants. Byrne tipped his hat. "My apologies, young lady. You have a rather refined accent. London?"

Lady Jane turned her face away.

They led Agostini out. Lady Jane covered her head with a pillow.

Chapter 36

CAPTAIN BALDASSARE CERUTI walked his chestnut stallion slowly toward the Mazzi estate. Tazio Zangara was at the gate. When he spotted Ceruti approach, he left his post. The other Zangara gang members were stationed about the grounds. When he arrived, they averted their eyes and walked in the opposite direction.

Salvatore Mazzi had suffered another stroke and was under Doctor Sprandio's care. Despite his physician's protests, Mazzi left his bed and met Ceruti on the portico.

Ceruti extended his hand. "Don Mazzi, my condolences on the loss of your son, Carlo."

Mazzi took Ceruti's hand in both of his. "*Grazie.*" He gestured for Ceruti to sit. "May I get you something?"

"A coffee."

Mazzi nodded to a servant who ducked into the house.

"I apologize, Don Mazzi, but I must ask you about Domenico and Bartolomeo Silvestri. They've disappeared without a trace. A workman on their estate said that they left about a week ago with two other men in a carriage. That's the last anyone saw of them."

"Could the worker identify the two men?"

"He described them as city types. Rough men." Ceruti gazed beyond the loggia. "Much like the men I see here on your estate."

The servant arrived with two coffees.

Ceruti said, "Do you know anything about the Silvestris' disappearance?"

Mazzi shifted uncomfortably in his chair. "I understand that the Silvestris became aligned with the Russomanno clan in Santa Lucia. So it's likely that the two men who were with the Silvestris were with that gang. The Russomannos are ruthless. Perhaps they fell out with the Silvestris and killed the brothers?"

Ceruti sipped his coffee. "Don Mazzi, I understand that you're about to purchase the Silvestri estate?"

"Yes, the property was taken by a bank in settlement of the Silvestri debts. The two properties share an important stream. We fought with Pero Silvestri in the courts over water rights. If we own the property that issue goes away."

"Water is a crucial matter for a farmer. Perhaps you had the Silvestris murdered?"

"Over water and a piece of property?"

"The Silvestris were on a vendetta. You would've done anything to protect your son."

Mazzi's eyes dropped. "Carlo was murdered after the Silvestris disappeared."

Ceruti leaned back. "Yes. That's true."

Mazzi's gaze drifted to the horizon. His face was pained.

Ceruti said, "The men on the property are from the Torre Annunziata Camorra?"

Mazzi reacted as if awoken. "They're just extra workmen."

"Did they kill the Silvestris?"

"Why don't you ask them?"

"Are you hostage to these men?"

Mazzi stiffened. "Never."

Leonardo's return trip to Italy was markedly different from his last. His clothes were unchanged, but he'd already assumed the mantle of a Mazzi. If there were stares, he looked back until the other passengers averted their eyes.

He was picked up by a carriage and taken to the Mazzi estate. When he arrived, Salvatore left his sick bed and embraced Leonardo. They went into a Great Room. Hewn brown timbers cracked with age supported a high ceiling above a travertine stone floor. Doctor Sprandio assisted Salvatore into a well-worn cloth chair and left. Leonardo sank into a leather couch. The seats were around a low table with bas-relief woodcarvings. On one side the mythological Athenian, Theseus, was pictured moving a great rock to recover his father's sandals and sword, symbols of his kingly birthright. On the other side Theseus was depicted weaving through the labyrinth in search of the Minotaur he ultimately would kill.

Salvatore said, "The Greek. Was it difficult?"

"I had help. A friend. I'd rather not say his name."

"But if the police arrest him, he could turn on you."

"We've been through a lot together. If he wanted to implicate me in a crime, he could've done so already. The police have no reason to suspect either of us. We have no apparent motive. My name is still Robustelli."

"That won't be for long. I've started the process for adoption."

"*Grazie*, Father."

Salvatore nodded. "I must speak to you about the men on the property."

"They look like the same bunch who were here before I left,"

"Yes. I made an arrangement with the Torre Annunziata Camorra to protect us from the Silvestris."

"Was it a financial arrangement?"

"Not exactly. Donna Zangara is head of the clan." Salvatore shifted in his chair. "She's a difficult woman. She has blood on her hands. She insisted we help her with future illegal activities. Perhaps I shouldn't have agreed, but I was anxious to protect us from the Silvestris."

Leonardo said, "What would you like me to do?"

"I want you to speak with her. We need to get these men to leave."

Leonardo's brow furrowed. "I'll try."

* * *

Leonardo tromped down the street steps toward the headquarters of the Torre Annunziata Camorra in Naples. A large rooster scurried across his path. He looked up to see Tazio Zangara at the doorway. Tazio led him inside.

Giulietta Zangara sat in her armchair and knitted. There was a dark gray pile of wool in her lap. Her work hadn't begun to take shape. When Leonardo walked into the living room, she gestured for him to sit and offered him a coffee. Tazio slouched in a wooden chair and looked at Leonardo like he was a carcass about to be butchered. The three waited to be served without speaking. The click of Zangara's metal knitting needles against each other was the only sound in the room. Zangara's niece brought coffees for the three of them and left.

Zangara didn't lift her eyes. "So, Tazio, Don Mazzi has sent me his bastard son."

Tazio let out a short chuckle. Leonardo straightened in his chair. His face got hot. He smiled. He took breaths to calm himself. He decided to present an air of confidence that wasn't confrontational. "I've come to discuss final payment for your service."

"You speak for Don Mazzi?"

"Yes, Donna Zangara. We purchased the Silvestri estate. We propose to sign the title of the land over to you. That would settle your claim on us."

The knitting needles stopped. "I don't agree." Zangara's stone eyes held Leonardo. "When we need financing, Don Mazzi will provide the funds. When we want cargo brought into Naples outside normal channels, Vincenzo will lend us his boat."

"But you failed to complete your end of the bargain."

Zangara jutted her chin. "How so?"

"Carlo was killed in New York."

The knitting needles started again. "I promised to eliminate the source of the threat to the Mazzis. The Silvestri brothers are dead. Carlo was in New York, beyond our security. Please express my sympathies to Don Mazzi for his loss."

Leonardo took a sip of coffee. "Captain Baldassare Ceruti of the *carabinieri* and my father have become quite well acquainted in the last few months."

Zangara's eyes locked onto Leonardo. If Zangara was a she-wolf, her teeth would've been bared. "Too friendly a relationship with the *carabinieri* could be deadly for you. Are you threatening me?"

A tingle went up Leonardo's back. He made an effort to control his voice. "Captain Ceruti asked my father about the men on our property. We haven't discussed our business with him. But he's no fool. We're concerned that if he sees your people on his next visit he'll make inquiries in Naples. Why take the risk to expose our relationship?"

Zangara continued to knit. "You're right." She turned to Tazio. "Remove our men from the Mazzi estate." Her lips formed a tiny smile. "You see? We can be reasoned with."

"*Grazie.*" Leonardo pulled on his ear. "We understand that you've settled with the Russomanno clan."

"What do you mean?"

"Tazio killed two of their people. We expected that the Russomannos would seek retribution."

Tazio glanced at his aunt. Zangara shifted in her chair.

"A lot of time has passed, and your nephew still breathes." Leonardo scrutinized Tazio. He avoided Leonardo's eyes. "In fact, no one from your clan has been murdered. That's a surprise to us. We wonder how the blood debt was paid."

Zangara said, "What are you suggesting?"

"Maybe the Russomannos received satisfaction in another way? Perhaps you protected Tazio and settled your debt by giving the Russomannos permission to kill Carlo?"

Zangara put down her knitting. "Signor Mazzi, this discussion is over."

Leonardo stood and tried not to rush out of the house.

Back at the Mazzi estate, Leonardo walked into the kitchen. He pumped out a tall glass of cool well water. Inside the Great Room, Salvatore waited. A blanket lay across his knees. He had a slight tremor in his left hand.

Leonardo plopped onto the couch. He drained the glass before he spoke. "She called me a bastard just as you said she would."

Salvatore nodded. "It was a difficult conversation?"

"I'd rather hand-feed a pit viper than deal with Senora Zangara. Tazio was there."

"You offered her the Silvestri estate?"

"As instructed. She refused, as you knew she would."

"Of course. These people aren't farmers. They don't work for their bread. They live off the sweat of others. So you played the Ceruti card?"

"When I brought up Captain Ceruti I thought *La* Senora would order Tazio to cut my throat right there and then." Leonardo put down the glass. "But the gambit worked. Zangara recognized the threat to all her business if the *carabinieri* focused on her gang. She told Tazio to remove everyone from the estate."

"Excellent. Zangara wants to be invisible to Ceruti and the *carabinieri*. Her men's conspicuous presence here was an imprudent risk. If Tazio ever takes over, the gang will be run by a *guappo* who'll try to write his exploits across the face of Vesuvius, and that ego will lead to his arrest and the *carabinieri* will hound Torre Annunziata into extinction."

The men sat in silence for a few moments.

"Father, I raised the suspicion that Zangara gave approval for Carlo's murder to protect Tazio and as settlement of the blood debt with the Russomanno gang."

Salvatore looked away. He brought a trembling hand to his face.

"She didn't deny it or even attempt false outrage. She ended our discussion."

"I never should've gotten involved with that scum. Poor Carlo."

"Don't torture yourself. No one could have imagined every twist of events."

Salvatore puffed out a breath. He patted Leonardo's knee. "At least this *merda* will be gone from the estate."

"You know this isn't over. *La* Senora will show up here one day with a demand."

"Yes, and you'll help me deal with it when the time comes. How would you like the Silvestri estate? There's a beautiful house. Perhaps you want to start a family?"

"That's generous." Leonardo sat back. "I'd like to have Nunzio as foreman for the property. He can live with me if he wants."

"I'm surprised by your request."

"As his son I couldn't please Nunzio. I never understood why. Despite the circumstances of his marriage to my mother, he provided for us and remained loyal to her. It's difficult for a son to learn that his father is just a flawed man. I understand Nunzio better, and I owe him."

"Nunzio is an excellent farmer and a hard worker. The property will be well cared for. And what about that girl, Azzura, you met in New York?"

"I love Azzura."

"You'll find that an American woman who speaks Italian is not the same as an Italian woman. Americans want to earn money and have independence."

"That's Azzura. I need to convince her that she can pursue her dreams in Italy."

"Remember that once a woman has a son, the husband falls to second place in her life."

Leonardo said, "The Mazzi name must live on."

"Yes. When will you return to New York?"

"There's still the open investigation of the accident on the *Gorjistan* and the death of the crew boss Murphy. Detective Byrne will arrest me on sight."

"Then remain in Italy."

"I must see Azzura."

"I'll hire the best attorney to defend you."

"You remember the *guappo*, Frank Rizzo, who cleared Carlo of the Tucker murder with Tammany Hall? I've been in contact with him."

Frank Rizzo, Big Jim O'Neil, Teddy Fitzpatrick and three other indistinguishable International Longshoremen's Association board members who looked like they had a platonic relationship with exercise shook hands around a huge oak table with emerald-green padded chairs.

Big Jim sat at the head of the table. Rizzo grabbed the seat on his left. Big Jim frowned and leaned on the opposite chair arm.

Fitzpatrick was on Big Jim's right. "Now that we've all met Frank Rizzo, I'd like to officially welcome him to the ILA board."

Rizzo said, "Thanks, Teddy, it's great to be here." Polite smiles reflected back. "I don't know how business is normally conducted, but I'd like to raise an important issue for me."

Eyes around the table widened. Big Jim daubed his face with a handkerchief.

Rizzo continued. "I think we can all celebrate the end of the bad old days when Italians were considered unworthy of the ILA."

Big Jim looked at the ceiling.

"But there's still some hangover from those terrible times we need to clear up."

Fitzpatrick said, "Frank, what's on your mind?"

"Even though the union was closed to Italians, I was able to negotiate a couple of memberships for two of my boys some months back. Not all longshoremen appreciated having Italians as members, and there was resentment in the rank and file. So when there was a terrible accident during the grain loading of the *Gorjistan*, and a fine man, Liam Murphy, disappeared, my two guys, Fontana and Robustelli, were arrested for murder."

Fitzpatrick ran his finger along the edge of the table. "I recall."

"Murphy's body was discovered in Istanbul buried in the grain. There wasn't a mark of foul play on him. Yet the police, under pressure from the union, continued to harass my people. I want the board to tell the ILA to allow the police to do their job without pressure. I'm sure that will end the matter for Detective Byrne."

Fitzpatrick sat back.

The other board members looked at Big Jim. His face looked like indigestion. He raised his eyebrows at Fitzpatrick

Fitzpatrick said, "Frank, now that Italians will enter the ILA, can we assume that strikebreaking is also a thing of the past?"

Rizzo smiled. "Absolutely."

Big Jim gave a curt nod to Fitzpatrick.

Fitzpatrick raised his hand. "All in favor of Frank's request?"

Everyone said, "Aye."

Fitzpatrick said, "We're in agreement. I'll talk to the appropriate people."

Rizzo brightened. "That's great." He slapped Big Jim on the back.

Big Jim jumped like he would regurgitate his breakfast. His eyes shot stilettos at Rizzo.

Rizzo laughed. "That's just great."

Leonardo's trip back to the States was as stressful as his voyage in steerage; he wanted the ship to fly. His plan was to return to New York a Mazzi, yet within days of completing the adoption process, he was conscripted for military service: three months of boring guard duty along the Austrian Littoral border. His solace was the faint scent of lavender on Azzura's letters, and the memory of their first kiss. Then her letters stopped. What happened? He worried about "Black Hand" violence. He worried about another suitor. In the darkest moments of the Austrian nights, he conjured up his worst fears. He'd rehearsed his approach to Ciro and Isabella so many times that he had dreams of their meeting. He was confident he'd convince them that he was the man for Azzura. But now, somehow, she was lost to him. Was this his punishment for the murder of Papanikolaou? The dead Greek's image still stuck in his head.

Leonardo's cables implored his Father, and Salvatore made the necessary payments and shortened his tour of duty. As soon as he was back in Naples, he booked passage to New York

Leonardo had cabled Azzura, but she wasn't at the pier. Leonardo hailed a carriage, and the top hatted driver whipped the horses toward Spring Street. When he entered the restaurant, Garibaldi barked and ran to him. Things looked normal. Leonardo breathed a sigh of relief. The dog squatted at his feet and Leonardo ruffled his fur. "That's my boy. Have you been a good watch dog?"

The dog smiled and flopped his ears.

Giuseppe and Leonardo embraced. Giuseppe held Leonardo by the arms and looked him over. "Hey, *walyo*, what an outfit. You look too rich to sleep in our little apartment."

"You can't get rid of me that easily. How have things been with the 'Black Hand' threat?"

"Terranova is in jail. Everything's quiet."

Leonardo said, "Thank God. Where's Azzura."

Azzura emerged from the back. Her face brightened, but she hesitated. Leonardo ran over and kissed her. She didn't kiss back. Tears welled up.

Leonardo said, "I missed you."

She made a half smile.

Isabella worked the dough. She shouted, "Azzura."

Azzura backed away. "You've been gone a long time."

"I'm sorry. I waited for the adoption to go through, then the military grabbed me."

Leonardo felt Isabella's glare. "*Buona sera*, Signora Medina. It's good to see you again."

Her tone was glacial. "*Buona sera*, Signore." Her eyes turned to her husband. She punched the dough as if it offended her.

Giuseppe said, "Azzura, are you going to marry this guy?"

She cast her eyes down.

Ciro wiped his hands as he walked over to Leonardo. "I'm not sure how to address you."

"I'm officially a Mazzi. Please call me Leonardo."

"Of course, Leonardo. I hope your voyage was smooth."

"It took too long." Leonardo smiled at Azzura. "Signor Medina, now I can answer your questions."

Ciro sighed. "Azzura is engaged to another man. Please respect that."

"What?"

"I've made the arrangements."

"But I love Azzura."

"It's best for my daughter."

"You knew I'd be adopted as a Mazzi."

"That didn't enter into our decision. You were in jail. You're associated with Frank Rizzo."

"I don't work for Rizzo."

"You want to take Azzura to Italy. She's an American."

"I have a beautiful home and property in Italy. We'll visit New York."

"The matter is closed."

"You can't do this."

"Signor Mazzi, I'm sorry that you're upset."

Leonardo turned to Azzura. "I love you."

Ciro stepped between them. "It's best that you leave."

"Not without Azzura."

Ciro stiffened.

Azzura said, "Leonardo, please."

"This isn't over." He turned and left. Giuseppe followed him outside. Leonardo was red-faced. "I won't lose Azzura."

Giuseppe said, "Isabella and Ciro's minds will be difficult to change."

"I don't care. I'll steal Azzura away."

"Calm down. You're not thinking straight."

"What am I going to do?"

"Ciro made a commitment. It's a matter of face for him."

"There must be a way to change his mind. Maybe I can pay the suitor to break the contract?"

Giuseppe said, "What about Isabella? She's the rock in that family."

"What have I done to make her hate me?"

"You're not Carlo."

Azzura raised her voice to her parents. "I won't marry Federico Rana."

Ciro said, "You accepted my arrangement. Rana is a good man with a trade. You'll be cared for."

"I was wrong to agree. I don't love Federico."

"I've shaken hands with him. It's too late to go back."

"You'd save face at the cost of my happiness?"

Ciro turned to Isabella. Her mouth was locked into a frown. Isabella said, "Carlo was a real Mazzi. Leonardo may be the offspring of Salvatore Mazzi, but he's a bastard."

"Carlo is dead. It was terrible. But it's time you stopped mourning."

"Have some respect."

"My refusal to marry Federico isn't about Leonardo. It's about me. I want to make my own choices. Leonardo's return woke me up."

Isabella pointed. "You never obey me. You made an embarrassing scene with Leonardo even though you're engaged. I hope Federico doesn't hear of it." She turned toward Ciro. "Did you see how that man kissed her in public?"

Ciro said, "Azzura, you need to forget about Leonardo."

"Papa, hasn't he satisfied your concerns?"

"I don't like that he was in jail."

"The police have dropped their investigation. They agree it was an accident. Poor people are easy to put in jail. The police were wrong."

"Leonardo would take you to Italy."

"I'm staying in New York."

Ciro sighed. He looked at Isabella. "I suppose I could speak to Federico."

Isabella crossed her arms. "Leonardo may have satisfied you, but not me."

Azzura's voice rose. "But what would you have him do?"

"There's nothing he can do." Isabella looked bereaved. She left the room.

Ciro caressed his daughter's cheek. "Give her time. Your mother will come around."

Azzura knew that her mother never would.

Leonardo met Frank Rizzo at the Mulberry Street Club. "*Grazie* for getting Byrne off my back. It's a relief to walk in New York without the Tombs hanging over my head."

Rizzo leaned his chin on his palm. "Now that I'm a member of the longshoremen's board, I want to focus on the docks, and I need to develop a legitimate income. If the newspapers portray me as a gangster, Big Jim O'Neil will have an excuse for dropping me from the board."

"I've spoken with my father about an export business sending goods to New York. There are lots of Italians here who appreciate a taste of Italy. Olive oil will be our first product, then we can expand. We've started a commune with other farmers in our region to press the fruit. We need a partner in New York we can trust."

Rizzo smiled. "Let's do some business." They shook hands

Chapter 37

EVERY DAY Leonardo received an urgent cable from Salvatore Mazzi. Salvatore lamented that Giulietta Zangara pressed him to finance the gang's illegal activities. If Leonardo didn't return to Naples soon, his birthright would be mortgaged and the estate would be bankrupt.

Azzura cancelled her engagement to Federico Rana at great embarrassment to Ciro. Rana wouldn't speak to him afterwards, and Federico's friends and family would no longer eat at Ciro's.

The breakup encouraged Leonardo, and he approached the Medinas for permission to marry Azzura. Isabella wouldn't speak to him. Afterwards he and Azzura sat on a park bench near the Mulberry Bend. There were no birds. Crocuses hadn't sprouted. The rain had created a bas-relief sculpture of brown muddy shoe prints on the ground.

Leonardo said, "Will your mother ever accept me?"

Azzura sighed. "She's set in her mind."

"Why is she against me?"

"She mourns Carlo."

"I can't compete with the dead. Do you miss Carlo?"

"I'm sad about what happened."

Leonardo took Azzura's hand. "My father's in trouble. I need to return to Naples. Why don't we elope in Italy?"

"You go. Take care of what you need to do. I'll be here."

"I want you with me. I have a beautiful house. It'll be empty without you."

"In Italy I'd feel like some sort of ornament. All my life, my parents have tried to control me. I don't want to exchange one cocoon for another."

"I don't understand. What will you do?"

"I'm leaving my parents' apartment. My godmother will help me. I'll sell food on the street until I have money for my own place."

"Is opening a restaurant more important than our being together?"

"Leonardo, I almost allowed myself to be forced into a marriage. Tradition would've trapped me like an insect under a glass jar. The stress opened my eyes. I won't be pushed into unhappiness."

"We can have a good life in Naples. I'll buy you a restaurant. You won't need to work."

"I want to prove myself, not live in your shadow feeling second class and obligated." Azzura squeezed Leonardo's hand. "You came to New York to be your own man. You wanted self-respect. My parents cared for me, but there was a price. They disregarded my feelings. In their minds I was too young to have a valid opinion. They shoved me in the direction they wanted me to go. Out of responsibility. Out of tradition. Out of love. Out of their having the power to coerce me. They told me to do as they wished or they'd disown me. They called my desires a disgrace. You want me to fulfill the role of an Italian wife, but that's not enough for me."

"Wouldn't you find fulfillment in children and my love?"

"Was that enough for your mother? From what you told me, she was trying to be her own person. She rebelled against the role her parents thrust upon her. She educated herself. She bore a child with a man she didn't marry. She lived with a man she didn't love. You were the center of her life. Even so, you left to find your own way."

"I abandoned her. That was a sin."

"You made the choice you had to make. You were compelled."

"You can't compare your choice to mine. I love you, and I want to take care of you."

"I love you, but I don't want to be your responsibility. You told me that your mother's marriage was unhappy. What if she'd stayed single? Might that have been better?"

"And survive on what? We would've lived in poverty and shame."

"Isn't that the sin? That your mother would've been condemned for her choice? A woman needs more than children to fulfill herself. Children leave. It's natural. I want you to respect me for myself, not because I'm your wife or a mother. Those things can be an important part of who I am, but not all. I'm not a child. I can make my own decisions. I want to make my own mistakes. That's how I'll learn and grow. I want you to love me enough to want what I want for me."

"To be like your godmother?"

"I admire Natalia. She cares for others. She's active in the unions and suffrage politics. I don't think she'll ever marry."

"Azzura, when I left Italy for America I was naïve. Somehow I thought I'd succeed. My optimism was my shield, and it sustained me through the worst disappointments. But now I know how crushing the world can be. That knowledge burdens me. I don't want to start anew. You don't know what the real world is like."

"I want to find out for myself. Do what you must in Naples, then come back to me. We'll face life together. We'll help each other."

Leonardo moved closer. "I won't be happy without you. Please come with me."

Azzura caressed Leonardo's cheek. "I think I know what your mother would say. She'd tell you that I'm the one for you. She'd tell you to stay with me."

"If I walk away from the Mazzi estate, the Camorra will engulf my father and bankrupt him. I can't be poor again. Not after what I've done."

Azzura's eyes widened. "What have you done?"

Leonardo looked away.

Azzura sat back. "Did you lie to me? Did you murder the Greek?"

Leonardo was silent.

Azzura's eyes welled. "I didn't want to believe it, but I knew."

Leonardo squeezed his temples. "Do you hate me?"

"I wonder now if I really know you. I told you not to commit murder and say it was for us. But it wasn't for us; it was for you. Don't you see what the desire for money has done to you? A gentle man has turned brutal."

"I'm not brutal. I'm my mother's son."

"You are what you've become." Azzura wiped her face. "I need to go."

Leonardo slumped. He watched her walk away.

It was Leonardo's last night in New York before his steamship left for Naples. Images of his mother came into his head, chasing him around the garden, reading Dante to him. He wondered if that would be the happiest time of his life. He thought about the day he left her in tears on the Naples pier, and his stomach soured.

He drifted off to sleep and had a dream. The day was overcast and enough moisture had gathered for the green fields to glisten with dew. The wildflowers were in bloom. Blue, yellow, and red smeared across the landscape like in his childhood. He looked out to the Bay of Naples. Emerging from the sea appeared the finely featured face of a woman. She rose from the surf, and the brine sheeted from her body. Her long dark hair curled in waves about her shoulders, and he could see that she wore a diadem of white flowers that bathed him in the scent of jasmine. She wore a gossamer blue dress, and the ocean lapped her bare feet with foamy white ripples. Her mouth moved. Leonardo strained, but couldn't hear the words; then she metamorphosed into his mother. Anna was radiant, like in her youth. She extended her arms to him. His feet were stuck. He pulled at his legs to get them to move. He felt a pressure in his throat, and he stretched to grasp her. He looked into his mother's eyes.

"Mama, I committed murder."

Anna's face saddened, and she dissolved into mist like a faded photograph. Leonardo awoke with tears in his eyes.

Azzura's father looked heartbroken when she announced she would leave. Her mother tore her hair, then for days wouldn't rise from bed.

Azzura bought a second hand pushcart with a kerosene burner to keep food warm. In the morning she met construction workers with coffee and sandwiches of potatoes, onions, and eggs. Afternoons she was back with macaroni and meatballs. Men flocked to her stand. Many lingered longer than needed. If their flirting was money, she'd be rich. She remained friendly, but focused.

Natalia arranged so that Azzura supplied food to union rallies. She met a lot of women. Everyone encouraged her to open a restaurant. She was having difficulty finding hiding places in the apartment for all the cash, and she started to search for a suitable place of her own.

The nurses at the Henry Street Settlement often asked her to talk to young girls who left home. She sensed admiration in their eyes, and she felt odd.

Eventually she reconciled with her parents, sort of. Ciro smiled when he saw her, but his eyes were sad. Isabella troweled guilt on her like concrete. In her few quiet moments she'd think about Italy. There were no letters. She hoped Leonardo was okay. Men attracted her, but there was no magic like their first kiss. She imagined apples didn't taste the same to Eve after the Garden of Eden.

Leonardo sent his carriage, and Caprice Sacco arrived at the Mazzi Estate. Caprice's hair was in a pompadour style under a wide-brimmed hat. She wore a low-cut, silky purple dress with a narrow waist. Leonardo wore a brown suit buttoned under his neck, a stiff-collared white shirt, and a light brown tie with diamond stickpin. He doffed his black felt homburg when he came down the portico steps to greet her.

"Signorina Sacco, I'm Leonardo Mazzi. *Piacere.*"

"*Piacere.*"

Leonardo led Caprice into the Great Room. He took the well-worn chair, she the couch. He dropped his hat onto the Theseus carved table.

Leonardo said, "You must be thirsty. May I offer you something to drink?" He held up a ceramic pitcher of blood orange juice.

"Oh yes. Please call me Caprice. I'm sorry that I'm late paying my respects for Carlo."

"It's kind of you to come all this way. You were at university together?"

"He once fought a duel for me."

"That was Carlo. I take it you were close?"

"For a while." Caprice shifted in her seat. "Isn't that a portrait of Carlo over the fireplace? You resemble him."

Carlo, with a classical distant and calm expression, dressed in military cuirass stood *contraposto*, arm extended and barefoot like Caesar Augustus.

"My father commissioned the work before he died."

"You lost your father as well."

"His heart gave out."

"I'm so sorry." Caprice sipped some juice. "Carlo's heroic portrayal is perfect."

"Yes. He was a man of honor. He defended his family in every way necessary. So did my father. A man must."

"I thought Carlo was an only child."

"We had different mothers. I'm adopted."

"This entire estate is yours?"

Leonardo gave Caprice a boyish smile. "Please excuse me, but I have an appointment in Naples. I want to hear more about Carlo's university days. Dine with me this evening. In fact, accept my hospitality; you'll enjoy a few days in the country. I'll pick up your luggage from the Grand Hotel Vesuvio on my way back."

Caprice's eyes were shy. "That's kind of you."

Leonardo tromped down the accordion steps toward the Torre Annunziata Camorra headquarters. He passed a couple of dark men in a café. They eyed him and whispered to each other. They started to rise, and Leonardo pulled back his jacket to reveal a revolver tucked into his belt. They receded into their chairs.

Tazio stood in the doorway. He held out his hand and Leonardo gave him the pistol.

"What's the English on the barrel?"

"'Colt Frontier Six-Shooter.' I purchased it in New York."

Tazio laughed. "Cowboy."

Giulietta Zangara greeted Leonardo with a motherly smile. "Signor Mazzi, welcome."

Tazio showed her the revolver.

"Return Signor Mazzi's pistol. We trust each other."

Leonardo took the chair opposite Zangara and her niece brought him a coffee.

Tazio handed him an envelope thick with currency. Leonardo fingered the contents.

Giulietta Zangara said, "You're pleased with your share from our last piece of business?"

"I provided the financing." They sat for some moments in silence. Leonardo cleared his throat. "Donna Zangara, you've had sufficient profit from our arrangement. I believe that my family's debt to you has been satisfied."

Zangara made a small smile. "Has it?"

Leonardo said, "My export trade with Frank Rizzo in New York is taking my attention. I intend to end our dealings in Italy."

Zangara sat back. "Perhaps you should include me in all your business activities."

Leonardo squirmed. "Please excuse me, but I have a guest at the estate."

At the doorway, Leonardo's toe caught on the door jamb, and he stumbled momentarily.

Tazio smirked. "Mind how you go." When he returned to the living room Tazio slouched in a chair. "Why do you give money to that aristocratic *sfacim*? You're not intending to release him from his obligation?"

"Tazio, one day Captain Ceruti will be transferred from Naples and Don Leonardo bastard Mazzi will lose his leverage on us."

"Ah, we cook him in warm water."

"*Bravo, Caro.*"

Leonardo raised his palm in farewell; Caprice turned in her carriage seat and waved the fingers of a gloved hand. The driver shook the reins and they were off. Caprice had shared his bed, but Leonardo ordered a black stallion to be saddled before the dust of Caprice's carriage had settled.

A workman snapped to attention. "*Sí, Padrone.*"

Leonardo's step lightened at the sound of his title. His estate couldn't be covered even in an entire day's ride. The sun was bright. Wispy brushstrokes of clouds painted a blue canvas. Leonardo rode the stallion past rippling green fields and trees bursting with abundance. Goats bleated above the sounds of the breeze and calling birds. The scent of jasmine was in the air. He sat high in his saddle. He'd done what he had to do, what a man needed to do. Even so, he wished he could think of his mother without angst in his gut, and the image of Papanikolaou's gaping skull wouldn't appear when he closed his eyes. He knew that Giulietta Zangara would eat him if she could, and he'd need to find a way to deflect her if Captain Ceruti left Naples. Zangara's enmity was the tariff of his inheritance. He shook concern out of his head.

His mind turned to Azzura as it had many times since they were last together. Their emotions had clicked from the start. There was an emptiness inside him of what could have been and anguish that first love won't be repeated. He wondered what she was doing. Should he see her? He'd rehearsed their meeting in his head many times. They'd embrace, kiss, and his heart would overflow. Azzura would want him to live in New York. He reconciled that if she was happy with herself, she'd be happy with him. He'd miss the estate, but he missed her more. Nunzio had proven himself able in managing the *fattoria*, and Leonardo could stay in New York and feel comfortable that the property was in capable hands. So why did he hesitate to see her? Did he fear she would spurn him? Did he prefer his fantasy to the possibility of polite disinterest? The debate raged in his head for months. At last, he took a deep breath. Could they be together again? He had to know.

END

More books from Harvard Square Editions

People and Peppers, Kelvin Christopher James
Gates of Eden, Charles Degelman
Love's Affliction, Fidelis Mkparu
No Worse Sin, Kyla Bennett
Anomie, Jeff Lockwood
Close, Erika Raskin
Transoceanic Lights, S. Li
Living Treasures, Yang Huang
Nature's Confession, J.L. Morin
A Little Something Richard Haddaway
Dark Lady of Hollywood, Diane Haithman
Fugue for the Right Hand, Michele Tolela Myers
Growing Up White, James P. Stobaugh
Calling the Dead, R.K. Marfurt
Parallel, Sharon Erby

CPSIA information can be obtained at www.ICGtesting.com
Printed in the USA
LVOW10s2247281115

464515LV00004B/337/P